The Sound of Birds

Joshua Lerman

To mom, for always being there.

Joshua Lerman

1 ➔

This driver license. I need to throw it away. Mary Ellen Rizner only exists in files and old, expired ID cards. Not a real person. Everyone calls me Mimi, but perhaps that's not the name of a real person either. The address on this card makes my skin tingle like being covered in little spiders. I live at 3222 Guilford Lane now, room sixteen, in Marion, Virginia. I hope I move soon. Not just move rooms, like I did a few months ago, but move away from this building, move out of this state. I can't stand the cold winters anymore. And I am so tired and fed up with all these people! Everything is so old and stale here. I am going to move to Florida or California or maybe even Hawaii where I can just eat avocados and mangos right off the trees. I won't need to worry about getting a job, which is good 'cause no one will hire me. Not with my history. And I'm getting older. According to this license I'm, uh…forty-three. Yowser. Maybe I can work in a cafeteria scooping up globs of foodstuff. I don't want to move to California. Too many fucking hippies! I don't want to be around hippies. Had enough of that when I was growing up and subjected to Mom and Dad's lifestyle. They shouldn't have been allowed to have kids.

I am sitting at my desk, looking through the window, through the blinds, which are angled so I can see through them, downward. The yard here is so manicured it makes me sick. It looks so unnatural, so fake. It's like something out of a nightmare, the squared hedges, the constantly mowed lawn, the purple and white petunias spaced out in exact measurements, set in mulched beds of perfect geometry. The rhododendrons, with bright pink flowers, lining the main walking path from the gate to the front entrance. Who are they trying to impress? Someone's family? No one should be subject to something so constructed, so construed. I have to get away from here, just to get away from that damn yard. And I can't live here anymore. I just can't. All the screaming.

I get up, walk across my room, out the door, down the hallway. I want to watch some TV. I think Judge Judy is on. TV mostly sucks; loud obnoxious people talking at you, or trying to be funny. But Judge Judy *is* funny.

All the walls in this place are painted mint green. It's a terrible color. Pastel, attempting to be subtle, but evoking the feeling of puking. If there was a way to measure how soothing or how irritating a color was, I am sure that this color would register very high in the irritation range. And they put it everywhere! Hospitals. Schools.

Out of the river, all ugly and green, came the biggest old alligator that I've ever seen! La na nana na na na nana.

I walk into the common room. Joan is sitting upright in the Lazy boy, staring off into space and Daryl, dammit, is in my place on the sofa! He *knows* that's my place during Judge Judy! These people! They are so dense, and they just don't care about a thing.

I walk over to the front of the sofa and stand over Daryl, crossing my arms below my chest. The remote is loosely cradled in his hand resting in his lap.

"Hi, Daryl."

"Hi, Mimi." Daryl is older. Older than me. He's an old black man who pretends he can't hear. Maybe it's all the hair in his ears. I think he can hear perfectly fine. And he's smart. He's just playing tricks on all of us, but everyone thinks he's stupid. Years ago he lost his job, and then he got depressed and he lost his house. He told me all that one afternoon after lunch, clear as day. I think he's a fake. I think he stays here 'cause he doesn't want to try to find a job again. Or he's scared he can't. Nurse Linda knows it. Yep. But she doesn't care. His eyes are big and brown, and always teary and yellow where they should be white. It's probably his meds. And his hair is half grey, half black and curly like a black person's hair and about an inch long.

"Daryl, give me the remote."

"What?"

"Daryl! I'm missing Judge Judy!" I smack his upper arm. "Linda!"

"Why are you calling her? Just give me the damn remote!"

"What?" his face contorts in a fake look of distress and confusion.

"Don't play dumb with me." I hit him again in the arm, harder this time. My palm stings like electricity. Shit. Didn't mean to hit *that* hard. Linda comes rushing over.

"Mimi, what are you doing?" she says in her high-pitched whiney voice. She should have been a mom somewhere in Minnesota. But she never married. Probably too picky. Or no one found her interesting. She would have made a good Christian housewife to some boring devout Christian man. But she isn't religious.

"I am trying to get Daryl to give me the remote!"

"You don't own the TV, Mimi."

"I always watch Judge Judy. Everyone knows that's the only show I watch."

"You can ask him nicely to change the channel."

"I did. He's pretending he can't hear me."

"Mimi, you know Daryl doesn't hear well."

"He knows that I always watch Judge Judy."

"If he doesn't want to change the channel, he doesn't have to. And I don't want you throwing a fit." She turns to Daryl. "Daryl?"

He doesn't respond.

"Hurry up. I'm missing it!"

"Mimi, it's not your turn to choose the channel." Her teeth gnash behind tight lips. She marches to the laminated sheet on the wall next to the TV. The peace accord. "It's Joan's time to choose the TV channel."

"Oh, Lord, help us all. She doesn't even *look* at the TV most of the time. She puts on Teletubbies or some crap and then doesn't even watch it and we're left having to sit in front of those damn asinine creatures, making stupid noises…"

"You are in one of your moods, Mimi. Did you take your medication today?" She stands right in front of me.

"Yes." I really haven't. Sometimes I like the medicine. It keeps my mind from being so agitated. But it also makes me so sleepy. Heavy. Groggy. It's more peaceful, but I feel half-dead.

"Now, let's ask Joan if she wants to watch your show. But I don't want you throwing a fit. You've been really good and you have that meeting with Dr. Jensen in a few days."

"I'm not worried. I'm a free bird. I can take care of myself and I'm sure I've demonstrated that in the past couple months since coming down to the second floor. And there is only one place to go after the second floor: the first floor and out the door!"

"Yes, well, Dr. Jensen will be asking you lots of questions and asking me and the psych techs lots of questions, so don't throw a tantrum now." Her sterile grey eyes admonish me.

"You don't trust me. You're going to tell Dr. Jensen not to let me out," I whine.

"You didn't take your medicine today. The difference is night and day. If you get released, you'll still be responsible for taking your medication."

"You're going to tell him that I'm not ready! I can see it in your beady little eyes! You don't trust me a lick!"

4

"Well, I don't want you hurting anyone, Mimi, that's for sure."

I am so angry I could scream! I could punch her! I could tear her ugly pink face to pieces! My lip is snarling. It's the ghost. The ghost hates Linda. I turn and walk away. If I don't, the ghost will try to rip her up. I walk past the nurses station and head back down the corridor. Linda is following me, goddammit! What does she think; I'm going to go hurt somebody! I'm not! I'm going to my room! Why is she following me? I can't stand her! The mint-green walls are blurry, as if they are moving, not me. I can feel the ghost in me, rising in my throat hot and sour.

The ghost entered me when I was seven years old. My parents brought me and Ethan, my little brother, to the Woodstock Festival. It was wet and muddy and crowded and I hated it. Our last full day, as we weaved through the crowd holding hands in a chain, I heard the most terrible noise, the most blood curdling scream a person could make. I looked to my right and this woman was on the ground, in the mud, screaming while these guys were trying to hold her down. She was writhing around like she had no bones. Screaming and pale, pale white. Her eyes were going all over the place. The guys were trying to talk to her and everyone sounded so scared, but I couldn't make out what anyone was saying. And all of a sudden, as if on cue, she turned her head and looked right at me. I felt the ghost go in me that moment. From her yellow snake eyes to my eyes and down into my stomach.

She lives in me. Sometimes I think I'm all messed up because my parents were unstable and I had so many bad knocks and that I just cracked. But, really, I know it's this damn ghost.

I start running fast down the hallway. The walls are of a luminous green tunnel. I am so fast. I run into my room, slam the door and jump onto my bed. If these doors had locks on the inside, I would have locked the door. But that wouldn't make sense to put locks on the inside with crazy people, now would it? Linda opens the door and looks at me. The ghost is swirling around in me. It makes me nauseous. Dizzy in the head. I want to cry and scream and puke. I want her to go away! Go away!

"Go away!"

She looks at me with condemning pity. I don't need her pity. I hate her pity. I need her to go away. Why doesn't she understand? Why doesn't anyone understand?

"Please, go away."

I start to sob. This is the one good thing that's happened to me in this godforsaken place. Lately I've been crying again. A good amount. The ghost goes away mostly when I cry. When I cry, it's me crying. The ghost doesn't cry. She is just venomous.

Linda stares at me. Finally she closes the door and I am alone. I don't want to be alone. But the ghost hates everyone. I need to learn to develop more pure good, a good heart, so the ghost can't live in me. When the light is bright enough, there can be no darkness. I read that in a book.

I'm glad to be crying now. It is cool rain falling on hot dry earth, or the earth before it cooled down two billion years ago: hot, molten, poisonous. The ghost has retreated to my belly. It sits heavy there like basalt. I am breathing. My body moves up, filling with air, and down, releasing the air. Up, filling with air. Down, releasing air. My head is still buzzing a bit, but this isn't bad. My room is hazy yellow and the air is heavy and thick. Dust motes float like wayfaring insect spirits in the striped shaft of light reaching in through the blinds. Birds are chirping and singing outside my window. I pray that one day I won't be indifferent to their songs.

* * * * * * * * * * * * *

Nigel is walking beside me. We are in a corridor on the first floor. I am wearing my only dress, sky blue with little silver and turquoise flowers and opalescent buttons. I haven't had a reason to wear it until now. Nigel is wearing his steel grey scrubs. I imagine the two of us walking down the aisle of a chapel, about to get married. How funny we look together in these outfits. We stop outside Dr. Jensen's door. Nigel turns to look at me. He is a handsome young black man. Clear creamed-coffee skin. Warm brown eyes that flash polished bronze when he smiles. Lips curling out like flower petals. I have often wished to be a hummingbird and to drink the nectar of that flower.

"Good luck, Mimi," he says. And without looking away from my eyes, he knocks on the door. We hear the small muffled voice of Dr. Jensen from inside.

"Come in."

Nigel turns the knob and pushes the door open, still looking me in the eyes, still wishing me good luck. He holds the door open for me. I walk in and look at Dr. Jensen sitting behind his big, wood desk. He is smiling big.

"Ah, Mimi, come on in. Come in and have a seat." With his whole hand extended, he presents a small grey chair in front of the desk. There is another grey chair just like it, against the wall to my right. The built in shelves on the wall to my left are filled with books. I make my way to the grey chair Dr. Jensen is pointing at with his hand. He is smiling big. He must be in his fifties, blonde hair thinning, round head. He is rather large. He isn't very tall, or very fat; he just…looks sort of big and full. 'Big boned' is what people would say, or 'meaty.' He is wearing a grey suit, a white shirt with a navy blue tie. He is smiling so big. I give him a quick smile back. He must know it was forced. I'm nervous. I sit in the chair and he stops pointing with his hand and he leans back into his bigger chair. I hear the door close behind me. I clench one hand with the other and start squeezing it rhythmically. They are dry like bone, like I had left them in a basin of talcum powder for three days.

"How's it going, Mimi?"

"It's pretty good."

"I haven't seen you since our last meeting five months ago."

"That's right." Like I keep track of these things.

He nods, looking at me scrupulously. His smile dims.

I take a breath. I need to relax.

His eyes focus and he looks directly at me. He takes a breath.

"You are clear why we are meeting here, Mimi, yes?"

"Yes." He is looking at me. "You are going to determine if I am ready for the outside world."

Dr. Jensen leans forward folding his hands on top of his desk, his fingers interlaced. "Of course the decision is mostly based on the recommendation of Dr. Westland and the reports from the nurses and techs." He studies me again. He doesn't know he is nodding his head ever so slightly, agreeing with his own thoughts. "What's your opinion, Mimi?"

"I'm ready, Dr. Jensen. I can take care of myself."

He studies me. I shift in my chair and squeeze my cardboard hand again.

"Nurse Linda's report says that you don't take your medication consistently."

Hot pressure, especially my head and my jaw. My teeth clench. Grind. Pressure behind my eyes. Don't water.

"This is very serious, Mimi."

My eyes coat over with water. I breathe through my nose. Heavily. Through my nose so he can't see how heavy I am breathing. But he can probably see anyways.

"Mimi?"

I take a couple more breaths before opening my mouth.

"Sometimes I don't want to take them. I can't feel anything." I wipe at my left eye. Water is dangerously close to leaking out. Shit. I take a quick full breath in through my nose to hold back this feeling. Mucous rattles high in my nose giving away all that I was hoping to conceal. I've become so goddamn emotional.

I take another breath, steadying myself. I take another.

"Do you remember why you're here? You hurt somebody very badly."

Venom.

"Yes, I remember!" she shouts.

I am panting a bit. He is looking at me. I sit up again.

"We can't take a chance of that happening again."

I am fighting. I keep myself steady. Breathing.

"It won't." My voice is trembling, "I am learning to control my anger."

He just keeps watching me. I am an animal behind glass.

"What does Dr. Westland say about your anger?"

"He tells me to notice when it's coming and to breathe."

"Have you been doing that?"

"Yes." Like three times already since I've been sitting here, buddy.

"And how's that going?"

"It's going well." I wonder if he can hear the trembling. Or see it.

He is looking at me, his eyes focusing and unfocusing as he goes back and forth between observing me and thinking about something. He is unconsciously playing with a black retractable ballpoint pen with his big, chubby fingers. He lets out an airy breath.

"Linda says you were hitting Daryl the other day. What was that about?"

"He was in my seat. I was upset, but I wasn't hurting him. It was like siblings. I wasn't trying to hurt him." The ghost got the best of me. I've never hit anyone like that before.

He nods slightly, tightens his lips together so they form a line, and reclines back in his seat. The pen still in his hands, hovering over his lap, elbows supported by the chair's armrests.

"And what do you plan to do when you leave here?"

"I'm not totally sure. Get a job. Work in a cafeteria. Maybe move to Hawaii."

"You won't be able to leave the state for a while. Not without a family member to take you in. You would go into a halfway house."

"Oh. Okay." That's fucking ridiculous.

"Do you plan to see your brother?"

"Maybe. I don't know. I'm not sure I trust him."

9

"I see. Trust. That's important," he seems to say to himself as he thumbs through papers on his desk. "Your brother...Ethan." Dr. Jensen looks up again. "He has shown concern for you, phoning every once in a while. He visited you on your birthday last year. It's important to have people who care about you."

"Yeah." Does he care about me? He used to. Little traitor.

Dr. Jensen looking at me. I look back. I wait. His eyes unfocus, trail off. Then focus in on me again.

"One more thing, Mimi." I widen my eyes, saying, 'Yes?'

"What of this ghost you used to carry on about so much?"

I take a breath.

"She's gone." I feel my voice clip at the end, my throat close as if not wanting to finish the sentence. But it was short and escaped. A lie.

"I see."

She looks out from my eyes whenever she wants. Anger. War. Hatred. Dr. Jensen is lying too because that lives in everybody. Maybe just more acutely in me, because of how she came into me.

"Well then, Mimi," Dr. Jensen smiles his big smile in his big grey suit, "that will be all. Dr. Westland and I will be in discussion and we'll share with you our conclusions."

I make a smile.

"You can leave now. Nigel is just outside the door."

I get up, feeling bewildered that it's over so quickly. I walk over to the door and turn the cool knob.

"Nice speaking to you, Mimi."

I turn back slowly, feeling dazed.

"You too."

I open the door. Nigel is standing there. I walk out and he closes the door behind me. He looks intently at me, trying to read what happened in there. I feel blank. Stunned.

"Ready for lunch?" he asks.

"Yeah," I say like a breath. Morning meds are taking effect.

We walk down the corridor of white walls. White walls on the first floor. We turn a corner and walk up a wide stairwell, stopping at the landing of the second floor. He takes the keys that are hanging from his belt and uses one to unlock the door to the second floor. He holds the door open for me. We are at the end of the corridor. Mint green walls. We walk side by side. I weigh 300 pounds. My vision is unfocused. Clouds.

"How'd it go with Jensen?" He is looking at me.

"They're going to discuss it." The words float out dead.

He nods slowly, then faces forward. We approach the dining room. He opens a door and I enter, startled to find the same old familiar, crazy scene of crazy people eating lunch together.

2 ➞

The thing I remember most about my childhood was our rust-orange Volkswagen camper van. For nine years it was our home, our mobile cave. We called her Bertha because Dad said that it was the quintessential earth-mama name. Bertha was a living thing to me, especially when I was young. Her headlight eyes. The VW emblem, her nose. Her smiling bumper. We all loved Bertha and she willingly followed the wild and restless will of my father from one town to another, from one music festival or Grateful Dead show to the next. We would settle down for a few months; Eugene, Bellingham, Boulder, but for reasons never revealed to me, we would suddenly leave. One day Dad would tell me to put my things in my bag and get ready to hit the road. I didn't mind it, all that traveling. It was all I knew. But somehow I could sense that I was living in a strange world, a separate world. Through various means I came to understand that there were things called schools and jobs and that most people lived in houses. We would stay at the homes of friends of my parents and if they had kids I would get drilled and when Ethan was old enough, he was included in the inquisition as well. Questions would be something like, "Where do you live?" "Why do you live in your car?" "Where do you go to the bathroom?" "What's that smell?" Ethan would look to me with nervous anticipation when the barrage of questions hit. I had usually fielded most of them at some previous similar conversation and ones I had trouble answering on my own, I would ask my parents once we left and were back in Bertha. By the time I was ten I was tired of the questions and would answer in a flat monotone, staring at my inquirers like a sleepy old hound. "We live in Bertha." "We live in Bertha 'cause Dad is Jewish and he has wandering in his blood." "We go to the bathroom wherever we want." "What smell?"

While other children had elementary school, Hanna-Barbera and soccer practice, Ethan and I had rock and roll, temporary villages and the road. Where other children had friends and relatives, Ethan and I had an assorted and rotating cast of characters who one day seemed like Mom and Dad's very best friend, two weeks later they were out of our lives forever. Bearded bikers wearing leather vests, bottle of beer always in hand, uproarious laughter that turned into coughing. Skinny women wearing lots of jewelry who slithered in their chairs when they were high, who couldn't grasp Dad's more intellectual conversation, and peering from beneath a veil of silk fabric would tell me in hushed tones that they were a psychic and could see my future. Nerdy guys who wore blue button-down shirts, slacks and black plastic rimmed glasses who liked to talk about how fucked up the world was and the government was and they never noticed Ethan or me, even when Ethan would tug at their trousers trying to talk to them.

I didn't really have parents. Mom and Dad were more like the stars of the psychedelic circus that was my early years. Dad was tall and gangly. He had a big nose, a big mustache and his large, round eyes looked like they were being pushed out of his head from the pressure of all the exuberance inside. He was an anarchist, an intellectual and a clown. And he was the ringleader. Mom was his lovely assistant, the Wild Woman seemingly completely untamed by society. She ran around barefoot and ecstatic, loved to scream and laugh at Dad's antics. She was lovely with her tan skin, amber eyes and pretty face. But she didn't even notice the looks and passes made by all the men when she walked by or the ones on adjacent blankets at concerts, who would lean over to our blanket to share a joint, always passing to Mom first. Dad was her man, and in her eyes there could be no better.

* * * * * * * * * * * * *

To this day I don't know why my parents originally named me with such a straight-laced, biblical name: Mary Ellen. It sounds like a Sunday school teacher's name, or a nun. Sister Mary Ellen. I was named after Mom's aunt Mary who she always said was a ray of sunshine, nothing but pure love, and Ellen Katz, a friend of Dad's in high school who smoked him out for the first time and slipped him a copy of *Living My Life* by Emma Goldman. So there you have it. Mary Ellen. But still, I imagine it was hard for them to resist the impulse to name me Moonflower.

Mimi, on the other hand, came in more typical Rizner Fashion. One time when I was six and Ethan was just a baby, the folks were on one of their LSD trips. When Ethan was very little, they did the responsible thing and would only put one magic square on their tongue instead of the usual two or three, only enough to cause 'mild' hallucinations, although you could never really tell what each batch would be like: how strong, how visual. This particular time the acid was coming on strong. Mom and Dad and Ethan and I were in the basement of some friend in Eugene, Oregon we had been staying with for a while. When they tripped, Mom and Dad would replace the light

13

bulbs with colored ones to help create the mood. Orange meant they wanted a warm, sweet, gooey experience, like honey. Blue was the sign that we'd be going to Saturn. Red was the underworld. On this occasion, the lights were blue. Mom and Dad were wearing their polyester psychedelic muumuus. Incense was burning. Pink Floyd was serenading us with haunting voices. Ethan was in his "cozy corner" with his toys in front of him. Mom was surprisingly capable of taking care of Ethan if he needed her, but it was my responsibility to look after him while they were tripping.

I don't remember the specifics of most of this trip, or many of them. They usually come on about thirty minutes after they placed the laced paper in their mouths. It was like a UFO landing. Strange. I could feel invisible waves. Everything would start buzzing. Mom and Dad's focus would start to change as they stared silently at carpet, walls or whatever was starting to kaleidoscope in front of them

This particular trip became very vocal. Sounds, and especially the sounds of their own voices, became the most amazing, curious and wonderful plaything on earth. Mom and Dad just sat like skinny, white Buddhas, draped in vibrant swirling colors, making noises. "Lalala laaaa laa laaaa lalalaaaa…" "Oooooo ooo ooo oooooo…." And my favorite, "zeeedahzaaahhahah zeeeeeedaaaaahh…" If they found a particular syllable, arrangement of notes or sound that really amused them, they would just crack up laughing. The vibrations were tickling them, is what they told me later. Well, they had been at it with their noises for a long time. Little baby Ethan, young as he was, was looking at me like 'what is going on with these people?' I could only shrug. Finally Mom started saying something more loudly.

"Ma. Ma." I turned. She was looking right at me. "Ma. Ma." She had this look like she was trying to reach out to me. "Ma. Mmma." She couldn't say my name. She stopped and swallowed. "Mmi mmi mmimmi." I got up from the cozy corner and walked over to her. Her eyes were opened wide. Horror movie wide. All that noise making and now she

14

couldn't say what she wanted to. I stood there next to her, looking right at her. Waiting. Her eyes like a cartoon. Finally she made a gesture, her fingers rubbing down her throat. I turned and went upstairs and into the kitchen. There was a used glass on the kitchen table. It looked clean enough. I dragged a chair from the table over to the sink for me to stand on. I filled up the glass, hopped down and went back down the stairs, remembering to shut the door behind me. I handed my mom the glass. She gulped half of it down before coming up for air, and then passed it to my father who looked surprised and uncertain with what to do with the object in his hand. Mom gave me a look. A little nod of the head, saying 'thank you.' But then, what she did say was "mimi." She smiled big and laughed at herself. "Mimi."

When they began to come down from the trip and regain their faculties, they joked and laughed about how Mom couldn't say my name. All she could say was "mimi." They pointed at me saying "Mimi. Mimi." This was hysterical to them. They said that they should call me that from now on, that it was meant to be. It was one of a very few "great ideas" they had when tripping that actually came to pass in real life. So my name was initially a joke born of an acid trip. How wonderful.

* * * * * * * * * * * * *

When I was fourteen and Ethan was ten, Mom and Dad decided that it would be in our best interest to settle down in one place until the two of us finished high school. It took them that long to realize that we might not want to follow in their footsteps, and become roaming pot dealers. I don't know how long they had been planning it, or what the decision making process was like. One day, sitting around the fold-down table in Bertha having a lunch of peanut butter and banana sandwiches, Ethan and I were informed we'd be "settling down for a while."

We landed in San Francisco, on Fell Street, right on the panhandle of Golden Gate Park. This location, they knew, would be advantageous for their business since all the hippies hung out in the park. We came July of '76 and just two short months later, I was enrolled as a freshman at Abraham Lincoln High School. What a disaster. Mom and Dad should have known that fourteen years in Bertha, eating, sleeping, driving down endless miles of highways with our god, Rock and Roll, would leave me completely unprepared to integrate into conventional society, especially at such a late stage in my development. I was under-educated and unsocialized. The education part was challenging enough. Dad taught me reading and writing as Bertha zoomed through the featureless grasslands of Kansas or Oklahoma, and basic math skills, but entry-level high school math is Algebra. It was clear after a few days that I couldn't wing it and I was put in remedial math with the slow and challenged kids. I was put in with this group not only physically, but also socially. I was doomed. I did not understand the rules of the education system. I did not learn the things that other kids learned in kindergarten. So I would do things like get up and go to the bathroom in the middle of class. The first time it happened was in English class. The teacher admonished me when I returned, 'reminding' me that I needed to raise my hand, ask permission and get a hall pass in order to use the bathroom. I stood there next to my desk as she spoke, my ragged clothes, my wild and tangled hair, the faces of the other students: disbelief, disapproval, disgust. I nodded meekly that I understood and slunk back into my chair, but it took several weeks to fully train myself in all the rules and expectations of this institution. Dad called it the cattle lot. Eventually I had the basics down. I raised my hand whenever I needed to speak, I didn't leave my desk without permission, I made it to class on time. But by then the other kids identified me as some wild, uncivilized creature; the Swamp Girl who just crawled out of San Francisco Bay to join them in their human world. I was not welcome. I did not act like they did, or talk like they did, or know the things they knew or played the games they played. They were used to hippies, it being San Francisco and all, but I wasn't merely one of those girls who wore tie-dye t-shirts and put daisies in their hair during lunch break. I was a freak, incapable of engaging in their conversations and smelling of mildew. And so I was gawked at, teased, harassed, and hated. A surprise swarm of daggers to suddenly realize how appalling I was.

Outside school, things weren't so bad. It took a while to get used to living in one place. After being in San Francisco for a couple months I became restless. The rhythm of coming and going was all I knew, and without the going, the ebb, it was like being on the down side of a see-saw, expecting to go up again, but instead, nothing, just sitting there crunched up, my knees too close to my shoulders. And things like certain buildings, certain streets, Marty's Sandwich Shop, my house, began to emit a glow, a presence. It was something I hadn't known in a place before: familiarity.

It did grow on me, this being in one place. The feeling of perpetual coming and going, in every cell of my body, finally receded, and in its place came a new rhythm. Routines. I got home from school around three and Mom would go pick up Ethan half an hour later. Dad was usually at Rebounded Books, the used bookstore he worked at twenty hours a week to supplement the family's income from selling grass and occasionally LSD. Working at scheduled times for another man was my father's definition of slavery. But there was a rent to pay now, and other expenses from city living.

Ethan and I did our homework until five or so, then we'd help Mom with dinner. It was never an extravagant affair, usually a grain or pasta, steamed or sautéed veggies and something for protein: a legume, cheese. We were vegetarian, but we ate a lot of junk food so I wouldn't say we were exactly healthy. Dad would come home before dinner was ready, deflated. It would usually take an hour and a joint before he found his usual gaiety. My father was a contradiction:

17

analyzing, thoughtful and well-read but behaved like a silly, rambunctious child. He believed trying to make too much sense of everything was the downfall of man, and that God was found in the nonsense. "That is where the bliss is,' he would say with a big ol' grin. I often feigned exasperation at my father's antics and horseplay and sometimes I actually was, especially in front of people I knew. Exasperated and embarrassed. But sometimes I played along and few things were as fun as joining Dad in his fantasyland. Ethan and Dad played all the time. Although Mom was always Dad's biggest fan, she lacked the theatricality to play the way Dad and Ethan could. Everything they did had an alternative story. They were suddenly pirates at the grocery store, fighting over the damsel (me) and stealing the booty (a melon) from each other, laughing and making a scene the whole time. Or they were Martians spying on the humans. On the rare occasions Mom called for a 'cleaning party' where we all had to chip in and do some scrubbing around the house they became Mexican cleaning ladies. Rosa and Rosalita would gabble away in their Spanish accents with rags in their hair, complaining about their husbands or how hard their work was. I was sometimes jealous of their bond, but I convinced myself that the jealousy was just disapproval of their antics. And so it became that.

Dad had to cut his hair after a few weeks of his job search, realizing that nobody wanted to hire such an unkempt man, even at used book stores and music stores. I cut mine after just three weeks of school when it became clear to me that I was a feral beast. Before we settled in San Francisco our wild, long, tangled hair was the mark of our little tribe. Now things were changing. My hair was shoulder length and combed every morning. Dad's was even shorter and also combed, parted to the right. Like Sampson, the power of Dad's smile and laugh had been diminished. Halfway through the school year, Ethan's teacher informed us that he had head lice and that his hair would need to be cut immediately. So only Mom kept her mane, a remnant of a past that was so different from our new

life. We might have never believed it actually happened if not
for her hair.

3 ➜

I am sitting at the little wood table off to the side of the
common room, against the wall. I have been playing solitaire
for almost an hour. I want to stop, but I can't until I have just
one good hand. Besides, I don't feel like doing anything else.

The TV is on, as usual. It's Ann's time to pick a station, but
there's nothing on at this hour of day but soap operas. She gets
a shitty spot, sandwiched between game shows and talk shows,
but I don't think she cares. She stares intently at the screen, like
because it is her time slot she owns the soaps. I can never
watch the garbage long enough to tell what's going on.

If only there was a space to put down this king, dammit.

Daryl is watching the TV too, but supposedly he can't hear
shit. I don't know who he thinks he's fooling. Joan is on the
couch, but she's too busy mumbling to herself to be paying
attention to what's happening on the screen. She can barely
ever stop talking, except when she's eating, and even then it's
only intermittent. Ann and her sometimes get into fights
because Ann says she can't hear the TV when Joan is sitting
next to her. It's pretty funny when they fight. They're like
squabbling hens.

Teddy is sitting in the recliner on the opposite side of the
room, reading a book under the window.

Damn, this game isn't going anywhere. Where the hell is
the three of diamonds?

Teddy usually reads science fiction. He told me he had a
big techie job. He used to wear a suit and tie and work with

computers and all. I guess everyone else is in group or in their rooms. Val is in group. Ann was kicked out of group for causing too much commotion. She's an angry little bitch. I stopped going 'cause I hated it. It was like dragging a dead horse through the mud, especially listening to Joan and Barbara try to explain something, or Dr. Westland or Dr. Owens trying to get somewhere with them for like half the session while the rest of us just sat there zoning out or trying to sit still. I got told 'stop sighing like that, please, Mimi' too many times.

Nigel approaches from the resident hallway. He comes right up to the table, looking at me, but I don't look up. He pulls out one of the other chairs.

"Mind if I sit?"

I make a slight movement with my head towards the empty seat. He swings one leg over the chair, puts his hands down on the table for leverage and sits. Ah, the energy of youth. He folds his arms on the table and leans forward, staring at me.

"Wanna play?" I ask.

"Sure. What's the game?"

"Gin. Ten cards."

"Alright."

I scoop up the cards and shuffle.

I'm a good shuffler. I riffle, slide shuffle and weave. Always in that order. I learned this all from Jared. He loved playing cards. And he learned it all from his grandfather who was a real hotshot, used to go to Atlantic City to play Blackjack, had a group of guys that he played with every week. I loved when Jared and I played cards together. It was one of our things.

"Table's pretty interesting, isn't it?" Nigel said.

"Huh?"

"The table. You haven't looked up from it since I've been sitting here."

"Oh. I'm tired," I say. It's the meds. I took my meds this morning.

Every morning and every evening I dutifully line up, like everyone else, at the nurses counter where the meds are dispensed. I put the little cup to my mouth and let the pills roll in. I take up the little dixie cup of water and throw it back. The nurse checks my name off on her paper. Some days I swallow the pills. Some days I smile at the nurse, walk away and spit the pills out in my room, in a napkin, and throw them out. I keep a stack of napkins in my desk drawer.

I toss a card towards him. It spins a couple times and stops in front of him. I slice one off the top and it sails down to the table in front of me. I repeat this nine more times. We pick up our cards and tap them on the table to get them all straight. We look at our hands and organize them towards a strategy.

Damn, my cards are all over the place. I look at Nigel. He is looking at his cards, hiding a smile. He has a good hand.

I flip the top card over and lay it next to the take deck.

He's still thinking he's doing a good job hiding his smile.

"Go," I say.

He looks up at me, eyes narrowing, then he turns his attention to the pile of cards on the table.

"You love your cards, Mimi."

"What else is a person suppose to do? I can't watch TV all day."

"Okay, okay. I was just making small talk, Ms Sassyfras, no need to take offense."

He puts a card face up on the discard pile.

"How's your ankle?" he asks.

"It's fine."

I pick up a card. Nothing I need. I put it on the discard pile.

"Maybe go easy during exercises today," he says as he picks up the card I put down.

"No, it's fine."

He puts a card down.

"Gotta be careful with those jumping jacks from now on," he says.

I don't respond. Jumping jacks are stupid. Easy to twist an ankle or hurt a knee. I will never do a jumping jack again.

I pick up a card. I can use this one. I discard a different one.

"Have you heard anything yet about the decision?" I ask.

Nigel lets out a sigh and frowns.

"They're not going to tell me before you, Mimi, so you can quit asking." He stares at me, a look of dismay. "If you ask me one more time, I'm gonna end up a patient here." He chuckles a little.

"It's your turn," I say.

He looks at his cards. He picks up a card from the deck.

"Shut up!" someone screams. It's Ann.

I turn to look. She's not yelling at Joan, she's yelling at the TV.

"Tell her the truth!" she screams with her rattling smokers voice, leaning in, pointing with two fingers like a gun. "Tell her!"

"Will you shut up!" I yell.

"Mimi," Linda warns, as Ann turns around to glare at me.

"Knock it off, Mimi," Nigel says as he crinkles his face like I'm such a bitter fruit.

I laugh to myself. Then look back at my cards.

Whose turn is it? What am I gonna do with this awful hand?

"Is it my turn?" I ask.

"Uh. No, I think it's my turn."

"Are you sure?"

"Yes, you put down that seven of clubs."

He's right.

He picks up a card, looks at it and places it strategically in the fan of blue-backed cards clasped in his hand. He puts another card down. I pick it up and put down another card.

I look over at the TV area. It's commercials, but everyone's eyes are still glued to the tube like they're watching some big event. Except for Joan. She is mumbling to herself and rocking slightly.

"Nigel, when are they gonna tell me?"

"I figure any day now. It's been almost a week." He looks at his watch. "Hurry up, Mimi. It's almost two, almost exercise time."

I look again at my cards, suddenly uninterested. How am I gonna win this stupid game?

4

By second semester I had had several months to digest the fact that I was a social undesirable. I had no friends and endured all the gawking and name-calling as best I could. Being at the receiving end of social torment is never an easy thing, and the deep hurt nagged like the searing sting of being branded. Even after the pain itself is gone, a phantom pain remains and echoes inside the canyons of carved flesh. One doesn't just make it mean nothing, like my mother told me to do. Instead I hardened my exterior. I would no longer cry in my bed after school. I became a crab.

I had decided when I was signing up for my classes the previous fall that I would try *Painting I* as my spring elective. I already knew how to make food for the family and use a sewing machine, so I didn't need Home Ec., and I had loved making little art projects in Bertha when we were on the road, so it seemed like a good choice.

The first day of class I went to the table that was in the corner furthest from the teacher's desk. I liked being in the back of a class because I wanted to avoid being in the sightline of the other students. You know what they say, 'Out of sight, out of mind.' I just wanted to be left alone.

Jared was sitting at the table with me. This was one of only a few good fortunes the heavens decided to bestow upon me. Jared had straight, brown hair, just past his ears, clear bright blue eyes like glacial ice and milk-white skin. He was pretty. And always smiling. Jared was the guy who transcended cliques. Everyone knew him and liked him. He was too wise to engage in the social games of adolescence, but it wasn't a conscious choice, like a thought, that he made one day. It was just who he was. Him sitting next to me in painting class was a presence brighter than the sun shining in the windows on a May afternoon, whispering the promises of summer break. He was somehow genuinely curious about everyone, including me. He also had a natural liking for everyone. I was a happy recipient of his benevolence. I had seen him around the previous semester, but I was sure he hadn't noticed me. Somehow when he looked into my eyes asking me about my life or making some joke about a teacher while we painted, I believed he had a special liking for me. This was not true. Not at first.

Jared was an awful painter. He struggled with proportions and depth and he couldn't produce the colors he wanted. He was a little frustrated, although he could make light of everything, like how Dad was back in the days of Bertha. I told him that his painting was delightfully abstract. Like Picasso, I said. I told him he was a natural, a genius. He would nod in sarcastic agreement.

"Yes. A genius. My art is too sublime to simply reproduce the material world on its own terms."

"You could make a fortune," I jested.

"It is not the money I am anticipating. It's merely the recognition."

While Jared had no actual talent to develop, something quite different was happening with me in that class. I delighted in my ability to render a realistic looking apple on my canvas several months into the class, and by the end of the semester I was working with complex objects like flowers in glass pitchers and shiny silver teapots.

While *I* was no Picasso, or a genius by any measure, I was talented and I learned fast. The teacher, Ms. Wilkinson, took notice and worked closely with me. I would stay after school several days a week and work on my paintings while Ms. Wilkinson did administrative tasks and cleaned up, making herself available for assistance if I asked for it. The other students took notice as well. Although it didn't raise me to homecoming queen status or protect me from insult in general, I gained a sort of respect (and dare I say admiration) in that class. It wasn't *me* that they actually admired but the work itself, and by association I was safeguarded by a cool respect.

Jared was my biggest fan. He praised with delight and wonder my pictures of calla lilies in a glass vase, my seashells on an old wood table or anything I did. He was truly amazed at how the globs of colored oil became objects that looked real enough for him to reach in and grab. He would have been welcome to take the lily of his choice, or any shell. I began to see Jared as more than just the nice, pretty guy who liked everyone and made everyone laugh. I saw a good, good heart, the source of all that jovial kindness. And with that seeing, I began to feel something. A longing. A longing to fall into that sweetness, my hands pointing together like a diver to split and penetrate his chest and go deep inside it. His pretty face seemed a heavenly thing; luminous and holy like the very first flower upon the earth. I began watching his hands, his arms. I watched the muscle of his calves twitch when he walked in shorts. I looked at his fair skin, his creamy alabaster skin and wanted eagerly to touch it. My heart would beat faster and I was afraid that he would notice me looking. But I looked anyway.

The three years leading up to ninth grade, after my childhood was over, were lost in a grey, nebulous no-mans-land, riding around in Bertha without ever a reflection or right of passage of the young lady I was becoming. Then, landing in San Francisco, surrounded by disdaining eyes, life began to be splattered with black and red: torment, confusion, a shredded soul. But now something new was arising. Now I had two things that anchored me, that were lights in my world: painting and Jared. And although class was only fifty minutes long, and after school painting only another two hours or so, the rest of my hours and days were also somewhat illuminated.

* * * * * * * * * * * * *

I remember the day I came home from school, after Ms. Wilkinson had called, asking Mom permission for me to stay after school to work on my paintings. It was a warm February afternoon, not so remarkable for San Francisco. Mom was waiting for me on the stoop. As soon as I turned the corner of our block I saw her there, wearing a faded pink tank top, bright orange pants and the brown sandals her friend got her in Turkey. Her huge mane fluttered in gusts of chilly wind that announced the inevitable end of the day's heat. Her eyes squinted from the glare of sunlight reflecting off of cars. She saw me too and immediately stood up and extended her arms in front of her, palms up, inviting me in for a hug. I was confused. It wasn't unlike my mom to want to smother us in embraces, but this seemed all too pre-meditated. I approached tentatively. As I reached the bottom step and looked up at Mom, her arms still reaching for me, she let out a shriek, unable to contain the anticipation of hugging me.

"What's going on?" I asked, suspicious. I didn't like her suffocating hugs.

"Come here!" she squawked, her smile about to explode her whole head.

"What happened?"

"Stop asking questions and come get a hug from your mama," she demanded.

What could I do? Turn and walk away? I ascended the eight or nine steps to the stoop and her hand grabbed my shoulder and yanked me into her body. Her arms wrapped around me as her body twisted back and forth in squealing rapture. My face was pressed into her shoulder and I smelled musk, moss and roses.

"Mom," I muffled with my mouth pressed into her flesh, "What the hell is going on?"

She grabbed my upper arms and thrust me out, holding me in front of her, beaming at me. Her eyes were suns and the gap between her two front teeth was fully revealed.

"Why don't you ever tell us anything?" she said shaking me slightly.

"Like what?" I asked.

"Ugh." She made the sound of light-hearted frustration as she whipped around, grabbed me by the wrist and pulled me inside. She led me down the hall and into the kitchen, right up to the kitchen table where she pulled me next to her and dropped my wrist. Right in the middle of the oval, unfinished wood table surrounded by four different chairs, sat a small, yellow glass vase with three daisies and right underneath, flat on the table, a set of paintbrushes in a clear plastic case.

"Ms. Wilkinson called," she said, "Your art teacher." I leaned in and picked up the brushes. "She wants you to stay after school so she can work more closely with you on your painting."

There were three round brushes, three flat square brushes, all of different sizes, and a fan brush. I opened the flap and felt the bristles. I hadn't been painting for very long, but I could tell the quality of these brushes was poor, probably from the toy store.

"She says you have real talent," my mother went on, her voice changing now. I turned and looked at her and saw an unfamiliar expression. She was still smiling, but in an almost sad, funny way and her eyes were coated with tears. She was proud.

"Thanks Mom," I said and leaned towards her a little so she could hug me. She wrapped me up in an embrace and started her twisting back and forth.

"Wait till Dad comes home. He is going to be elated."

And he was. We went out for pizza that night. For several weeks it seemed that painting was all that anybody wanted to talk about. It made sense. Hippies didn't want their kids to become lawyers or CEOs. They dreamed of social revolutionaries, little enlightened buddhas and anti-establishment artists. But I wasn't a painter with a purpose. There was no social discourse going on in my *Apple and Orange on Green Tablecloth*. And I never had any inkling to share my paintings. Painting was merely my drug. I felt good when I painted.

5

I met Donny in April, about a year after moving to Richmond, Virginia, at the Tapper Tavern. I was never a big drinker; the stuff is poison, but a person needs *something* to do on a Saturday night once in a while.

Most of my time, back then, was spent going out for a sandwich or a cup of coffee, reading books. I used to read all the time. I would also go for walks, usually in parks. Being outside was good for me, and not being around too many people was good for me. I have had some friends over the years, and a couple of boyfriends, but they all receded into the electric fog that is life, existing just outside the circle of my experience. And I paint. Or, I painted. I haven't painted since coming to the hospital, although I make pictures with crayons a lot. My room is covered with them. Maybe I'll paint again soon. I don't feel strange when I paint. When I paint I am not there and the ghost is not there. It is just the painting.

I got a job cleaning offices in Richmond. It was good work for me, not having to have much interaction with people. People think I'm strange, then I feel strange. Cleaning the offices was late at night and I worked only with an older Korean lady who didn't speak any English.

Anyways, I met Donny in the Tavern that night. I was sitting at the bar, my head turned up at an uncomfortable angle, staring at the TV, watching the baseball game. I couldn't give two shits about baseball, but people look at you funny if you're just sitting in a dark bar staring at everyone as they stare at the TV or talk with each other. It makes them uncomfortable. Sometimes they think you're a prostitute.

Donny walked up beside me, but I didn't pay him any attention because it is a rare thing for people to want to interact with me. I probably figured he was just coming to get a better look at the game, or he just happened to come over to that part of the bar. But he didn't sit. He stood there. I turned my head some and my eyes the rest of the way, so I could get a look at this person standing right next to me, to see what he was doing. He caught my glance, he had been looking right at me. I quickly turned back to the TV. I felt heaviness in my belly and light in my head.

"Excuse me, young lady?" How charming.

"Yes," I said, just half turned back at him, looking not at him or the TV.

"Hi, Darlin'. May I sit here?"

I looked. He was big, six foot four, and strong. He was real close to me.

"Oh, sure," I said quickly, then glanced back at the TV.

He sat down in the stool next to me and put up his hand, sorta how Jesus does when he's blessing someone, but Donny wasn't blessing anything. He wanted a beer.

I looked over at him. He *was* big. He was wearing a plaid shirt and an old blue baseball cap with white stitching that said 'North Richmond Tigers.' The hair revealing itself from underneath was grey. Even in a dark bar, lit mostly by the TV, I noticed some discoloration on his skin and a few lines. It's hard to tell with labor men but I was pretty sure he was older than me, maybe fiftyish.

The bartender, barely visible in the darkness behind the bar, part of that darkness, approached wiping his hands on a rag. Donny called the man, 'Fred' and ordered a Budweiser. He turned to me again and he caught me looking at him and he smiled. I made a little smile back.

"My name is Donald." He stuck his hand out.

"I'm Mimi." I put my hand out; we joined hands in between us. My hand was enveloped in his big hand. His was rough and he gave me a little squeeze.

"It's a pleasure, Mimi." He smiled all cunning, one side of his closed mouth stretching more than the other, dipping his head down and a bit to the side in a bow, his eyes locked on mine. Charming. But I saw him for what he really was. I had us both fooled. I sometimes don't know what I know. I don't let myself know. Denial. I could have chosen to end it all right then. But I suppose I wanted something from him.

I tilted my head in a little bow too and gave a demure smile. I have had plenty a man walk away after talking with me for just a few moments. They see I am a torn woman, all torn up and neither here nor there. But sometimes they couldn't see it, or they don't care and sometimes they were just as fucked up as I am and all these types of men will take me home for the night. Sometimes we stay in touch for a week or a month or off and on over the course of a few months. A couple of them I have even called my boyfriend. Nothing like I loved Jared, though. And Donny was the opposite of Jared. He was not the svelte pretty boy who could look right into my heart. He was a beast, a big loud animal. And that turned me on. I knew after just a few moments of talking that he was going to take me home. He couldn't see how torn up I am.

"I haven't seen you here before, Mimi."

"No. I've been here once before, but I'm new to Richmond."

"Is that right? Where'd ya come from?"

"Well, I've lived in lots of places, but before moving here I lived in Poolesville, Maryland."

"I ain't heard of it."

"It's a small town, 'bout forty minutes north of DC."

He nodded slowly, eyes glazed. He was somewhere else. Maybe thinking of the small town he grew up in.

Then he was back.

"Mind if I smoke, Mimi?"

"Go right ahead."

He reached into his shirt pocket and pulled out a pack of Marlboros, of course. Cowboy cigarettes. He flipped the lid and presented the pack to me, eight or ten cigarettes lying straight and obedient in their box.

"No, thank you," I said. He grabbed a cigarette by the butt with the fat tip of his orange-brown stained thumb and middle finger and in a flash it was in his mouth and he was lighting it with a match. He puffed in a few times, fire and light beat like a heart. Smoke gathered at the end of the cigarette and around his mouth. Three puffs: one, two, three. Then he pulled the cigarette away from his mouth and exhaled a strong cloud, like a steam engine.

I was surprisingly calm. Usually a person so close would have me sweating and squirming and talking nonsense and I would need to leave. But Donny didn't scare me. He was so cool and so solid. I don't think he cared much about anything, anything except his country and his family and beer. His teeth were big and stained yellow, I could even see it in the dim bar light. He sat with his big back hunched over, and he held his cigarette and drank his beer like they were natural extensions of himself.

"What had you move to Richmond?" he said.

I am always wary how much to share with people.

"I just needed a change. Poolesville was too small."

He nodded slowly, understanding. He looked at me with a half-mouth smile. "You got work or family here?" he asked.

"I got a job," I said quickly, "How 'bout you? What do you do?"

"I work over at the tobacco plant. Drive a forklift. It ain't glamorous, but it pays the bills. And I'm a native Virginian and tobacco is our history. It's in our blood." He was still smiling. He took a swig of his beer, then looked back at me and gave me a little wink. I gave him a half smile back and shifted in my seat. Then he gave me the wolf look. It was the look that said I was a rabbit and he was hungry. I looked down at the coaster I'd been fidgeting with, swallowed hard.

"Well, I'm glad you decided to come to Richmond." He was speaking less loudly. This was less formal, more private. "I hope you don't mind me saying, but you are quite a pretty lady."

I tried to control the bashful smile, but couldn't. Heat gathered in my chest, ran up to my face and ears.

"Thank you."

He looked at me strong and intentful. I stopped smiling. I almost melted off my stool. Testosterone is a powerful force. He glanced over at my empty glass.

"Can I buy you another drink?" His face so close. Ready to bite.

"Sure."

"Whatcha havin'?"

"Vodka tonic."

He put up his hand up like Jesus again.

"Fred," he called.

The bartender, tall, dark features, emerged from the darkness behind the bar.

"Another vodka tonic for the lady and I'll have another Bud."

"You got it," the bartender said, then he turned and disappeared. Donny chugged what was left of his beer. He put the bottle down with enough force to make a noise, making a statement, 'done', and he let out an 'ahhhh.' Imbecile.

He gave me a smile again and I gave a little smile back, then ran my fingers through my hair, glancing back up at the TV.

Fred came back with our drinks. He looked at me when he set mine down in front of me. My heart jumped. I looked away.

"Thanks, Fred," Donny said. Then he held up his beer, looking at me and said, "To new connections."

I took my drink up.

"To new connections," I said.

We clanked our glasses together and raised them to our mouths. He swigged, I sipped.

* * * * * * * * * * * * *

Making love to Donny that first night was a warm, sweaty spring breeze after a long winter. I hadn't had sex in years and having his big, heavy body on top of mine felt so good. Weight. Matter. I was there. I existed. Big heavy bodies do that; bring me into myself. He smelled like meat and tobacco and beer and salt. He tasted like smoke and salt. It was the earth, dirt, ground. His fat tongue talked to me inside my mouth, and so he was there too. I was there and he was there. I was there with somebody. It was the sweetest feeling I knew, making love to someone. His big hands touched and grabbed all over my body, saying 'Here is your arm, here is your breast, here is your thigh, here you are.' His furry chest, his belly resting in the curve of my back. Him being inside of me, us moving together, making sounds together. It's the best thing I know.

I didn't sleep much that night, but it was heaven. He was warm and heavy in the bed. The mattress sunk down underneath him pulled me in like a black hole. I was bounced like a giddy kid on an inflatable trampoline every time he shifted or turned. He snored like a moose singing.

The next morning I woke up before him. I lay there for a while, listening to him breathing, looking around the strange, bare room taking form in the morning light. After about thirty minutes I decided to get up. I raided his fridge and made him a breakfast of eggs and toast, tater-tots, OJ and coffee. He woke up and entered the kitchen groggy and loud like the beast that he was, and pleased to see food all made for him, made by a woman.

6

Gail, my social worker, is sitting on the bed with me. I like Gail. She is older than me, maybe sixty, with short brown hair, a bob, warm brown eyes magnified behind spectacles. She is short and usually wears jeans and a turtleneck under a sweatshirt, or just the sweatshirt on hot days.

I know why she's here. I can tell from the look on her face that the news is bad. I can also tell from her averting eyes that she knows that I know. I want to scream, but I'm not going to. I want to cry, but I'm not going to do that either. I was hoping for it, my freedom returned. But I'm not getting it. The ghost is upset. What right do they have to keep me prisoner here? My stomach is throbbing.

"Now, Mimi, I spoke with Dr. Jensen and Dr. Westland and it was a very difficult choice for them, but they decided that…"

"They're not letting me out, I know," I interrupt, startling her. She bites her lip and blinks and slowly begins speaking again.

"That's right. They've decided…"

"I know," I interrupt again, "They think I'm dangerous. They think I'm gonna go around bashing people's heads in." Now I can really feel the ghost. Fire. Burn this all away.

"Mimi," Gail says more firmly, "you need to demonstrate that you can control your anger. The nurse's report says that earlier last week before meeting with Dr. Jensen you hit another patient."

"Goddammit!" I cry out, "I was just trying to get him to move. I didn't hurt him."

"You have to restrain yourself from any physical contact like that. Dr. Westland says that you are making progress in anger management." She looks at me quizzically through her circular spectacles, waiting for me to say something, to assure her that things are, indeed, going in the right direction. Like she's my parent or something. My teeth are clenching tight, grinding back and forth. A wild cat pacing in its cage.

"Are you making progress with your anger, Mimi?"

"Well, I haven't killed anybody here yet," I say.

34

Gail puts her hands on her knees and shakes her head. "Mimi, I only want to help you. I'm not trying to patronize you. Your anger is the issue that keeps you here. You need to be honest about it so we can all work together on getting it under control."

I breathe out, and turn away towards the window. My body relaxes some.

"Yes. I'm making progress," I tell her.

"Good." She slaps my thigh with approval. I let out a chuckle. She's a funny little lady. A little, old mouse, with her little bones and little body, her brown rodent eyes, sniffling nose and short brown hair, slightly messy. People can be so animal like. Ethan is a turtle, his round head and little triangular nose pointing down like a beak, the thin line underneath, just a slit, an opening where lips should be. One summer I did a whole series of paintings on Ethan the Turtle. I transposed his face, exaggerating its turtle-like qualities, onto all these turtle bodies. I painted Ethan the Turtle sitting on logs, eating guppies, and one of him trapped in an aquarium looking frightened. He hated those paintings. It's my grandmother's face too. My mom's mom. Turtle genes.

"I have to go now," Gail says, "I have other patients to visit with."

"Okay," I say, still looking at the window, the sunlight so bright through the blinds I can't see out of them. "Thank you."

"You're welcome." She stands by the door, her white sweatshirt has Minnie Mouse on it. She carries a shoulder bag with her folders in it. One of those folders has my name on it. I am somebody's case. A nut case.

"Everything is going to be okay," she assures me.

"I know," I say only half present, thinking about what the papers in my folder say.

"Take your medications," she adds.

"I will."

She opens the door quietly and walks out. The room is empty. This room. My room.

* * * * * * * * * * * * *

Oh man. This chicken is dry and chewy. Probably microwaved. Yuck! And the string beans are watery. And the bread taste like saw dust. Prison food. On the other side of the table, Joan, who always looks like she is about to cry or just finished crying, is eating with vigor. Ann is staring at her with her usual spite. Poor Joan has to room with that little she-devil. Daryl looks like he's enjoying his meal fine enough, with that usual absentminded grin plastered on his face.

"Pretty gross, eh Mimi?" I feel an elbow poking my forearm. It's Teddy.

"Yeah," I exhale.

"I haven't eaten such disgusting food since I went to Spain as a vegetarian years back. I don't think they grow vegetables in Spain. I remember we went to this vegetarian restaurant there and I ordered something that in English was called 'Three Soufflés.' Soufflé, my ass. It was jell-o! I kid you not. Carrot jell-o, spinach jell-o…and I'm forgetting what the red one was. But whatever it was, it was the most disgusting thing I've ever tasted in my entire life. Even worse than this crap." Teddy raises two soggy string beans on his fork, dripping water. "I mean, come on! Did they just open up a few cans and throw the beans in a pot, water and all? Couldn't they have at least strained the beans? Who the hell gets a job as a cook when they clearly don't know anything about cooking?"

"Can you please eat your food with your mouth closed?" Ann yells at Joan, "It's disgusting, all the noises you're making! How am I supposed to eat?"

"I'm not making any noise," Joan whines. She talks strange, high in pitch, full, heavy with effort.

"The hell you're not! Teddy, isn't Joan making all these noises while she's eating with her mouth hanging open like a damn sow or something?"

"Well how am I supposed to eat with you always yelling?"

"I'm not yelling! I'm telling you to stop fucking eating with your mouth open! Have some consideration for other people!"

"I don't think she can help it, Ann," I chime in.

"Help what? I'm not doing anything. I'm just sitting here trying to eat my lunch…"

"Mind your own damn business, Mimi."

"…starts yelling at me and now I don't even want to eat my lunch 'cause…"

"Why do they lock the witches up with the crazies, Mimi?" Daryl says smiling a huge smile, looking at me. "It's just like Salem. Still no place for a witch in this godforsaken world."

What in the hell is he talking about?

"…and even when I try to just go to my room, Ann always comes in when I'm eating and starts yelling at me, and I just loose my appetite, because it gives me a stomach ache when I'm being yelled at. I never yell at my children. Never. John yells at them. He yells at me too. He yells more than Ann. But, you can ask my children, I never yell…"

"Will you shut up!" Ann rasps. "I should have my own room. With my own damn TV!"

"But I'll tell you, Mimi," Teddy says, his eyes glazed looking but not looking at the fake flowers at the center of the table. "The whole world is just a puzzle. It's code. I am supposed to figure it all out. I foresaw it. The endgame. But so far, I've failed. It's not an easy undertaking, trying to solve the Great Enigma that God has put before us. Perhaps I still have time. But time is running out. The world is sinking deeper and deeper into darkness." His sandy blonde hair is starting to give over to grey. His skin is somehow always Florida tan and his eyes are small. He looks at me with those dark, tiny, black orbs and I get goose bumps. "All the sages and profits say the answer lies in love…or compassion or some version thereof. But that is thus far just a word, a concept. It is its application I am struggling with."

"Joan, shut up."

"…there has never been a time when I didn't let you have your way, except when you want to change the channel when

I'm watching TV, and that just isn't fair because I only get one hour every other day to get to pick the..."

"I am going to stab this fork into your head."

Maybe I should call Nigel over. My bones are quivering. Sickness is everywhere.

"Do you know what love is, Mimi? I mean, has anyone ever been able to define it? So how does it exist if we can't even define it? Maybe we just made up the idea of love to make us feel ok about our lives."

"Uh huh." I nod my head in agreement. Chills. He creeps me out.

Teddy puts his hand on my forearm. "Have you ever felt love? Either given or received?"

I'm afraid to say anything. My throat is full.

"Ouch! You pinched me! Ann pinched me!"

I turn to look at Joan, clutching her hand and holding in to her breast. Ann is staring at her, pointing her chin up towards her, lips clamped tight. Daryl turn towards me, his eyes wide, amused. "It's you and me, Mimi, locked up with all these crazies."

I stand up and grab my plate. Teddy takes hold of my wrist. "You've barely touched your food!"

I stare, my mouth hanging open. His eyes like a cobra. A little forked tongue flickers from between his lips.

"I..."

He let's go and chuckles, "Hey, at least it's not Spinach 'soufflé.'"

I take my plate and quickly walk to the bus counter. I set my dish in the tub and walk towards the double doors.

"Hey Mimi, done so soon?" Nigel asks. I walk by, unable to speak or even look at him. The doors never looked so wonderful.

7 →

School let out for summer and I felt like a drowning animal being plucked back onto dry land. Finally I could breathe. I was back in my element. The constraints of bells and walls and the judgmental stares of my peers receded away into temporary oblivion and the freedom I had always known was mine again. Mom suggested that I get a job to help out with finances or at least do volunteer work to keep myself occupied. I kept saying that I would look into it, but by mid-July it became obvious to us all that I would be doing no work, outside of helping around the house.

This was not only my first summer in a stationary home, but also my first as a teenager with the freedom to explore the city and do whatever I pleased. I had always had that freedom, but being in one place that I had come to know, gave me a very long tether. On the road, I didn't like to venture too far from the family, especially after getting lost at concerts a couple times.

Not having friends made this freedom less exciting and trouble invoking than it sounds. My days were spent in Golden Gate Park with a book, or taking random buses around the city to find thrift stores, used book stores and antique stores that sell random old pieces of jewelry, home décor stuff like genie lamps supposedly form Persia and antique scales and letter openers. I sometimes figured I *should* get a job so I could start buying some of those adorable old trinkets that transported me to another time and place just by looking at them. But that buying power would have to wait. I valued freedom over things.

On my random excursions through the Victorian wonderland that is San Francisco, I would sometimes visit Dad at Rebounded Books in North Beach. He was always happy to see me, lifting his head out of a book when he heard the little bell on the door and beam into a huge grin when he saw that it was me entering.

"Well, if it isn't my little cat." That is what he liked to call me. And I think he saw me as very catlike.

"Hi, Dad"

"How's it going?"

"It's okay."

"You having an adventure?"

"Yeah." I could tell he wanted to hug me. I didn't like being hugged anymore.

"Are you reading anything good right now? We have books!" Big goofy grin.

"*The Scarlet Letter*."

"Oh, that *is* a good one; takes a look at the terrible, arbitrary rules a society can make based on fear. And how that's been awful for women."

"Uh huh." My eyes wandered. There were no customers in the store full of dusty old books on old shelves and piled up on the floor.

"Did you see your mom today?" Dad asked.

"Yeah. Her and Ethan were going to some friend's house." He nodded. "Hey, Dad, can I get a couple bucks to go to the Goodwill and get a skirt and a sweater?"

"A sweater?"

"For the fog. I want a light sweater I can carry around with me and throw on when the fog rolls in. It's so cold."

"It is," he said as he dug his hand into his pant pocket, "There's nothing like summer in San Francisco to have you miss summer. Do you know the quote by Twain?"

"Only because you've told me like ten times."

"Well, excuuuse me." Dad said putting his upper lip over the lower one and making his large bug eyes pop out even more than usual, weaving his upper body like a giant real-life jack-in-the-box! I giggled, which brought a smile to his face. Then he stared out the large window and some inner shadow eclipsed the smile, his face melting as all the muscles relaxed and eyes went blank. "I was thinking of all of us hitting the road again for the rest of summer, going south maybe, or up to see Uncle Carl in Bellingham, but your mom convinced me it would be too much to have to start all over from scratch again, looking for a house and a job." He handed me a few crumpled dollars, then looked down at me trying to find his smile again. "Get yourself a bite to eat too."

"Okay." I saw Dad as a dog chained to a stake in a backyard. Mom always said that Dad needed to travel because he had Jewish blood, a natural nomad. I looked hard at my Dad, trying to understand this urge. It was as mysterious as the sea, the stars, where the wind comes from. He would not choose this motionlessness if he didn't think he had to. He was doing it for Ethan and me. But it was too late for me. Here was his fifteen-year-old daughter wandering through her life in complete solitude, without a friend in the world and no map of where she might be going. I didn't even realize how lost from the flock I was. I just knew that I was different, and I was sad.

My two little lights, Jared and painting, carried me through summer. Warm winds fluttered through me, a delightful hunger that was new and strange. I channeled it almost exclusively to fantasies of Jared. I also saw other boys and men with this warmth, but eye contact scared me. What if they saw me, saw that I was a dumb and wild thing, a freak?

My painting improved some, I thought, as summer granted me the time to slow down with it. I hadn't even realized I had been rushing. Ms. Wilkinson said my work evoked extraordinary emotion, that it was almost tactile. I began to see what she was talking about and started attempting new techniques and styles, exploring the medium and myself. My painting helped me to see and say what I could not say. Ethan didn't mind the easel in the middle of our room. Sometimes he would sit on his bed quietly and watch me paint.

Like all things do, the summer of '77 came to an end. As school neared, I felt a tightening in my belly, constricting in my throat, electricity in my jaw.

The Sound of Birds

* * * * * * * * * * * * *

Tenth grade. The first day of school I was quiet and laid low, once again choosing seats in the back of the classrooms, hoping to avoid any unwanted attention, which was basically the only attention I got. The day went by slowly and in the manner I had expected and feared, characterized by disdainful glares, obvious gossip and the occasional object being flicked at me. Seventh period remained in the forefront of my mind the entire day, the peaceful island that awaited me. But when I walked into the large art room at the end of Building II, my relief suddenly turned into surprise and delight. Sitting at the large, square drafting table, the same one we had sat at last spring, was Jared. He looked up and smiled at me. I smiled back nervously. I had no idea how he had been admitted into Painting II, or why he even wanted to be there. I decided that he wanted to have that time together again, and that Ms. Wilkinson was doing me a favor; perhaps she knew he was a muse for me.

I walked over and he patted the circular stool next to him, inviting me to sit down. I obliged, containing the excitement of super-novas, folding it into a neat, calm package so that I could hardly even feel it myself.

"How's it going, Mimi?"

"Good. How are you?"

"I'm good. Did ya have a nice summer?"

"Yeah. It was alright."

"What did you do?"

Oh shit. I tried to think of something interesting. "Mostly just explored the city. You know, going on little adventures and stuff."

"Sounds cool."

"How 'bout you. What did you do?"

"Well mostly worked at my dad's office doing random jobs that nobody else wanted to do. It sort of blew, but I made some money. Other than that, you know, hung out, got stoned, went to a couple shows at the Great American. Went with my family to Connecticut to see my grandparents for a couple weeks. That was alright. I don't know. It was all kinda not very eventful."

"Yeah, mine too."

We both just sat there awkward for a moment.

"Surprised to see me here?" he asked.

I grinned. "Sort of."

"Well I had to pull some strings. I convinced Ms. Wilkinson that I was the genius behind all of your painting, that my unsteady hand, a genetic condition, keeps me from actually being able to execute skillfully all that I see in my mind, but that I tell you what to paint and you use your steady eye and hand to put on canvas what was conceived in my own soul."

I giggled.

"I think she bought it," he added.

"Obviously. You couldn't have gotten in based on your own paintings."

"Ouch. Well, the rose has thorns, does she?"

I gave him a 'beware' look.

"Okay. Lesson learned."

Ms. Wilkinson closed the door and began to address the small class. She welcomed us back, handed out a syllabus and explained what we could expect to be learning in Painting II. I listened intently, but also kept some of my attention on Jared. He doodled and organized his binder with all the new papers he had received in his classes on this first day of school. It was comfortable, us sitting next to each other. Comfort with someone who wasn't my family. This was new and stirring with the energy of two beings entering proximity; chambers opening, lights coming on. A house to be explored. His. Mine.

* * * * * * * * * * * * *

So it came to pass that in tenth grade I had a friend. But an enemy also emerged. Although just about everyone except the nerds and dorks had at it with me, one girl in particular took it upon herself as if it were a career choice to make me miserable. Her name was Francis Capparelli, and although I had seen her parents at school functions and they seemed nice enough, I was sure that Francis was not of this world, but came from the dark, hot depths of Hades, a demon in the form of a teenage girl.

As fate liked to have it with me Francis (her friends called her Franny) was in three of my seven classes. She wasn't the prettiest girl, or even the most popular, but somehow she was able to elevate her own status by pushing down on those around her: standard Newtonian Physics, also known as The Rising Bitch Theory. It is "cool" among teenagers to be mean and sour, and humans in general, it seems, haven't evolved beyond the old idea of a pecking order. So then what of those that don't peck? I had little abrasions all over. My feathers were completely tattered. Craziness, I tell you. This was the first time the thought of suicide actually entered my mind, and I've thought about it from time to time my whole life, although not in any serious way. More like fantasy, just wanting to escape from torment. I would walk to the ocean sometimes after a hard day, like a zombie, hollowed out, and think of just walking right into it, just keep on going right into its icy, black embrace.

Francis' tormenting was relentless and tactics were varied. Everything from name calling to throwing pieces of crumpled paper at me in class. She would bump into me when I stood in front of my locker getting books for my next class. One time my face hit the edge of the locker door and gave me a badly bleeding lip that took weeks to heal.

My hate for her was a cauldron of boiling acid. The ghost lived inside that cauldron, and when the heat turned way up and the acidity almost dissolved this whole world, the ghost arose like vapors and once released was almost impossible to contain. The things it would say. The pictures it would show me in my mind. Truly gruesome. She would swim and fly around in me for hours, me walking home from school mumbling what a fucking bitch Francis was, images of her getting run over by buses, beheaded, falling from the top of a skyscraper.

When these horrific images first came into my mind, I was startled, thinking they were coming from me. I felt wretched guilt even while I was burning in malice. And shame for being such an awful, awful thing. But then I remembered how there was a ghost inside me, and that relieved some of the guilt.

That night at Woodstock, after I had seen that woman on the ground, an albino python, and the ghost came into me, Mom and Dad were getting all our bedding ready in the tent, and I asked them.

"What happened to that lady on the ground?"

"What lady?"

"The one who was white. The one making all those noises." They had to think about it. This was Woodstock; there were a lot of white ladies on the ground making noises.

"The one they were trying to calm down. She was in trouble," I said.

Dad showed a spark of understanding. "Oh, that lady. She's okay. Don't worry." He straightened out the last blanket and sat down cross-legged on a corner of the cozy square he and Mom created. Mom sat on some pillows in the opposite corner. Ethan crawled from next to me over toward her.

"Why was she doing that?"

He hesitated, then gave a look of surrender. He thought Ethan and I should always know the truth, no matter our age, no matter how scary. I learned all about Vietnam and death and poverty when I was very young.

"She had a very bad acid trip," Dad finally said. I thought he meant she fell down and was hurt. I was somehow not satisfied with that answer.

"There was a ghost inside of her," I told my parents. They looked at each other. Ethan in Mom's lap reached with his little hand and tugged on her paisley blouse.

45

"Maybe," my father said. And that was the end of it. Forever. For them. I wanted to tell them the ghost went inside of me, but I was afraid to. I was afraid the speaking it would make it more real. I was afraid of the fear and worry I imagined coming into their eyes.

Ethan slept in between them and I slept on the other side of my father. I tried to give myself as much room as possible. It felt hot and suffocating to sleep in the big pile the three of them enjoyed.

8

Donny courted me like a Southern gentleman. Well, like a redneck trying to have good manners was more like it. He picked me up in his F150, always opened the door for me (that stopped as soon as I moved in with him) and brought me out to dinner at burger joints and The Sea Lobster. I acted like a Southern lady....well, more like pretended to be a redneck gal, and never made my opinions of his life and tastes known in those days. I was happy to have company and I didn't want to ruin it by telling him he was a brute and an ignoramus. I fell into a role, not realizing I might get caught in my own game. I thought I was doing the right thing.

So I was, during that time, a girl from southern Virginia in mannerisms, speech and how I lived my day-to-day life. I was riding shotgun in a pickup truck to bad restaurants, dank bars and nowhere in particular. Donny was sly and charming and I just liked it when he put his big hand on my thigh and squeezed, like he was trying to juice me, like I was something tasty. This life was fakin' it in a way for me, but it was more real than being buried in another book, or staring at the TV from dinnertime till bedtime.

Sometimes Donny would ask me what I wanted to do. He would shoot down some of my ideas, like roller skating, saying we would get ourselves killed, but relented to go paddle boating a couple times. And bowling was something we both enjoyed. One time I even got close to beating him. I started off with a strike that game and rode that good luck or confidence or whatever as far as it would take me. By the fifth frame Donny was actually getting scared. I bowled another strike.

"Oh, man!" he complained, "It's so unfair. This is all luck. Those last two pins just fell over on their own accord."

"Why can't you just admit I am beatin' your butt."

"Cause I've seen you bowl before and you're awful."

"Maybe I'm a bowling shark and I just wanted you to think I was awful."

"If you was a bowling shark we'd have bet on this game. And you would have some form to your throw. You just tiptoe up to the line and release the ball with a prayer."

"Well, if you know what's good for you maybe you should start praying too." I smirked, a pious angel.

"If you know what's good for you you'll wipe that smile off your pretty little face," he grinned, looking like a wolf. Hot. But I couldn't let my defenses down.

"You gonna talk all night or are you gonna bowl?" I said.

He narrowed his eyes. "I'm gonna kick your butt from here to kingdom come." He swaggered up to the approach, his fifteen pound scarlet bowling ball curled up to his chest, his eyes narrowed so that pins was all he could see. He took a breath, then began his four step march, the red ball swinging back, his last two steps increasing momentum. The ball flew by his right leg and he released it, his arm still pointing at it all the way down the lane. The ball made a slight curve, then curved back in and slammed into the pins, all ten pins flew around in a brief tornado of chaos, falling like killed things, sounding like pride, and Donny turned back towards me pumping his fist like he's punching someone in the stomach. "Yeah!" he bellowed.

He swaggered down to the pit where I was sitting on the wide bucket-seat plastic chair, a dance in his swaying body. "Did you see that?"

"No." I said, oblivious and innocent.

"No?" he roared, "How could you miss it. I just schooled all ten of those pins. And you."

"Oh, I wasn't lookin'. I was looking at my shoes. They're sorta cute being red on one side and blue on the other and the number on the back. How much do you think they cost if I wanted to buy 'em?"

"I hope you're joking."

I shook my head, "I love a nice pair of shoes."

"You don't seem like a fashion type." He looked at me suspiciously.

"Well I'm not. But I do like a cute pair of shoes."

"Why don't you march those little shoes up there and try and get your lead back."

"That's a good idea. Stand back." I used my forearm to move him aside, but of course I couldn't move him an inch. I picked up my purple ball, stood on the approach eying down those pins, and sauntered toward the lane, tossing the ball out in front of me. It made a thud as it hit the fake wood floor and slowly spun down, too far to the right. It knocked over only 2 pins. And that was the beginning of the end. Donny, from that point on, increased his lead, frame by frame. He teased me some, but also could see that I was getting frustrated, even with me doing my best to hide it. So he became playful and flirtatious, slapping my butt, saying naughty things about what my consolation prize was going to be.

And so it was. Along with the opportunity to cook him breakfast once again.

* * * * * * * * * * * * *

Donny's house was modest, a two bedroom rambler on the outskirts of town, red brick with a brown front door and shutters. The front yard was a grass square, backyard same thing except with a maple tree in the far right corner. The neighborhood was more of the same: chain-link fences, some with dogs, others with plastic kiddie pools or inflatable baby pools. A few old metal swing sets. Driveways with parked trucks or old Buicks or Chevys, streets lined with crabapple trees, patches of grass browned by the hot Virginia sun, the same shrubs under every house's front windows.

Donny liked his lawn to look nice. He mowed and watered it in the summer, on the weekends. It was a symbol of pride for him and spoke of his character. An American flag was mounted next to the front door.

On the inside, beige carpets covered every square foot except in the bathroom and kitchen. All the furniture was either a relic from the 70s and 80s or characterless Ikea stuff. Décor was sparse. On the coffee table in the living room was a framed picture of his niece and another one of him with his brother, Lyle. And the trophy. The only thing on any of the walls was a framed poster celebrating the Washington Redskin's Super Bowl victory from some years ago.

The living room had a sliding glass door that led out to a concrete slab in the backyard, that Donny called the patio. There were four lawn chairs, a small plastic table with an ashtray and the grill. This is where Donny would sit and drink his beers on hot weekend days and warm evenings after work. I moved in with Donny after just three months, and on the weekends, the only time we were off work simultaneously, I would join him on the patio and sip iced tea or lemonade and watch the blue jays squabble, the sparrows flit around and over the chain-link fence the neighbor children play. And almost invariably one of the parents would emerge from the screen door to yell at one of their brood or all of them. 'This is America,' I thought. Donny and I didn't talk much, and that was a good thing. I could play the quiet card. It's when I say too much that I get myself into trouble. He didn't care about my slumpy posture or the way I averted my eyes, or at least he didn't seem to and he never said anything about it. I imagine I looked like an abused animal, and maybe he thought that was the case, or maybe he just didn't think about it at all. Hanging out on the patio, having sex, dinner together on the weekends, this was basically all we did together. Donny had convinced me to go get my driver's license, and I did, so I began doing the grocery shopping and running errands while Donny watched sports games at home or at friends' houses. I also scrubbed and organized everything. I can be a little obsessive about how neat and organized a place is…except when the ghost is active. She doesn't care. She is a mess. To me what Donny and I had was not a romantic relationship; it was an arrangement, a trade. We both abated, to some degree, the loneliness of too much solitude and gained the availability sex. I got security. I didn't want to end up homeless again. Donny got cooking and cleaning and an errands girl.

When late summer came I saw even less of Donny. The Richmond County Softball League had a fall season because many of the guys couldn't wait until spring to play again. Donny loved his softball. He told me all about it one day when we were out on the patio. I had never seen him so impassioned about anything.

"I've been playing with the league for fifteen years," he told me. "I used to play baseball when I was young, but they don't have baseball leagues for adults. Just softball. But I love softball." He rambled on and on. I had my sunglasses on so he couldn't tell I was only half listening. I was more interested in the three crows sitting in the tall pine tree in the neighbors' yard, watching the three children play with a hose, spraying each other, shrieking their little heads off. Suddenly a loud 'whack' scared the crows and they flew off. That sound was the screen door slamming shut due to a strong spring that was probably new. The children's mother, wearing a peach colored dress and white apron, stood on the landing of the concrete steps leading up to the back door. She had her fists on her hips.

"Tommy! Quit spraying your sister with that hose!"

"But she likes it, Mommy," a little voice responded.

"If she likes it so much then why is she screaming like that?"

Tommy was silent. Donny was still talking.

"I play second base now, 'cause my gun just isn't what it was." He kept on yammering, the neighbor lady kept on yelling at poor little Tommy, the sounds of lawnmowers and weed-whackers and a jet plane filled the air. Others would call this a quiet Sunday afternoon, but it was not quiet and it stirred the ghost in me. My head was buzzing with all the commotion. My vision became unfocused. I was drowning in it. I interrupted Donny's monologue:

"Why is she yelling at her kids like that?" I asked. He looked stunned, caught off guard, tackled from left field. His mouth hung down.

"I guess 'cause they're misbehavin'," he finally answered in an aggravated tone. "And her name is Sharon. You should go introduce yourself, Mimi. You've been living here for almost two months."

"I don't think it's necessary," I said, "I don't think we have anything in common."

"It don't matter, it's courtesy. What's wrong with you?"

"Nothing's wrong. I just don't feel like pretending. I don't want to have to wave and shout 'Hi, Sharon,' with a big old fake grin every time we're in our backyards at the same time. Or worse yet, she'll realize I'm not interested in being her friend and she'll start despising me."

"That's ridiculous. Sharon and Paul are good neighbors and I don't want anything to ruin our good relations. Next weekend we're gonna go over and introduce you." He just wants to show me off, I thought. But I didn't say anything. I didn't want to argue. Sharon had gone inside and the crows, those dark sentinels, were back in the pine.

"Two years ago my team won the tournament. We won nine to seven in the championship game and I had three RBIs, so you could say that I won the game for us."

I smiled flatly behind my sunglasses.

51

9 ——→

I am sitting on the olive green couch watching Judge Judy. She cracks me up, always snapping at everyone like the whole world is full of bumbling idiots, and she, the queen of the land, is the only person with any wits and has to set things straight. She loves being the boss. Alpha wolf.

I don't read as much these days. I seem to have lost my ability to focus since I lost my head. I read simple things occasionally like *The Alchemist* and *Their Eyes Were Watching God*.

Daryl is sitting next to me, staring at the TV with a big grin. Is he watching Judge Judy or smiling about something else? If he can't hear, what's he so entertained by? The crinkles on her brow when she is yelling at someone through her thin red lips, telling them how it is and how stupid they are and how they better shape up? He looks at me, still smiling. I don't smile back. He is a nice man. A nice, nice man. But he's a liar, a fake, and that just rubs me the wrong way. He dips his head in a gesture of 'How do you do?' I press my lips together and glare at him, shaking my head.

He shakes his head and chuckles, his belly bouncing.

"Mimi Rizner, you somethin' else."

I fold my arms over my chest.

"How'd you lose your hearing Daryl?" I ask, bitter mocking.

"What?" he says, the smile leaving his face as he leans in so he can maybe hear me or read my lips.

"Real funny, Daryl," I say.

"What's funny?"

"You are Mr. Funny-head."

"Okay," he says, smiling and shaking his head some more as he turns back to the TV.

"You know, Daryl, I can see right through your whole charade. You do know that, don't you?"

He turns and looks at me sternly. "Did you say something?" The capillaries in his yellow eyes buzz like electricity.

I swallow hard. "I said I can see through your charade. I know you're not def."

"Mimi," he leans in, his breath like coffee and vinegar, "you don't know nothin'. You so lost in yo'own spatterin' mind, you think you got it all figured out, but that ain't the voice of wisdom going off in yo head, it's the clamorin' of judgment."

What?

How dare he.

"Look, Mimi," his face softens, "I like you. You got a lotta potential. But give it a break sometimes." He exhales through his nose. Quiet. Except for the TV. Daryl smiles and turns back to the watch the show. A cool breeze on the side of my face. I look to the far wall. All the windows are closed, of course. That was strange.

I rotate to face the TV again. Judge Judy is almost over. I wish Nigel was here; I want to talk or play poker. But Hillary is on duty right now. She'll play cards, but she's not good company.

I'll draw.

I get up from the couch and walk past Hillary sitting at the little wood table. She has curly blond hair that she usually wears in a ponytail, green eyes and bright peachy skin. She always has eyeliner on, and lip-gloss, and purple eye shadow to accentuate her green eyes. I don't know who she's trying to look pretty for around here.

"Where you going, Mimi?" she says loudly, smiling.

I stop. "I'm going to my room to get my crayons."

"Okay. Hurry up. You don't want to miss Days of Our Lives." She beams like a proud pre-school teacher. I must be fifteen years older than her, but she talks loud and simply to me on account of me being a patient here. It's like she thinks we are a bunch of autistic five-year-olds. Totally patronizing, but I've learned to just accept it.

I walk down the corridor looking at each door as I pass by, whispering the names of who lives on the other side.

Joan and Ann

Barbara and Holly

Janitorial closet

Nell and Latisha

Val…

Val's door is open. I stop and peer in. She is sitting on her bead, filing her nails. She notices me standing there. She looks back down to her nails. "Hi, Mimi."

"Hi, Val."

Val is young. Twenty-three, I think. She is pale, almost translucent, and has dark brown hair that is black from her ears down because she used to dye it before she came here. Her nails are painted black and she is awful thin. I try to encourage her to eat more. She picks at food like eating is not a natural thing to do, like her body doesn't really want it. I can't imagine never being hungry. I'm no fatty, but I have a healthy appetite.

"You want to color with me?" I ask.

"Sure," she says looking up. Whenever she looks me in the eyes, it always looks like her eyes are saying 'Please, help me.'

"Okay, I'm gonna go grab the crayons. I'll be right back."

I walk briskly the twenty or so feet to my room. I have no roommate. They don't fully trust me here.

I head over to my desk, under the window, next to my bed. I open a drawer and grab my big box of sixty-four crayons and about ten pieces of computer paper. I wish I could paint, but they won't let me. Maybe they're afraid I'll empty a tube of paint down my throat, chocking myself to death, or that I'll poke someone's eye out with a paintbrush. But I'm not looking to off myself. And I've only been violent that one time. I turn swiftly and shuffle back to Val's room.

"Ready?" I say.

"Yeah." She always seems like she isn't fully there and talks sorta breathy and moaning, like everything is stupid. She puts the nail file into the top drawer of her desk, scoots off the bed and onto her feet. She walks zombie-like towards me, feet dragging, shoulders hunched up towards her ears. She looks at me, her dark irises surrounded by yellowed whites, surrounded by dark circles, surrounded by the white of her face. Concentric circles. A bull's-eye. I would paint her, but she probably wouldn't like what she saw – what I saw – a sickly waif. White, black and lavender, her colors. And a little yellow. I smile at her. Her eyes close half way and one side of her mouth spreads about a centimeter to the side. That's her attempt to smile back.

We walk down the corridor side by side. Her skinny legs in tight black jeans move unsteadily, like the whole twig tower of her could just collapse any second. I don't know how much of her sluggishness is due to medication and how much is due to the heavy way she holds the world. We reach the little wood table off to the side of the common room. Hillary is still sitting there.

"Oh good, you're back," she says, "Oh! And you brought Val with you. That's great!"

We are silent. Val is a raven, unamused. She dislikes Hillary more than Linda.

"Well, sit down already," Hillary says.

"We work better in private," Val says.

"Oh, alright." Hillary gets up. "Y'all can have the table. I'll go sit next to Daryl on the couch. He ain't such a sourpuss." She looks at us.

Val and I are silent.

I give her a sardonic smile. Hillary's face droops, then she turns and walks over to the couch.

Val and I sit down. I put the paper in the middle of the table and set the box of crayons next to it. Val takes a sheet of paper and sets it in front of her. I do the same. Val pulls back the lid of the crayon box and those good little soldiers of varying degrees of pointiness and roundedness are all standing up straight, begging to be used, to be realized as they're spread across the paper. Val grabs the gold crayon and starts making long back and forth strokes across the bottom of her paper, filling it all in, solid gold.

55

I hover my hand above the pointy and round heads. Some of them say 'Pick me! Pick me!' but I don't know what I want to draw. I look inside for images. I see plants. Marijuana plants. I see bats. The Washington Monument. My stomach starts to twist. I don't want this unsteadiness right now, the watery, murky emotions.

"Aren't you going to draw something?" Val mumbles.

"I don't know what to make."

"How 'bout a portrait?" Val loves my portraits.

I hear Hillary laugh.

A sign. I will draw Hillary. I reach in the box and pull out all the pinks, peach, orange-yellow, brick red, and violet for shading. I grab a couple yellows and sienna for her hair.

I start with her oval face. She's pretty. She was probably popular in high school, a cheerleader. Probably a sorority girl in college. This is an odd place for a cheerleader to end up. Maybe she thinks she's cheering us back to sanity.

I draw her eyes, making them rounder and larger than they actually are. I want to exaggerate her springy disposition. I will have her curly hair coil out in all directions, not contained by the scrunchie as it usually is. She wants to be a wild girl. She wants to dance on tables topless. I chuckle. After this picture I will make an action picture of her dancing on a table. I'll make a little Hillary series.

"Mimi," Val says suddenly, "How come you're in here?"

"I told you, Val, I hurt somebody."

"Who? Who did you hurt?" She always speaks slow, like a real southern girl.

"A man. Someone I was living with."

"Your boyfriend?"

"I'm not a teenager, Val. I don't have boyfriends. But, yes, we were together...sort of."

Val looks at me all serious, like a teenage girl trying to extract a secret from her best friend.

"What did you do to him, Mimi?" she asks softly.

"I don't want to talk about it. I can't even think about it. My head is already buzzing. Now what's that you're drawing?"

She takes a moment, her half-dead-person eyes looking for something in me. I don't know what. I've got nothing for her. I raise my eyebrows. She looks down at her artwork.

"Oh. This is me on the yellow brick road. Except I'm not on my way to the Emerald Tower, pretty as it may be. I'm going to find the Wicked Witch of the West. I want to find out what makes her tick. And I'm hoping she'll teach me to fly on her broom."

Her picture is quite good. The figure is well proportioned. The trees lining her golden road are alive with a whimsical movement flowing up their trunks, dancing through their bare limbs.

"I like it," I tell her.

"Thanks," she says, but intoned more like 'whatever.' She is looking down at the table. "Did I ever tell you how I got in here, Mimi?"

"Yes. You tried to kill yourself."

She doesn't speak for a moment. I hear the TV commercials. So loud. Like I can buy your fucking Tide anyways!

"My step dad did things to me."

"I know Val. You told me. I'm sorry. He can't hurt you now."

She stays quiet, head hanging down, her face almost touching her bony chest.

"What's it all for?" she asks, "No one seems to know. Do you know, Mimi?" She pulls her head up and looks at me, waiting for me to turn into some fount of wisdom. But I hate that question. It belongs to the realm of the dead.

"I think we just need to make it what we can. Find our pleasures." I tell her. I want to say love, and to express our higher nature, but I'm not sure I fully believe that. I have tried and I can't seem to find my higher nature beyond the webby tangle of my own questions. She lowers her head again. Do I tell her what I think she wants to hear, or what sounds soothing, or what I really feel? "You know, Val, somehow I think it's all worth something. I have memories that remind me of something about life, that it is profoundly good at its core, even though I usually can't touch it anymore. I always hope I will one day. And if not, and if it's not even true, than I have the mess that I have and that's what I got."

"I think it's all meaningless," She mutters.

What else can I say?

I take a breath.

I extend my hand and place it on the meatless talon that is her hand.

She takes a labored breath, quick and strong.

She looks up and pulls her lips over to one side about a centimeter, a smile. She pulls her hand away and starts drawing a grey-green castle in the background of her picture.

10 ➤

Tenth grade went on slowly. I endured my social torment and focused hard on my studies. I resolved that I would not be in special education classes for my last two years of high school. I realized that I was no dummy and learned quickly the grammar, basic math and algebra I needed to catch up with my peers.

Jared's light was ever growing in warmth and proximity, although seventh period was all I got of him. He would smile and give a subtle wave of his hand or mouth 'hi' as we passed in the hallway, but we never stopped to talk with each other. He was of a different caste than I was. One time, however, he did stop. Francis was standing in front of me, right in my face, not letting me go to my next class, telling me how disgusting I was. Out of the corner of my eye I saw Jared walking towards us slowly, noticing what was happening. I tried to say 'help' with my eyes. He approached with his relaxed, friendly grin.

"What's up, Franny?"

"Not much. Just giving Rizner a piece of my mind."

"Huh. Sounds boring. Wanna walk me to Biology?"

She looked again at the revolting creature in front of her.

"Sure," she said, turning away slowly so I could get a good dose of the spite in her eyes. They walked off, arm-in-arm, and I resumed breathing.

My paintings continued to develop. We began to focus on landscapes, bringing in photographs to replicate and sometimes we would set up our easels on the school lawn to paint the semi-urban landscape around our school campus. That year I painted my favorite piece I ever made in high school, and perhaps ever. It is of a lady in a grassy field. She is wearing a simple beige dress, walking away from the viewer, towards the horizon in an endless field of waist high grass. It is late afternoon in late summer; the light is rich, golden, fulfilled. The grass is waning yellow after having dropped its seeds. The chestnut-brown haired woman can see the Byzantium purple silhouette of mountains off in the distance, under clouds rendered bright liquid gold by the low sun. Light this bright always looks liquid. And it is very ancient, the light of the first day mentioned in Genesis. It is the light that comes before all things, before matter, and it knows all the eons and all that exists within them.

I called this piece *Woman in a Field*, but I had a secret name for it: *Death*. And I liked to imagine my own death just like this, serene and beautiful, witnessed by the liquid light. And mysterious. Who knows what lies beyond those mountains.

"She seems lost, but okay," Jared said, "Maybe even hopeful."

I nodded as I listened.

He squinted like a critic from the *New York Times*.

"I think she's looking for someone," he continued.

I just remained silent. I liked hearing his interpretations of my work. And we both had a great time interpreting his work.

59

"It's a band of munchkins and magic squirrels hunting for Dorothy in Kansas," I said of one of his pieces called *The Cavalry*, both of us laughing.

"No, it's children of an alien race who teleport themselves to Earth, without their parents knowing, so they can ride stolen horses. The owner's dogs are chasing the little bastards." We both cracked up. I enjoyed these games of interpreting his paintings almost as much as I enjoyed painting itself.

"It's what *really* happened during the New York blackout."

"It's Han Solo and Chewbacca and their friends as kids playing on their home planet, known as Splatter."

* * * * * * * * * * * * * *

Our first floor flat was rather bare, and felt old and dusty. When we first sold Bertha and moved in, the two-bedroom living quarters felt huge to me, but by the middle of tenth grade, being an adolescent girl, I needed to not be sharing a bedroom with my little brother, endearing as he was. And it seemed as though every footstep, every word spoken, every cabinet door closing in that small flat was occurring right next to me. Sitting alone in my room, reading a book, I felt intruded upon by the conversations happening in the kitchen of which I could hear every word and outburst of laughter and talk of all sorts of weird things like aliens and crystals and sex and politics. No matter how hard I tried I just couldn't tune it out. And I became uncomfortable with Mom and Dad's business once I understood that it was illegal and basically frowned upon. The few times I complained Mom told me I was a grouchy hermit and that I needed to learn some tolerance. I tried. I really did. But they didn't make it any easier. Especially Mom. She was so loud.

Velocity was food to Dad. After only a year-and-a-half of being "settled," Dad was starving. He seemed to me to have become a completely different person. The exuberance that had defined him had been replaced by a sluggishness. He always complained of being tired. His once bulging eyes now remained half hidden behind pink eyelids. His body hunched, almost totally into itself like a roly-poly, when he sat at the kitchen table with Mom separating larger quantities of pot into dime bags and eighths. Perhaps Dad's waning enthusiasm is what brought on my parents sudden dabbling with MDMA. I was no longer used to them in such altered states, they hadn't done psychedelics since we settled is San Francisco, and it made me recoil. They would blast music like funk or classical and lay on each other on the couch, Mom running her fingers through Dad's hair, both of them making moaning noises and laughing with open throats like they were going to start drooling, Mom doing her laughing that becomes shrieking. They would end up in their bedroom having sex. Ethan and I could hear every moan and groan and scream and slap and laugh and the things they were saying to each other. Ethan didn't seem to mind too much. He would sit there grinning in amusement and even giggling when mom would scream or say something absurd, quickly cupping his hand over his mouth so they wouldn't hear him. I, on the other hand, didn't appreciate being invited into what I thought should be their own private domain. My body reacted to it, and that made me uncomfortable. The only good thing about it all was that it was nice to see my father smiling again, which he was when they were high on the stuff.

One rainy Saturday afternoon in February, Mom and Dad were high as kites on their new chemical candy. They were playing some weird game where they got in opposite corners of the room and slowly crawled toward each other. They would meet in the middle of the room, still on hands and knees, and kiss. They called the game "Anticipation" and as Mom looked at Dad moving so slowly towards her, eyeing her with passionate hunger, she would scream with rapturous torment. By then, I knew that other people's parents didn't do this sort of thing. Other people's parents worked in offices and for fun they went out for dinner or to a museum or a cocktail party.

Only *my* parents got high and crawled around on the floor like oversexed preschoolers.

"Let's go," I said to Ethan. He looked at me with surprise. "Where?"

I thought for a second. "Let's go get hot cocoa."

Ethan looked unsure. He was so adorable with his round face, his light coloring, his strawberry blonde hair.

"Alright," he decided, realizing he would not be able to join in the games Mom and Dad would be playing that afternoon.

We put on our coats and hats.

"Dad, can I have a few dollars? Ethan and I are going out for cocoa." I probably didn't need to raise my voice. They weren't that far gone yet.

"Sure," he smiled, looking up from his quadrupedal position, "My wallet is on the counter."

I took the money, found my umbrella and Ethan and I walked out.

"Bye," we called behind us.

"Have fun," they called back.

It was barely raining, but I decided to use the umbrella anyways. My coat was wool and I didn't like the way it smelled when it got wet. Ethan stayed close to me, holding my other hand. I loved it when we held hands. I liked being a big sister. I liked being *his* big sister.

"You're mad, aren't you?" he asked, "That's why you wanted to leave."

"I'm not mad. I just don't feel comfortable being around them when they're high."

"You looked mad."

"Well, maybe I was frustrated."

"Should we make dinner tonight?"

"Probably. I doubt they'll be in the mood."

"Wanna make pizza on English muffins?"

"Yeah!" I pumped his hand with excitement. He put a little skip in his step.

We walked on for several blocks.

"We can get cocoa here," Ethan said as we walked by a little diner.

"I like going to this café on Haight. They use real cocoa, so it's not too sweet."

"I like it sweet."

"Trust me, you'll like this too. And it's really neat in there. All these college kids are hanging out. I like to watch them."

"Do you have a crush?"

I did. But not on any of the college kids.

"No. They're just hip. They're all reading fat books and wearing cardigans and funky patterned shirts. You'll see."

We got to the café and I let go of Ethan's hand. We were too old for that in public. He didn't take offense because I needed to close and shake out the umbrella. We walked in and Ethan took a look around this dimly lit den full of armchairs and old end tables and big wood tables surrounded by rickety chairs. Everything was brown and orange with some red and yellow. On some nights there was live music there, usually just a guy or girl with a guitar singing folk standards and some originals.

I glided over to the counter where the super cool handsome guy with sideburns and brown hair to his shoulders and a mustard colored sweater looked at me in his 'ain't life awesome' manner, smiling, bobbing his head to some imaginary beat. I smiled back.

"How can I help you two fine young people?" He smiled at Ethan, totally stoked! Ethan smiled back, delighted by the familiar friendliness. This guy was like so many young men we met on the road, at a show.

"Two hot chocolates, please." I said like I was ordering the finest caviar.

"Right on." He turned to make our drinks, put them on the counter and said, "A dollar, fifty." I reached into the coat pocket and pulled out the five dollar bill I took from Dad's wallet, smoothed it out a bit in my hands, and held it out for him. He took it, punched some buttons on his register, causing the drawer to open and handed me three singles and two quarters back. I slid one of the dollars into the glass jar next to the register for tips.

"Why thank you, little lady," he said almost cowboy-like.

"Right on," I responded, trying to sound hip myself, bobbing my head just a little.

Ethan was looking at me like, 'Who are you? Why are you acting this way?' I gave him an awkward little smile, then handed him his cocoa.

"Come on, let's go sit on the couch."

We sat there on the couch, the brown upholstery made of thick yarn, sipping our cocoas, Ethan's legs not quite touching the ground. He was not at all interested in this warm den-like environment that I likened to some nest or hive ruled over by the Queen of Cool. Nor did he stare, like I did, at all the young men and women, heads buried in books, taking notes or talking casually about politics, current events and music, the low buzz sometimes spiked with a sudden outburst of laughter.

Suddenly the door flew open with more energy than usual and in flew, I could not believe my eyes, Jared. The weather outside had become more intense, rain shooting about like bullets in the blasting wind, shifting its course every few seconds and delivering this new presence. He glided right up to counter and unfazed by the young man's cool mystique ordered his drink. A bubble was trying to arise in me, to run up my throat and escape my mouth, and in that bubble contained the word "Jared." But I was nervous. I closed my esophagus at its base. What if it made him uncomfortable to see me in public? What if he chose to ignore me? I sat up straight, staring at him, eager, a bubble in my throat. I reached out with my eyes instead. He paid for his drink and made for the door. I sat up straighter, the bubble almost escaping from the inertia of my movement. He stopped suddenly. He turned around and walked back to the counter, putting some coins in the tip jar. I heard him say, 'Thanks.' I didn't hear the cool cat say it too, but he nodded his head, smiling in approval. Jared turned unconsciously, scanning the room. Our eyes met. His friendly blue eyes. I smiled shyly. He was surprised. Then excited. He floated over to me with a big grin.

"Hey, Mimi," he said.

"Hi, Jared."

"What's up?"

"Oh, not much. We were bored, so we decided to come out and get some cocoa."

He looked over to Ethan. "Aren't you going to introduce me to your son?"

Ethan giggled. I felt a little embarrassed. I always forget the whole introduction thing.

"This is Ethan, my little brother."

"Hi, Ethan. I'm Jared."

"Hi."

Jared reached his hand out and Ethan met it for a shake. I could tell Ethan was charmed, his face glowing shyly as he looked up at this pretty boy smiling at him. I guess Jared had an effect on all the Rizners.

"Mind if I sit?"

The question sounded strange to me. I shook my head slowly, unsure if I was answering correctly. He sat in the wooden chair next to me and we made small talk about school and different people and Movies. He also asked Ethan about school and his life, making sure he felt included.

"What are you doing for dinner?" he asked me.

"I don't know," I said.

"Yes you do," Ethan interrupted, "*We're* making dinner."

I swallowed, "Oh yeah."

"Oh, okay," Jared said, "I thought maybe we could go grab some pizza."

"We can!" I said with unchecked excitement. I quickly deflated myself trying to conceal my feelings.

"What?" Ethan looked at me like I was talking in Chinese. He wasn't used to me being dishonest or breaking plans with him.

"You can make dinner without me. Just put some sauce and cheese on the English muffins, preheat the oven to 350 and cook them on a baking sheet for ten minutes."

"But I don't want to…"

"Ethan, come on. I want to get pizza with Jared."

"Well, me too." He was serious. He wanted to come.

"Someone needs to cook for Mom and Dad."

"Your parents make you cook for them?" Jared asked.

Ethan opened his mouth to speak.

"They're sick," I said quickly. Ethan looked at me like I was speaking Chinese again, crinkling his forehead. Jared looked at both of us like something fishy was going on. I tried to look innocent and naïve.

We all sat there with those looks.

Finally I spoke, putting my hand on Ethan's shoulder. "Can you handle it so I can go have pizza with my friend? You go out with your friends all the time."

He looked down at his shoes.

"Please?"

"Fine," he relented.

I fought the smile muscles in my face. "We'll walk you home," I said.

"Let me finish my coffee," Jared said, "Maybe by then the rain will have died down again."

"You drink coffee?" I asked, surprised and a little awed.

"Yeah," he said with a sexy, devilish smile, "It taste so good with cream and sugar. Have you ever had coffee ice cream? Well it tastes like that. And I get a total buzz from it. I feel like I could run through walls."

I smirked uncomfortably, hiding all the warmth I was feeling inside me. Ethan perked up. It's no wonder both of us eventually became coffee addicts with *that* sales pitch.

The weather never calmed. We walked back to my house through the rain and driving wind which tried to yank the umbrella from my hand, turned it inside out and spun me around with it all the way home. Ethan thought it was hysterical and Jared chuckled too. They fared better than me without umbrellas. By the time we got home, I decided to take off the wool coat and change into a rain slicker. Jared didn't get past the entryway; if it wasn't raining so hard he wouldn't have gotten in the door. I was terrified of him encountering the folks, especially high. Luckily, all the gods must have heard my silent, desperate pleas as we approached the house because they were in their room like I had begged for. Ethan was sad to not be joining us, but this was my time. The truth was Mom and Dad could have had something simple like granola when they came down, or even made the pizzas themselves. I was glad Ethan didn't think of that.

Jared and I shouldered our way through the wind to Luca's Pizza. Most of the kids in our school went to the pizzerias on Haight Street. Maybe that is why Jared chose Luca's. What he said was that Luca's has awesome pizza, an undiscovered gem.

We ordered at the counter. I got two slices of mushroom (I always got mushroom). Jared probably got onion and garlic or pepperoni. We sat and talked about painting and painting class and how quirky Ms. Wilkinson is, the big glasses she wears and how she giggles at her little puns. He asked me why I never go to the roller rink and I made some excuse about being afraid to fall and break my head open.

He looked at me intently.

"You know what I like about you, Mimi?"

No. Tell me.

"You're smart. Not smart like academic smart, just smart. Everyone at school seems so naïve, so immature."

I sat there with what he said like it was an object. I held it. Looked at it. Let it come inside me. I sipped my Fresca through a straw. He dipped a French fry into a puddle of ketchup and chomped it down to his fingers, shoving the end into his mouth. I wanted to tell him that I not only liked him, but that I loved him, that I was in bliss that we were hanging out together. It was as if fantasy actually does come to life. But I knew better than to say all that. That much I had learned about social convention; don't say everything you feel. Play it cool.

67

"Thanks. You're smart too."

He gave a wry smile.

We talked more about school and our families. He was so intrigued about my life pre-high school. I didn't tell him much. There is so much to tell about those years on the road. The menagerie of circus-like characters who came in and out of our lives, confrontations at small town diners, acid trips, weeks spent on the beaches of Baja. Adventures within adventures curled up within the seashell of memory, seemingly now only a dream of another realm. I told him a couple good anecdotes, to whet the appetite of his interest. His jaw hung down as I drew out the tale of when four year old Ethan unknowingly ate two whole ganja cookies, and spent the next two days thinking he was a cat, walking around on all fours, meowing, rubbing up against people's shins. Mom and Dad were seriously concerned on the second day when there was still no recognizable trace of their son behind the kitty.

He told me a little about his younger years, summer camp, his family, but kept dismissing everything as boring. I thought it all sounded cozy.

The rain had stopped. It had gotten dark as soon as we sat down to eat. We were there for a long time. Eventually Jared walked me home. We climbed the stairs and stood on the stoop leading to the two flats of my building. I wasn't sure what was next. A kiss? No.

"Alright," he said touching my arm briefly.

I decided to be brave.

"There is something else I like about you," I breathed out quickly, "You're really nice." I must have looked so earnest, even desperate. He just smiled kindly.

"Aw, thanks." He touched his hand to my arm again, like a pal. "Alright, well, goodnight."

"Goodnight," I said, sad that this was ending.

"See ya at school."

"Okay."

And with that he turned and left. I walked slowly up the stairs, holding the rail, which I never did. I opened the door and walked into my flat with its smell of wood and emptiness and reefer and musk. The lights were low. Ethan was in the living room working on a jigsaw puzzle, waiting up for me. Mom and Dad were in their room. Ethan was happy to have me home. He loved the family. His love was like a glue. It was a safe feeling, for him, to have the whole family together. It's what he was used to. When I ended up leaving San Francisco, Ethan was distraught. He thought I was breaking up the family. I suppose I did.

The next day my parents drilled me playfully with questions. Who was he? Was he my boyfriend? Did we kiss?

Mom was thoroughly entertained. I was frustrated, mostly because the answers were not what I wished they were. Dad played along too, but he had crashed pretty hard from the MDMA and his tiredness was back, a cloud, a dark visitor, perhaps a ghost of his own.

11 ➤

It's strange how people do things they know are no good for them, things they know are going to end in a bad way. Like heroin, or drinking too much in a night, or eating that third piece of dessert. That's how it was with Donny. Somewhere in me I knew all along that we were not a good match. I knew that he was boorish and our beliefs were conflicted. And I knew that deep underneath that cool exterior lay a reservoir of anger. I knew all of this and yet I kept on moving things forward with him. Maybe it was mostly the sex, but it was also companionship. A person needs these things. A person thinks too much when they are all alone. I had been alone for a very long time and even though I was scared of living with someone, I was more scared of the deep pit of loneliness I

69

have fallen into repeatedly in my life. So I didn't admit to myself that I knew what I knew about Donny. I'll never lie to myself like that again. Not that I'll get the chance. Nobody wants broken things.

He wanted things to work. At his age having a woman around to cook and clean and have sex with was a true blessing, easing his life substantially. He had had several relationships since his wife left him ten years before I showed up, but I don't know anything about these women or what happened with his wife. Donny is not one to talk about his personal life or his feelings.

So generally, in the beginning, he was good to me. He worked days and I worked nights so we only saw each other on the weekends, really, and for about an hour between him being home *from* work and me leaving *for* work. We would usually eat dinner together. Sometimes he'd wake me up for sex in the mornings, only an hour or so after I had fallen asleep. He was good humored and liked to call me Mimi the Beaver Lady on account of my overbite, and we would laugh. Heaven knows my parents were not the type to strap braces on their kids' teeth. That would be like putting up the proverbial white picket fence right in our own mouths. I teased Donny back calling him Donny the Doughnut Eater on account of his belly. But we didn't really laugh at that. Maybe it was my delivery.

I knew that the two of us didn't have much in common, that we weren't actually connecting. But maybe all his needs were being met and it was just me feeling that. Donny never read and he was quite conservative politically. He didn't like to hear me talk about what was on my mind much. He would start to busy himself or make some grunting noise and I knew that that was his signal that he was done listening to me. Sometimes he would say things like, "Mimi, you are a strange bird," or "I'm not in the mood to hear your kook talk." That was in the beginning. Towards the end he had a harsher way of expressing how he felt about me. "Crazy bitch!" "Fucking she-devil!"

Early on, I managed to feign fragility and sickliness for my erratic behavior. I had lived with Donny a little over two months before my birthday rolled around. He took me out to dinner that night. It was his idea of a 'nice dinner.' The Rib Shack. We got dressed up. He wore khakis, a white shirt and a navy blue blazer that he probably owned for twenty years. He didn't put on his baseball cap, which he always wore. I had bought myself a birthday present the previous day, the first dress I'd owned in years and still my only one, knee length, sky blue with silver and turquoise flowers all over it, a few opalescent buttons from the middle of the chest up to the collar. Size 6 like I've always been. Putting it on, I felt strange, trying to doll up. I spent some time in front of the mirror, bushing my hair more than I usually care to, and put a silver barrette over my left ear.

As we drove down West Broad Street in his pick-up, heading into town, I wondered what reality I was living in. Who was I, a forty-something cleaning lady, sitting in a pick-up truck with my forklift driving man, in Richmond Virginia? Why did I let this happen? I felt a heaviness in the pit of my stomach that didn't leave me all night. I realized I was in the wrong life, like wearing somebody else's clothes. But where was *my* life? Donny put his hand on my thigh and looked at me. I turned to him and forced a smile that I'm sure looked condescending; my lips didn't even part. But Donny couldn't read between lines. Heck, Donny could hardly read at all! I faced forward again and watched as the traffic lights and little brick strip malls increased in frequency. I put my hand on Donny's hand, the one resting on my thigh, because I felt like I should. If I didn't, a space would have opened up, a distance that would have been recognized even by Donny. Most of me was not there, with my hand. It was just flesh, not a point of connection. But it was enough for Donny.

We parked in the large parking lot of the Rib Shack, full of pick-up trucks, little Chevys and Fords and a few long, shiny Cadillacs. As we walked to the entrance, Donny put his big hand around my upper arm. I had sort of liked it when he did

71

things like that before. It had been sexy. But on this night it felt different. It hurt. And I felt like I was being imposed upon. I started feeling lightheaded and I could feel the ghost stirring inside me, hot and wanting to push Donny away. We walked in and a bubbly blonde hostess wearing all black greeted us, a bubblegum pink smile and chirp of 'Hi!' If Dad could have seen me there he would have rolled over in his grave.

"There's two of us," Donny said.

"Do you have a reservation?" she asked.

"No." Donny said, looking a little embarrassed.

"Okay, well, no problem, we have a few tables open," she reassured us. She glanced at the map on her podium, grabbed a couple menus then looked up and flashed us a bright, white smile. "Okay, right this way." Her voice was like a fork scraping the bottom of an aluminum pot. It made my fillings hurt. She hugged the menus to her plump breasts and walked in a hurried swagger through the dining room. Donny followed and I brought up the rear, looking down at the floor and Donny's cherry brown loafers, avoiding all the stares from the other diners. People always look when someone new enters a space; human behavior. Then they start their mental list of judgments.

"Donny!" I heard coming from our left. "Donny!" Our train suddenly stopped. We all turned to the table just at our left.

"Rob!" Donny shouted for the whole world to hear. I jumped. Donny leapt by me, knocking into me a bit, and shook hands with a man with red hair and a red beard, dressed just like Donny was except he was wearing jeans, instead of khakis. As he stood there, I decided he was closer to my age than Donny's. Sitting next to him was a woman also about my age with frosted hair, silver jewelry and a hot pink cocktail dress. She was smiling up at the guys, chewing on gum. I stood by quietly and I could feel our bubbly hostess begin to go flat with impatience.

"Hi, Rhonda," Donny said warmly.

"Hi, Donny," she said in her rural Virginia accent, "I haven't seen you in forever. How you doin'?"

"I'm good, I'm good."

"Well, that's good. We should all go out for a beer sometime and catch up," she said.

"Yeah, let's do that," Donny smiled.

"And who is this beautiful lady behind you?" Rob asked.

"Oh." He pulled me forward by the arm. The air felt thick as water. "This is Mimi."

"Well, hi, Mimi," Rhonda beamed, "Nice to meet you."

"Nice to meet you," I managed, although I'm sure it was as audible as a mouse's sigh.

"Nice to meet you, Mimi," Rob said as he stuck out his hand. I put my hand in his and he gave me a warm squeeze and a little shake.

"It's Mimi's birthday," Donny said.

"Oh, happy birthday," they both said in good cheer.

"Your table is this way," the hostess interjected.

"Okay," Donny said obediently. "Well, gotta go."

"Well, wait a minute," Rob said. "We haven't started eating yet. Maybe we can have that beer together now."

"Yeah," Rhonda cheered.

"Is there a table for four open?" Rob asked the hostess.

She looked around the room and pointed to one being bussed. "That one will be open in a minute," she huffed.

"All right then," Donny said with a smile. My skin tingled all over, the room suddenly cold.

"Well, wait a minute," Rhonda broke through like a sunbeam. "It's Mimi's birthday. Maybe she was hoping for a private dinner with Donny." Everyone turned to look at me. "Mimi, were you wantin' a private dinner or can we join you?"

What is a person suppose to do in a moment like this? The truth is, I didn't want either. I wanted something far away, to be on a beach with a book. But this world is not built on honesty. I certainly didn't want to be in such close company with strangers. But saying no to them, denying these three what

73

they wanted, would take more self-esteem and confidence than I had.

"No, no. Come join us," I said as loudly as I could so they could hear me.

"Alright then," Rob said enthusiastically.

"You can go ahead and seat yourselves when it's all ready for you," the hostess said and she set our menus down on Rob and Rhonda's table and hurried back to her podium where there were already people waiting for her.

When we all sat down together, my insides were moving around and twisting themselves into knots. I was perspiring some and probably turning colors.

"You alright?" Donny asked me quietly.

"I feel a little sick," I admitted.

"What's wrong?" Rhonda asked.

"I just feel a little nauseous."

"Well, drink some water," she said, "Maybe they have chicken soup on the menu."

"I'll bet some beer will help you," Donny said and they all laughed.

"It'll definitely help me," Rob joked and they all laughed again. I have been criticized in my life for being too serious, but this type of humor is not funny; it's primitive.

I started to drink my water and all those damn familiar feelings came rushing in. Disconnected. Being completely untethered to everyone and everything. Here I was again, floating away to nowhere. A balloon inflated with fear. Was it just high school that did that to me? Or all those years of living in a van and not learning how to relate to people? Or is it all the ghost?

"What did you do for your birthday," Rhonda asked. I looked up, startled to have the attention on me again.

"Oh not much. I cleaned. Went out for coffee and read a book." They all sat there staring, mouths slightly open, Rhonda nodding a bit.

"Who did you have coffee with?" she asked.

"Just myself." Again the staring.

74

"Don't you have family?" she asked. I wasn't sure how to answer that.

"I have a mother and a brother in San Francisco."

"A mother and a brother," Rob repeated enjoying the rhyme. "I left my heart in San Francisco," he sang.

"Is that where you're from?" Rhonda asked. I didn't know how to answer that one either, but I decided to give the simple answer.

"Yes."

"San Francisco," Donny announced, "nothing but hippies and faggots." He made a spiteful face like all those hippies and faggots had done something terrible to him, like kill his mother. Rob nodded in agreement, hanging his head. His mother obviously met the same fate.

The waitress suddenly appeared at our table.

"Good evening, everyone!" she beamed. "So, I got your twos order," she said pointing her pen at Rob and Rhonda. "Your beer will be right out." Then she turned to Donny and me, "Are you guys ready?" Donny wanted us to decide quickly so our food didn't come out too far behind Rob and Rhonda's. That would have been torture for him. But I didn't even have a second to look at the menu.

"Yeah, we're ready," Donny said, "I'll have the full rack of ribs." The waitress scribbled on her pad.

"Rice, mashed potatoes or French fries?"

"French fries."

"Soup or salad?"

"Soup."

"And for you?" she asked, wax museum smile for me.

"I, uh….um…do you have chicken?"

"She'll have half a rack," Donny interrupted. She nodded as she scribbled.

"Rice, mashed potatoes or French fries?"

"Uh. Mashed potatoes." What happened to my chicken?

"Soup or salad?"

"Salad."

"Alright then," She smiled. "Anybody need anything else?"

"A Budweiser," Donny grunted.

"Alright." Scribble. "And for you?"

"I'll just have water."

"Alright then. I'll be back in a minute with everyone's beer." She smiled at us, put her pad and pen in her apron pocket and hurried away. We were quiet for a moment then Rob said:

"My cousin has a poodle named Mimi." How does a person respond to *that*? I was looking down at the table, the white butcher paper tablecloth. My insides were static electricity, my head was whirring and crackling. I didn't know what to do. Cry. Scream. I couldn't think of a response.

"Oh," I said.

Conversation resumed in its rowdy manner. After a moment I stood up and managed to say audibly, "Please excuse me." I went to the bathroom and stayed there a long time. When other women came in I would look into the mirror and pretend to fix something that fell out of place; loose strands of hair, lipstick on the corners of my mouth, eye crust. Very normal things to see going on in the ladies room at The Rib Shack. I was even joined a couple times by other women, wiping and tucking things back into their contained places. When I finally got back to the table, the three of them had their beer and Rob and Rhonda had their ribs. I sat down hoping they wouldn't pay me much attention.

"You okay, honey?" Rhonda asked, chewing, barbeque sauce on the corners of her mouth.

"I'm fine," I said, "Just a bit nauseous."

"Maybe you're pregnant," Rob joked. Donny's eyes widened in fear.

"No. I'm just not feeling well. I'll be fine."

The three of them continued to banter and joke and laugh and I just felt smaller and smaller. My head began to hurt. I started feeling hate towards Donny and Rob. It was the ghost. The ghost hates imbeciles. They all continued to order more beer. Our food came and Donny dove in like a rat in a trash heap. I nibbled, but could barely eat. The three of them got

louder and louder. I was bombarded; attacked by the noise and
the stupidity. I excused myself again, and this time went
outside for fresh air. I stayed out for a very long time. To my
surprise, Donny came strutting out the front door. He stood
right in front of me.

"What's going on?" he asked, obviously frustrated.

"I told you. I don't feel well."

"You're embarrassing me in front of my friends."

"What do you want me to do?" I whined.

"I don't know. Staying at the damn table would be a start."
I sighed.

"I just don't feel well."

He grunted.

"You are a strange bird, Mimi," he said with a vicious
scowl. "I'm going back in. You might as well too, it ain't gonna
do you any good just standing out here." He turned and walked
back inside. I followed after a couple minutes. When I got back
to the table, everyone was quiet. Rob looked uncomfortable.
Donny looked angry.

"You okay?" Rhonda asked. I almost cried.

"I just don't feel good," I whimpered like a little girl.
Rhonda turned to Donny.

"Donny, why don't you take her home," she said, "She's
obviously having a hard time." Donny grabbed his napkin
from his lap and threw it down on his plate, the ribs only half
eaten. My plate was barely touched. Donny started scooting
out of the bench, pushing into me. I slid out and stood up and
Donny stood right next to me, almost knocking me over.

"It's been a pleasure," he said sarcastically to Rob and
Rhonda.

"We'll go out for beers soon," Rob said.

"You feel better, Mimi," Rhonda said, "Happy birthday."
I managed a little smile for her.

"Thank you," I said.

Donny charged through the dining room and gave the
hostess his credit card. He signed the slip and walked out the
door and to his truck in the parking lot. I followed a few paces

behind. The whole ride home and the whole rest of the night Donny didn't speak to me. But the next time we were both awake and at home together, a few days later on account of our schedules, he acted as if nothing happened. And so did I. Although something shifted on the inside. The empty space, the place between us where we were unable to connect, was beginning to get filled…with resentment.

12

He is a young Santa Claus, a beneficent Nordic man with balding red-brown hair, a red beard and an omnipresent smile showcasing his little white teeth with ample spacing. His forest green shirt, his orange, brown and gold paisley tie look like throwbacks to the seventies. There is hardly anything on his desk, save the note pad he is writing on, a glass with a few pens in it, an amethyst and a photo of his wife and son on a park bench.

I sit comfortably in the soft, brown armchair in front of his desk. I decided to dress up today. I just felt like it. I am wearing the silky cream-colored blouse I had bought at Sears while living with Donny in Richmond.

Dr. Westland and I are just talking casually and he is asking me the same questions he always asks in our twice-weekly meetings: How am I doing? What have my thoughts been like? How does my body feel? Am I taking my medications? Have I had much anger come up recently? He says that we should meet three times a week since I stopped going to group, but that hasn't happened yet. I guess he's trying to fit it into his schedule.

When I first started meeting with Dr. Westland I wouldn't say much, just tell him what I thought he wanted to hear, what

I thought would get me out of here. But recently I started telling him the truth. It just feels good. I saw a therapist a few times of my own inclination back in Philadelphia, but that felt so clinical and sterile, frightening. Dr. Westland is more like a friendly uncle, although he's probably in his mid-forties, maybe a couple years older than me.

He talks to me too. He tells me about his wife and his son and how he plays tennis competitively in an adult league. We have a running joke about how I'm gonna join when I'm good enough and we're gonna play together. "Mixed Doubles" is what he calls it, meaning a team of one man and one woman. One woman. That's me. A grown woman. My own woman. Here, in a mental hospital.

"How's that backhand coming, Mimi?" Dr. Westland smiles.

"Oh good, good. Some of the other teams were watching me practice and they were shaking with fear."

"Nice. I want to win that trophy next year." He feigns direness.

I lean in with tiger eyes. "It's in the bag."
We chuckle.

"So, how's your ankle?" he asks, seriously now.
"Its fine. It was just hurting for a few days. I just twisted it."

"That's good," he nods, "And have you been coloring?"
"Yeah. Not so much. When do you think I'll be able to get my paints?"

"I told Linda to try to retrieve your paints. I don't know what the hold up is. You could ask her."
"She hates me."

"Linda is not the malicious monster you make her out to be."

I raise my eyebrows.

He coughs up a quick laugh. "I've worked with her for years. She's a good nurse."

I twist my mouth over to one side and narrow my eyes.

He looks at me.

"You know, Mimi, I've been working on getting some funding to have an art therapist back in here. I think you would really enjoy that."

"Does that mean I could paint?"

"Yeah, I'm pretty sure she works with paints."

"That would be so nice."

He smiles. Behind him the walls are faint blue, no doubt meant to be soothing. His red beard stands out against the blue like a fire suspended in air, and his blue eyes are sparks, lightning glittering, crackling. How did he get like this?

"Mimi, the technicians' report says that you still aren't taking your medications consistently."

"I hate my medicine."

"Doesn't it make you feel better?"

"Um, sort of. But it also makes me so tired and groggy. I can barely function."

"Oh. Well that's not good." He is a birdsong, filling the meadow, just after a rain. "Let's lower your dose a bit."

"Okay." This could be good. A lower dose. Maybe it will help. Something still doesn't feel right, though. I think I just don't like the idea of being on medication. Feels like an indictment.

"And how has the anger been this week?"

What? Oh. The anger.

"Okay." I shrug.

"No big outbursts?"

"No."

"Have you been feeling it much?"

"Not really."

He nods slowly and scribbles on his yellow note pad.

"So have you had a chance to practice the breathing this week?"

"Hmm. I've been practicing a little. If I get agitated with something. Or with Nurse Linda."

He breaks a big smile.

I can't help but let one side of my mouth curl up in a sly smirk.

He scribbles on his pad, then starts flipping through it. He slows down and reads the pages.

"Mimi, what about the ghost? I haven't heard you mention it in a while. Is that still happening?"

"Well, she hasn't been very active."

He taps the pen against the pad like a drumstick. "And tell me what happens when the ghost is 'active?'"

I shift in my seat and look up at the ceiling.

"Well. I can feel her in my belly first. That's where she lives. And then she comes up through my throat. If I can't keep her down she starts yelling and sometimes takes over my whole body." I look at Dr. Westland. He is looking back. He is here, with me. "She is hateful. She is…" His eyes widen, thirsty for this juicy telling, that will help him label me with some pathology, jot it down on his yellow pad, put it in my file. But I don't care. "…evil. She plays out pretty gruesome images in my mind. And her thoughts are awful. When she is around the world gets darker, edges harden, shadows breathe. And these shadows seem to be able to be in people too. Most people."

He is barely moving. Just looking. What is that soft look behind his eyes? Fear? Compassion?

"She's been with me since I was pretty young, but got more active when I was in high school." My life skips by like a flipbook. I shudder. "The worst was when I moved to DC and I was homeless. I was really fucked up then. It felt like she was in control. It's hard to tell what's her and what's me when she is really active." I sigh. "Then I had a pretty hard time towards the end of living in Poolesville. She was always around and I was a foul creature. Everyone in that town hated me. I had to get out of there."

"And what did you do when she was really active like that?"

"Well. She would talk a lot. She would say hateful things out loud. Yell sometimes." I laugh. "I'm sure I was quite the scene."

He gives me a sympathetic smile.

My stomach sinks.

"But for the most part I was helpless. I mean, I didn't hurt anybody…" Oh.

Dr. Westland has no expression on his face. But of course he knows.

Crying is coming up. I put my hands to my face. Stuff this. No. Let it.

A couple sobs come out.

A wail. Like an ambulance.

More sobbing.

"Mimi."

I slowly take my hands away from my face. There is a box of tissues suspended in front of me, a white box with a blurry water-color-like iris on it and a tissue steaming out the top like a plume of smoke. Dr. Westland is leaning over his desk, holding the box out for me. I take it onto my lap and pull a tissue out, which is instantly replaced with another one, like magic, like I hadn't taken a tissue at all. But I had. It's in my right hand. Illusions.

I don't need the tissue. There is no fluid to wipe away. The tissue is in my right hand, the box is cradled on my lap with my left. There is too much stuff in my hands. It is stifling. I put the box on Dr. Westland desk. Dr. Westland looks at me. I sit up in the chair and wait for him to speak.

"Tell me, Mimi, why is the ghost so angry?"

The answer comes quickly and unexpected. "She is really upset."

Of course.

Dr. Westland nods. "I see." He puts his hands together and they rub together slowly. "So we need to figure out how to make her feel better."

I have never thought of that. In my best fantasies, she leaves like a rainstorm leaves, as it will, suddenly moving on, and all that is left is sweet quiet. I've been waiting for that, desperately at times, for so long. But this idea is new. And how do I do it?

"This week, Mimi, I want you to be a brave explorer. And a diplomat. I want you to go inside yourself, to your stomach, and talk to the ghost. Ask her why she's upset."

I nod slowly.

There is a new feeling inside me. What is it? Like standing on the bow of a ship, an old ship. I am the statue. A maiden. Before me an absolute vastness. And something, hidden in its hazy blue expanse, to be found.

13

Everything changed after that day. I never asked Jared what changed for him, what went on in his mind, but it didn't matter. He had made some choice. Our pizza date solidified an actual friendship…or something. Jared began talking to me outside of class, in the hallway. We often spent lunch together, went off the grounds to get sandwiches and steak fries. I'm sure he put up with a lot of shit. The most popular kids stopped associating with him, although he never really lost his reputation as the nice, funny guy that everybody likes. But his attention turned from the larger social scene to something more specific and subtle: me. I was in heaven. Life was suddenly flooded with light penetrating between the clouds. Optimism found a place for itself in my inner pantheon. And so did a sublime feeling that I suppose was contentment. I was still ridiculed and gawked at, and later simply ignored by the other students. But I had a balance now to the negative.

"When am I gonna get to meet this kooky family of yours?" Jared asked one day in Painting class. I was focusing

83

on the front side of a wood cabin I was painting, squinting my eyes, lost in the minute greens, umber and white visible in the wood in the photograph sitting upright on my easel.

"Wow! Far out, Mimi."

"Thanks."

I used my tiniest-bristled brush, a 00, to apply the white, which might have been mold on the wood.

"Did you hear me?"

"Um…yes. You said you want to meet my family."

"Yeah. I want to meet these people. After all the stories, they're becoming like mythical characters to me. I'm starting to wonder if you're spinning tales."

I looked hard at the photo of the wood cabin in a little meadow, surrounded by trees, but I was losing my focus.

"They embarrass me."

"I don't care. Mimi, I won't think anything less of you, no matter how crazy they are."

I looked up at him. He was sincere. 'What's the worst that could happen?' I thought. I pulled my mouth over to one side, looking at Jared, trying to imagine a worst-case scenario.

"Okay," I say turning back to my painting, "Why don't you come over for dinner tomorrow night."

"Really?"

"Yeah, really."

"What time?"

"Umm. We usually eat around seven."

"Okay! Rad! I'll be there."

I swallowed hard, and felt a little lightheaded. But worst-case scenario was that he would see my folks for the nuts that they were. No damage. I knew he wouldn't judge me for it.

"Hey wanna see my painting?" he asked.

I slid my chair away from my easel and leaned over to look at his work. I laughed. His eyes and mouth opened in smiling shock to my reaction, causing me to laugh even harder.

"Mimi," he said like I was being naughty.

The assignment was that we all got a photograph from a magazine or postcard of a landscape and we had to paint an exact replica. Jared, of course, got the most challenging photo in the blind draw: a pasture full of cows, a barn, a large complicated farmhouse with tons of surfaces and details, and trees and clouds taking up the rest of the space. The whole thing looked like melted wax. So surreal.

"Those poor cows," I laughed.

He slapped my thigh playfully but hard, the look of disbelief still on his face.

I wanted to kiss him.

* * * * * * * * * * * * *

Jared arrived right on time. He was wearing a brown and black polyester button up shirt and brown slacks, holding a bouquet of white daffodils. I was a little surprised. I was wearing the same thing I had worn at school. As much as I had learned about civilized living, which occasions called for dressing up was something I still hadn't grasped. And my parents were no help because they didn't even think about it. Formalities were archaic in their world.

"Hi," he said.

"Hi," I managed, still trying to figure out what was going on with his outfit.

"Can I come in?" he smirked.

"Yeah," I smiled, coming back to my senses. I moved to the side so he could enter and shut the door behind us. He looked around.

"Pretty sparse," he said quietly. I nodded, not understanding that he was talking about furnishing and décor. I walked him down the hallway and into the kitchen with its mismatched chairs. Dad and Ethan were sitting at the table, Dad beaming at us when we entered. Mom, standing at the stove, shrieked ecstatically and charged Jared with her arms out in front of her, palms up. She gathered him up in a tight hug, twisting him back and forth. He bulged his eyes out at me, pretending like he was being squeezed to death. I giggled quietly.

"Oh my god! It's so nice to meet you, we've heard so much about you." She pushed him out and held him by the arms in front of her, looking closely at him, smiling her big smile, eating him up. She turned to me and acted serious, "Good job, Mimi. He is adorable." Her smile broke open again, taking wicked pleasure in knowing that that comment probably made me uncomfortable.

"Here, Mrs. Rizner." He lifted up the daffodils, slightly mangled from being caught in the hug, a.k.a. Mom's ecstatic death vice.

"Oh my gosh, they're beautiful." She removed her hands from his shoulders to take the bouquet. "What a sweetheart." She looked at him adoringly, then turned to me. "Yes, Mimi, you can marry him."

Oh, god.

"But please, Jared, don't call me Mrs. Rizner, call me Sal. And this is Mimi's dad, Jack."

Jared walked over and shook Dad's hand, Dad smiling sincerely.

"And you've met Ethan." Mom continued.

"Hi, Ethan. How's it going?"

"Good." Ethan looked surprised, probably by all the formalities. Guests were usually Mom and Dad's friends and we didn't do introductions when they came over to smoke a joint. If they were new, and they wanted to know our names, they'd ask. Or if we wanted to, we'd ask.

"Well, why don't you both sit down; dinner will be ready in a minute. I'm gonna put these flowers in water."

Dinner was nothing special. Spaghetti with marinara sauce and mushrooms, steamed broccoli, salad and bread. Jared ate with polite vigor, and conversation went as expected: jovial, full of inquiries and smattered with a few moments that were embarrassing for me. After dinner Dad asked Jared if he smoked grass and when Jared answered yes, Dad pulled out a joint, lit it and passed it across the table to Jared. My eyes nearly popped out of my head.

"No!" I said. Everyone looked at me, Jared holding the joint six inches from his mouth. I felt silly and didn't have anything more to say, but the quiet of the room resounded with my disapproval. Jared passed the joint back to Dad and after a moment the tension released.

"Oh, I'll take that," Mom said grinning, further dissipating any lingering discomfort. Dad held out the joint and Mom pinched it with her thumb and forefinger, put it to her lips and sucked the smoke in, the cherry growing brightly as it crawled upward.

I leaned towards Jared when no one was looking and quietly asked him if he wanted to see my room. Jared courteously thanked Mom and Dad for dinner and we excused ourselves from the table, Mom giving us the cheesiest grin of approval for what she saw as teenage lust. But I didn't know how Jared felt. And I measured my high hopes with a good deal of realism. Either way, he was my friend and I wanted to spend time with him. I led him to my bedroom and covertly locked the door. Ethan would have to entertain himself for a little while.

Sitting on the edge of my bed, not looking at each other, he began to speak, "You know, Mimi, this is kinda…weird…for me." His thumb was stroking the top of my hand, as it rested in his palm. It sent goose bumps up my arm. Magical little creatures swam around in my belly. My arm looked so dark next to his. I tried to hold his eye contact. What was it that he wanted say? He couldn't be my friend? No. In fact he couldn't say it in words at all. He leaned towards me and as soon as I realized what he was trying to do, the little creatures in my belly shot upward and exploded in ecstasy, swarming my face. He put his lips on mine and I sat there unmoved like a corpse. I didn't know what to do! But he wanted to kiss me. He pecked at my lips, sucking gently. Just the bottom lip. Then the top. Then both again, trying to see what lays between, enticing me to open up. I pursed my lips slightly and met his kiss with my own, feeling his soft, wet mouth. He was speaking, but not with words, trying to share something with me. And ask me something. I met his eagerness with my own. Our lips parted now when we kissed and it was like trying to drink his very essence. His tongue entered my mouth and rubbed against my tongue. It came back and did it again. Tantalizing me, saying 'Hello, Mimi.' I greeted him the next time he entered, welcoming him. This excited him. It excited me to excite him. He pushed me down against the bed and drank rapturously from my mouth. Embodied in our very tongues, we danced in the dark place between us. He put his hand on my side. He went under my shirt, and explored my skin. My stomach pulled in at first, but then released. I put my hand under his shirt, on his stomach. His hard body was muscle and bone. I felt his abs, running my hand over them, up slowly, and down, my fingers feeling the space between each muscle. His hand moved up farther and cupped my breast. Something in me relaxed, opened, like gaping for air. Air circulated in me. And light. Images of prairies on a warm spring day kept entering my mind's eye, even a cabin too. Afterwards I wondered if I had been seeing our future. Ah, the dreams of little girls.

We didn't have sex that night. I wouldn't have been ready and he didn't even try. But something happened there in my bedroom. Souls met. And it was a divine meeting. It was stars in alignment, a constellation that had always been there, only its shape never before traced, never noticed or named.

He didn't sleep over. But I was awake when the sun rose, floating not on a bed of cotton and coils, but a bed of ecstasy, and in that moment I knew what the poets know and what the birds of dawn know: that the rising of the sun is a majestic and cosmic gesture beyond what the human mind can possibly comprehend. I can tell you that it is futile to try. It only gets one all tangled up. But I suppose the mind is relentless like a little dog pulling on its bone, giving a guttural growl as you try to take the bone away, needing, just needing to hang on to some conceptual understanding. The sanctified reality of life itself exists like a humming ocean unknown, below the dense smoky layer of ordinary perception. Lovers and poets penetrate it at times.

* * * * * * * * * * * *

Jared and I were officially lovers, or 'boyfriend and girlfriend' or 'going out' as we liked to say in high school. Perhaps Jared saw something more valuable than reputation. We held hands in public, kissed in public, spent most of our free time together. And I guess that although the other girls might have been surprised, they couldn't have been altogether shocked. After all, I was quite attractive after I had gotten cleaned up. I have my mother's nose and mouth and body and my grandfather Isaac's turquoise eyes.

Jared didn't plummet to the depths of social rejection from dating me, nor was I elevated to some esteemed sense of arrival among my peers. Instead, we were mostly treated with indifference and slipped into a pseudo-obscurity. We existed together in our own bubble, surrounded by a few of Jared's closer friends. I even made a couple friends, or warm acquaintances, in the last two years of high school.

14 ➤

I began to get more comfortable living in Donny's house. I was most comfortable when he wasn't there. I converted the shed into a painting studio. It was a small space, maybe six feet by eight, but it was enough for me to sit in front of my easel, with all my supplies, stacks of canvases leaning against the walls, a couple baskets with my paints and brushes. It took some convincing, but Donny finally relented. After all, it was basically empty except for the lawnmower, the weed whacker, a shovel, a rake and a hose, all of which remained in there among my paintings.

The time also came when I decided to try talking Donny into redecorating the house. After all, it was supposedly *our* house at this point and I could barely stand the barren walls and lack of color. It's hard to have a sense of yourself in an environment like that; everything just blends together in a beige soup.

It was a Saturday afternoon. Donny just got home from a softball game. I was sitting on the light brown couch playing solitaire when I heard him come through the door.

"Hey, Doll," he said. He was chipper. He obviously won his game.

"Hi, Donny." I stood up and we kissed. I liked it when he was happy. It made this little arrangement so much more bearable.

"You won," I stated.

"We did more than win; we kicked their scrawny asses, those damn Morris' Motors. I don't know how they beat us in the spring playoffs."

"Well, good job." I said. He looked at me with happy eyes, happy not only that he won, but happy that I was there to share it with. When he looked at me like that, I was sorta happy too.

"And how was your day?" he asked.

"Oh, you know. I took the bus and got coffee at Perly's and read my book, then just spent the afternoon here."

"Okay. We'll let's celebrate. You deserve a beer for having such a boring day."

I chuckled.

We went to the kitchen and got ourselves each a can of beer.

"What's for dinner?" he bellowed.

"I thought maybe spaghetti and meatballs and some roasted carrots and a salad."

He made a grunting noise. "When's it gonna be ready?"

"I don't know. Sevenish if I start now. You hungry?"

"Starving," he sighed, looking pathetic.

"I'll make you a sandwich to hold you over."

I pulled the white bread, sliced turkey, mustard, mayo and tomatoes out of the fridge. I had to teach Donny that the fresh turkey in the deli section of the grocery store is better than the packaged stuff. I also tried to get him to start buying fresh bread instead of the weird, white pre-sliced stuff full of preservatives, but he said it was too expensive and besides, he liked his bread more. Get *that*. I think he was just headstrong.

After making him his sandwich, we sat at the kitchen table, an old plastic relic that was meant to be outdoor furniture. I looked around the room. A generic plastic wall clock, like the kind in offices and schools, hung above the sink. A porcelain pig sat nearby on the old laminate counter. He had told me it reminded him of his mother, which made me laugh inside because I could see the resemblance, but he meant that it was hers and she liked to collect porcelain farm animals, especially pigs. There was mail on the counter, and a mug with pens and pencils and a small screwdriver he used to fix his reading glasses, which seemed to need a lot of fixing. But that was it. We were surrounded by white walls, the grey linoleum floor, white fridge, white table, a mustard yellow counter, old stained cabinets loosing their luster. It was enough to make a person want to bang their head against the white walls.

"I went four for five today," Donny told me, puffing himself up in his seat, the sandwich in his hand looking like an hors d'oeuvres he could eliminate in one bite.

"Huh?" We often spoke different languages.

He was frustrated. "I was up to bat five times and got on base four of those times."

"Oh. Good job." I forgot to put on a show. I was zoning out. His face sank. He could tell I didn't care. He chewed his sandwich like it was stupid me he was chewing up.

"You know, if you'd start coming to my games, you'd start understanding what it's all about."

I sighed. "I'm sorry, I just don't have the patience for sports."

"You have the patience to sit on your ass all afternoon."

Neither of us spoke.

He drank his beer loud to prove that he wasn't uncomfortable. And that he was right.

I sipped on my beer.

"Let's go to the fair tomorrow," he said, suddenly enthused. "It's only here for another week."

"Alright. But no playing the game where you can win goldfish. I don't want pets to take care of."

"Don't worry. I'm all you got to take care of."

"That's more than enough," I mumbled out the side of my mouth, pretending only to be talking to myself.

He drank more of his beer until the can was empty. Then he got up.

"Want another beer?"

I shook my can, as if to show him how heavy it was with beer, but he wouldn't have been able to tell, of course. Sometimes a person does things that don't make any sense.

"Mine's still full," I explained.

He turned and walked to the fridge and got himself another beer.

"I'm gonna have a smoke. Wanna come out to the patio?"

"I need to get dinner started. I'll be out in a bit."

Donny went outside and I gathered his plate and washed it. Then I turned the oven on. I took out the bag of baby carrots and the meatballs the supermarket already had prepared and put each in their own baking dish with a little olive oil. I sprinkled salt and rosemary on the carrots and put both dishes in the oven. Then I set a pot of water on the stove for the noodles and put an empty pot out for the sauce.

I walked out to the patio with my beer. Donny was relaxing, listening to the birds and probably replaying his moments of glory from the game.

The corner of his mouth twitched into a smile as he heard the crack of his bat hitting the ball. I shut the screen door behind me and it woke Donny up from his daydreaming. He made a groaning noise, like waking up, and he stretched his fists into the air, beer in one hand. I came around and sat in one of the other chairs.

"Nice evening," he said.

I nodded and noticed at the fence to our right the neighbor's cocker spaniel, sniffing about, raising his leg once or twice to pee.

We sat in quiet for a long time. It was nice. I looked at the big man who gave me shelter and was a warm body that I could let my own body get close to. It was nice, that part. I figured in that moment that maybe I actually would be around for a while.

"Hey, Donny?"

"Yeah?" he looked at me from under the brim of his baseball cap.

"I think I want to do some redecorating."

He scowled. "Redecorating? I ain't got the money for that."

"I'll pay for it. It won't be much, just a new kitchen table and some nice drapes…"

"Naw. We don't need no redecorating."

I felt stuffed with air. "I need to do it, Donny. I can't live like this."

"Like what?" He looked at me, squinting his left eye, disapprovingly.

"It just doesn't have any charm to it," I said, my voice getting high pitched.

"The answer is 'no.' The last thing I need is a woman redecorating around here. Before I know it, I'll be sleeping under flowery blankets and the whole place'll be covered in pink frilly shit."

"Donny!" It was the first time I raised my voice to him. He looked stunned, then curled his face up like a bulldog. But I went on, "If I'm gonna live here, I need to be comfortable too.

93

Everything is so beige, so blah. It won't be much. I'll put up some of my own paintings."

"Your paintings aren't exactly pleasing to look at. Half of them I can't even tell what they are."

"I can't stand how empty and beige it all is! There is no decoration at all, unless you count that goddamn baseball trophy in the middle of the coffee table.

"It's a *softball* trophy," he snarled.

"Whatever. It's fucking tacky."

He sat up and grabbed my arm, squeezing ferociously. His eyes bulged. He turned purple-red.

"There ain't gonna be any redecorating and that's final. You got it?" He yanked my arm and continued pulling. It felt like it was gonna rip right out of the socket and the pain shot all the way up to my ear. I couldn't speak and I couldn't even look at him. So he knew he won, and he let my arm go. I pulled it back into my body and held it. It was hot where his hand had been. We both sat there for a while, him calming down and me not knowing what to do with myself. I got up and went to finish making dinner.

Everything was hot: my arm, my neck, up to my ears. Then crying happened. Or at least tears. A broken dam. Tears fell into the water cooking the pasta and during one moment I dreamed that they would become poisonous to Donny and after eating dinner his insides would start bleeding and he would die a terrible, painful death. I felt guilty for having this vision as soon as it passed through and knew that it was the ghost. The ghost can be so morbid.

During dinner I was silent, and of course Donny's insides didn't rupture. He was silent too. Donny never apologized for anything. The next day we went to the fair. My arm had three little circular bruises. I was quiet, but cordial. We ate cotton candy and played a few games, but neither of us had a good day and didn't win anything. I told him that the rides make me sick.

I kept inside a shell for a couple weeks before relaxing and letting myself have fun with him again. Donny's temper didn't go away however, and he hurt me on several occasions. But what was I to do?

15

"Here, Val, try some of these potatoes. They're really good." I scoop three big spoonfuls onto her plate. I'm not surprised she isn't eating the meatloaf; it is wet and tasteless. And I don't think she likes meat.

"Thanks," she says in her breathy half-dead way. She only says it 'cause she's programmed to, like all of us, and her way of saying it, lacking even a milligram of sincerity, makes that truth real obvious.

She jabs one of the little, square potato chunks with her fork and pulls it up to her mouth, chewing cow like, her eyes glossy and distant.

"How are they?" I ask.

"They're good," she says staring off into god-knows-where. Her hand comes to rest on the table. The fork slips out and lies on the table under her hand. She is still chewing and staring off.

"You okay, Val?"

She finishes chewing the little bit of potato in her mouth, swallows and turns towards me. "Yeah," she says. She stares intently at me and finally there is a connection. "Mimi?" It's like she's talking in her sleep.

"Yeah?"

She breathes out through her nose. "I think I took too many Xanax."

My heart jumps. "You do?"

"I don't know. Maybe." She is talking so slow. Confused.

"How many did you take?"

Her mouth is open and a small puddle of drool is forming behind her bottom lip. She takes a breath in and a little life returns to her eyes momentarily.

"Um. Four."

"Why did you do that?" That was stupid.

She lets out a tired sigh.

"I was feeling anxious."

Oh god. "Well then you take *one*."

She sighs again. "I know. I was really, really anxious. I couldn't breathe."

"How did you even get a hold of four?"

"That's dangerous," Ann interjects from the other side of the table. "I'm gonna tell Linda." I hadn't realized that other people might be hearing us.

"No." Val whines half-heartedly.

"She's fine," I say, "We don't need to involve Linda."

"What do you know? She overdosed on her meds. That could kill her."

"I'll stay with her. If she gets any worse, I'll tell Nigel."

Ann swivels her head, looking around the room. "Linda!"

"Goddammit you little shit!"

"Fuck you, Mimi. Linda!" she calls out again.

Tornado inside me. Jaw is clicking. Breathe.

Linda comes over to the table.

"What is it, Ann?"

"Val overdosed on her meds."

Little snitch.

"Val," Linda demands, her icicle eyes piercing flesh. "What did you take?"

Val is stiff.

"Val! What medications did you take?"

Val doesn't speak. Joan is mumbling, frightened like a girl just woken from a nightmare.

Linda's lips tighten up so you can barely see them. "If you don't talk, I'm gonna send you off to the hospital, is that what you want?"

Val is still silent and motionless. The room is swelling with curiosity and anxiousness.

"Give her a second," I demand.

Linda shoots me a steely look, but I stare right back at her. She looks again at Val. I look at Val. All eyes on Val. Someone at a table behind me starts yelling. The room is getting more agitated.

"Val," I say, prodding her.

She licks her lips and smacks her lips together like she is chewing. She looks at me. "I took four Xanax."

"Oh, goddammit, Val." Linda says.

The room is becoming thick with chatter. That person behind me is still yelling. The young men who serve the food are frozen, staring at the commotion.

"Val, come with me." Linda walks around the table and grabs Val by the arm, pulling her up out of the chair.

"Shouldn't she eat?" I say.

"Mimi, please." She starts pulling Val away as fast as Val can drag her feet along the grey industrial carpeting.

"Where are you taking her?" I ask

"I need to check her vitals, Mimi. Chill out." The two of them slowly make it across the dining room and through the swinging doors.

I look around the room. People are gossiping, rocking, moaning, laughing. It's like dominos around here. One disturbance causes a chain reaction. Like a school of fish. A flock of birds. Strange birds. Nigel is calming down the old woman who was screaming.

Ann shakes her head in disapproval.

Barbara hisses like a rabid snake.

Teddy has his elbows on the table and his face buried in his hands.

Daryl has an entertained smile on his face.

* * * * * * * * * * * * *

I might as well try this. I have to do something. If I want to get out of here, I have to do something. At least show Dr. Westland and Dr. Jensen that I'm trying.

I lie on my back, on my bed, on top of the covers, my little generic blue quilted comforter. The blinds are closed. The overhead light is off. It is dark, like chocolate brown and cool grey mixed together. As dark as it can get while the sun is out.

I take a deep breath. It is time to embark, to be an explorer. I am going to seek out the ghost. To ask her why she is hurting.

I take another deep breath.

I don't know how to do this.

How do I do this?

Dr. Westland said go to my belly. That's where she lives.

I take another breath and feel my belly swell. It is tense from the activities at dinner. I can feel her moving around in there like pushing her way through pipes that are just big enough for her to move through. I take another breath. She knows I'm coming. But she is pretending not to know. Not to care. The breathing is taking me in. Deeper. She moves faster. The pipes are getting banged up a little. I can catch her. By the tail maybe. She is wearing grey. She always wears grey. She has no feet. She always flies. She moves faster. She is gone. No. She can't disappear. She is only hiding in a dark place. I can feel her breathing. Come here. Come here and show yourself.

Nausea. Acid comes up with a scream in my ears from the inside, dizziness like being lost in a hall or mirrors. She grabs me, shakes me, screaming. Why? Why her? Why is it all like this?

I breathe. Metal in my mouth. My head is caving in, like aluminum getting crumpled up. Can I crumple up? Scraping. Crushing. I am inside of her, burning.

I have to breathe! I can't! She's pushing on my chest. How can I? How can I betray her, invalidate her? It's not my fault. How could I be different? She's in me. Everyone is haunted. By what? What is she? What is it?

Where am I? What am I? I'm disappearing. Oh, god, help!
I scream loud. My throat ripping.
I'm disappearing!
Screaming. Everything turning red again. No!
The door swings open.
Talking.
Nurse Linda. Hillary.
"Mimi!"
"Mimi! What's going on?"
"Get some Haldol. Injection. Now!"
Nothing is real!

* * * * * * * * * * * * *

Omnipresent smile. How does he do it?
"How's everything?"
Here we go. Same cursory inquiries.
"Fine."
My face is tight.
"Fine?"
Well, I didn't go to the Bahamas, Mister.
"Yeah, fine."
"Okay." He taps his pen on the yellow pad, purses his lips.
"I heard you had a rough moment last night."
My bottom lip quivers.
He is waiting for an answer. If I open my mouth I might
cry.
His little white teeth glisten like pearls behind a copper wire
beard.
"Are you feeling better?"
I open my face just enough to let a "yeah" push out like
steam, then tighten it back up again.
"That's good."
I curl my lips in. A plug. Steam behind my eyes.
Dr. Westland is just watching me.

What can he really do for me?

He opens his mouth, "Mimi." He sits up in his chair, "Let's do some breathing together."

If I could open my mouth without my face exploding I would say "no." Shaking my head might even be enough to loosen what needs to stay tight. So instead I follow his lead, put my hands in my lap, close my eyes and start breathing through my nose. It's an effort. How do I stay alive if I can barely breathe?

"Can you go slower and deeper?" Dr. Westland asks.

No.

I force a deep breath in and it escapes too fast for me to control. I suck in another breath, and hold it. I open my mouth and it all just spills out like a dragon with no fire, just hot air.

I can't take another deep breath. My lungs feel already filled. I put my lips together like I'm gonna whistle and squeeze out any remaining air. Maybe I'll never be able to take an in-breath again. Subconscious self-suffocation.

My lungs suddenly call air back in, filling up. The air falls out. I open my eyes.

"I can't do this right now."

Dr. Westland opens his eyes slowly, serenely.

"Okay." His voice is smooth like warm oil. "Fair enough."

He stares at me placidly. I can't hold his gaze, my eyes bouncing from his eyes, to the wall, his eyes, the window, his eyes.

"Mimi, can you tell me anything about last night?"

Ugh, god.

I sigh in disgust.

"I..." the crying wants to come. Who cares.

My eyes fill with salt water; the sea within. My nose is itchy.

"I tried..." my voice is shaky with crying. Not what I expected. "...to do what you said. I tried to ask the ghost why she was upset."

"Good. Good job."

What? For losing it?

"And what did you find out?"

Nothing.

"She is scared. Afraid of being seen. And touched." I am realizing this as I say it.

"Why?"

"She's just scared."

Dr. Westland nods.

"She thinks the world is a cruel place."

He gives a sympathetic smirk, still nodding.

"She's confused."

"About what?"

"Everything. What it's all for. What's real. Who she is."

His eyes widen.

What more is there to say.

"Pretty heavy stuff this ghost is wrestling with."

"Yes." A tear comes out, hangs on my cheek. For the ghost.

"Let's have compassion for her," he suggests, one step behind me.

A river. A big, strong, sweet river. Tears dripping and falling.

Yes. Compassion for her.

He reaches back and grabs the box of tissues with the purple watercolor iris and hands it to me. I take it. I pull out the tissue that has hovered in mid float, hanging like smoke on a smokestack for who knows how long, waiting for this, its time. I wipe off my cheeks with it, wipe my nose. I crumple it and dab the corners of my eyes.

"She's just trying to defend herself."

"I'm sure."

I sniffle in. "Should I try to talk to her again?"

"Not now." He leans forward. "I want you to practice the breathing, Mimi. Everyday. Even for just five minutes. You have to learn self-control. And to establish some peace for yourself."

I sniffle, probably looking like a little pink piggy.

"Okay," I say, squeezing the tissue ball in my hand.

The Sound of Birds

* * * * * * * * * * * * *

I'm on the couch sitting next to Val. Ann is on my other side, Daryl is on the recliner, falling in and out of sleep, a sudden snore every few minutes followed by him sitting up, looking around, smacking his lips and settling back into the recliner, beginning the whole cycle again. It's evening time. Sitcoms. No one ever laughs at them, except Hillary who's sitting at the little table behind us with Nigel and Joan, who's been bobbing her head lately, chewing on the inside of her mouth.

Val completely disappears when she watches TV. She says she hates TV, that it's completely moronic, but when she's watching it, she gets completely absorbed.

"I can't stand this show," I say.

"Uh huh."

"That little girl is so bratty."

"Totally."

It's been getting darker earlier. The outside light faded a while ago and the blue glow of the TV became the dominant light source. Soon Hillary will flip on all the fluorescent lights, which she is prone to do. Don't wanna get stuck in the dark with all the crazies.

The TV light against Val's pale face changes every few seconds with the changing camera shots.

"Wanna draw?" I ask.

Her mouth, which has been hanging open a bit, closes.

"Um…" She is registering what I said. "No."

"Do you want me to leave you alone?"

She turns to me. "No. Sorry. I was thinking."

"'Bout what?"

She bites her bottom lip. "Tomorrow. I have a meeting with Jensen."

"Wow. You're due up for one of those?"

"Yeah." She suddenly looks pitiful. "I hope he lets me go. I'm done with this place."

Good luck. You just OD'd on your meds a couple days ago.

"Good luck."

"Thanks"

Poor girl.

I put my hands on my thighs, my jeans. "Well, I can't sit here in front of the boobtube anymore." I stand up and walk over to Nigel, Hillary and Joan at the little table. Three seats. All taken. "Joan, you want my seat on the couch?"

"No," she bellows whale-like. "I'm gonna go to my room."

Yes. That was easy.

She pushes herself up.

"Goodnight, Joan," Hillary beams.

"Goodnight," Nigel joins in.

Joan shuffles away down the women's corridor.

"Wanna play cards, Nigel?"

"Hmmm. A few hands."

My cards are still on the table from earlier.

"Wanna play, Hillary?" Nigel asks.

"Oh, sure."

Oh, god.

I smile.

I sit down and take the box, empty the cards out onto my palm and begin shuffling.

"What's the game, girl?" Nigel asks.

"Poker. I need the money."

"Well if we played for money, you'd certainly be rich and I'd be penniless," Nigel smiles.

"Good thing for you we don't then," I wink.

"Yes. And for Lucille."

"Who's Lucille?" Hillary asks, speaking louder than necessary.

"Lucille's his pooch," I tell her, slide shuffling the deck.

"Yep. And she eats enough for me to need a second job, let alone lose all my money to Mimi in poker.

103

Hillary blurts out a forced laugh.

I widen my eyes; she is annoying. I start to deal. One, one, one. Two, two, two. I love the motion of the cards spinning on the table as they slide into place, joining the cards already dealt like a little family, all waiting to be picked up and revealed.

When the dealing's done we pick up our cards and organize them in our hands. I look mine over. Not bad. A pair of tens to start.

"Oooh, y'all better look out," Hillary announces, shaking her shoulders in a slow motion shimmy.

"Hillary, ain't you ever heard of poker face?" Nigel jabs.

I grin big.

"That's only necessary if you're gamblin'. Since we're not, I'm just gonna gloat how bad I'm gonna kick your behinds."

Nigel closes one eye, jesting to measure her up with the other. He suddenly throws down cards. "Three please."

I deal out three more to him.

"I'll take one," Hillary says as she lays a card onto the new discard pile. I deal her one card. I discard three myself, and take three new cards. Oooh, look at that! Another ten. Haha.

"Okay, whatcha all got?" Nigel says putting down his cards face up. He has a pair of sevens.

"Two pairs!" Hillary beams showing her cards.

"Can y'all be quiet!" Ann shouts over her shoulder. Nigel and I make little guilty-scared faces at each other, then smile.

"What do you got, Mimi?" Hillary says in hushed tones.

I put my cards down. "Hey, where did all the chips go?" I joke.

"What? You won?" Hillary looks over my cards. "Darn it!"

I gather up the cards and begin shuffling again.

"I can't believe you won that one. I thought I had it for sure," Hillary rattles on, "What a stinker."

I deal five cards to each of us.

We all pick up our cards and start organizing them.

"Oh, great!" Hillary complains, blowing air out from between her lips. "This is awful. Mimi, you are not allowed to deal anymore."

My hand; I have nothing to start. I'll keep the king and the jack.

Nigel is staring intently at his cards. His big bottom lip hangs down. It looks soft as good bedding with satin sheets, like I could crawl up and lay cozy on that lip. It would feel so nice to kiss him, to get lost in his mouth, to have those soft lips sucking on my nipples, making them hard. Him kissing all over my body with those soft lips, licking everywhere with his big soft tongue.

Things are getting relaxed down in my crotch. Steamy wet and tingling. I better stop fantasizing.

"Two cards," Nigel says throwing down two of his cards.

16 →

The first week after school let out sophomore year, Jared asked me if I wanted to go camping. I didn't know what to say. I wasn't sure what that meant. When he explained it to me, I realized it was basically the same thing I had been doing my whole life, only in a tent instead of a van. But it didn't matter what it was he was proposing we do. Anything with Jared sounded like a good idea.

We left on a Thursday. Jared borrowed his mother's Ford Pinto and we drove up highway 1 with the windows down and our hands and my feet hanging out the windows, Aerosmith and Jackson Browne blasting on the stereo. My body was electricity. Dry grass blazed gold in waves of reverent bowing. The ocean on our left sparkled and the sun glare reflecting off its surface was almost blinding.

Jared wore sunglasses, bobbing his head and slapping the outside of his door to the beat of the music. I also bobbed my head, less exuberantly than he, and I slapped my hand on my thigh. He turned and smiled at me a couple times. This was his domain: freedom, rock music. He was more like my dad than I realized. I was observing the way the hills slanted and rolled down into the ocean and decided that I would paint a series of the California coast.

When we entered the state park where we would be camping, the first thing I noticed was all the redwood trees. There weren't many old growth; people cut all those down, but the forest still had a spirit of magic and majesty.

We parked at our campsite and got out of the car. Flying insects glistened in the sunlight, playing zigzagging chasing games around the tree trunks. Cicadas buzzed and rattled in the canopy, and this, combined with the intense heat, put me in a trance. As I stood there in my daze, watching all the movement within the hot stillness, Jared began unloading the back of the car, pulling out our tent, blankets and the box of food, water and cooking supplies we had brought.

He laid the tent out on a flat area, then while kneeling on one knee looked up at me.

"Are you gonna help?" he quipped.

I realized then how far away I was. I closed my mouth, swallowed and blinked my eyes a few times. I couldn't talk for a moment. I staggered over to him and kneeled down next to him. He looked at me first with a smile, then with an eyebrow raised.

"You okay?"

"Uh. Yeah. It's hot." I held on to the edge of the flattened tent like he was doing, then looked at him, waiting for the next cue. He just smiled with amusement.

"What?" I smiled back.

"Where did you just go?"

I had to think about it. "I don't know. The sound of the insects in the trees, it made like a net. Everything was buzzing, vibrating, and there was a rhythm like a looping. Like 'wa-wa-wa-wa-wa.'"

He looked at me strangely. "What you just said doesn't make any sense at all."

I giggled. "Me either."

He shook his head. "Come on. Help me get this tent up." We erected the blue and grey Coleman tent that he bought with money he saved from working at his dad's office the previous year. It was a bit cumbersome. This was only the second time Jared had put it up. But after a little bit of fumbling, we got the thing together. We threw our bedding into it, which I set up nice and comfy for us while he drove the stakes into the ground. When I was finished I looked at our little nest of blankets and smiled. This must be how mama birds feel, I thought. I crawled backwards out of the opening of the tent, and stood up still smiling.

"All done."

"Right on," he said, "Let's get some firewood."

"You wanna have a fire right now? It's crazy hot out."

"No. It's for later. This way we won't have to worry about it if it starts getting dark and we're out hiking or something." Jared was extremely practical, especially for such a joker. He always said it was because he was a Virgo.

I pursed my lips over to one side and nodded slowly, happy to let him be the boss.

We gathered wood and put it into four different piles: kindling, sticks, branches and logs. It brought back memories of the countless times we parked Bertha at different state parks or campgrounds and we would "live" there for a couple weeks at a time. My parents would have Ethan and I help out with collecting the wood. Of course they would *always* "lose track of time" and begin gathering at dusk, hurriedly trying to get enough for the evening's fire. I remember seeing my parents emerging from the woods in the almost dark, the whites of their eyes glowing like animals', hoping the wood piled in their arms would last a few good hours.

All that seemed so far away as I unloaded a handful of sticks into their proper pile, then wiped my hands on my shorts and ran my fingers through my straight, smooth, shoulder length hair. Jared dropped some large logs down on their spot and wiped his hands off against each other, then on his jeans.

He put his fists on his hips and looked down at the carbon that would fuel our fire.

"That looks good," he declared.

I nodded in agreement.

"Let's go for a hike," he said. He changed into his hiking boots and I put on my sneakers. We filled a canteen with water from a plastic milk jug and put it in a backpack along with some trail mix, his bird identification book, my sketchbook and a couple of pens and pencils.

We hiked through the redwoods, cedars and oak, the smells filling me, cleansing me. Birds called back and forth, fluttering in the treetops. The feeling of rock and hard earth under my feet, the crunching of twigs, every once in a while the rustling of a small creature foraging for its dinner. These little things were full of life and gave me a subtle euphoria.

A part of me wanted to run off the path, just run in the woods as freely as the birds and animals, like I used to. But I was content to follow behind Jared on the narrow trail, a byway for humans to get from one place to another, even out in 'the wild.'

We stopped a couple times to sit on a boulder and eat trail mix and drink water and kiss. I would just look at him and wonder if he felt about me the same way I felt about him, if he adored me.

Back at the campsite Jared got the fire going as I chopped the potatoes and carrots and wrapped them in aluminum foil. When the burning wood created enough coals, I put the two foil pockets on the edge of the fire, along with a pot of water for pasta and another with canned tomato sauce.

Dusk came and we ate our dinner at the picnic table. The potatoes were still a bit hard in places, and we forgot to bring salt, but we ate with voracious appetites due to how we exerted ourselves. After dinner we played cards within a small circle of light created by a kerosene lantern. I loved watching him shuffle. He was a real pro. I thought it was sexy.

After cards we just sat by the fire on a big log that Jared had dragged out of the woods. He put his arm around me and

I leaned into him. We exchanged stories. He told me how his mom had fought with his dad because she wanted a career, but he wanted a housewife. He told me about his grandfather who took him fishing and taught him endless card games and tricks. I told him more about Bertha and our escapades around the country. I told him about the time I got lost at a Grateful Dead concert when I was seven and found myself hanging out with some other family, sitting on their old woven Pendleton blanket, and thought that maybe I was just going to end up with them if my own parents didn't find me. He was so intrigued by my life and really liked my parents. I began to understand how they might seem cool from an outside perspective, but I was resentful of them for being so different. I would have enjoyed his upbringing much more, I was convinced, to have lived in one house, and to have gone to school and have friends. To have them over to chat and play. To have learned basic grooming, for christ's sake. But Jared tried to convince me that my freedom was an ideal beyond what most people could ever dream of, working their whole lives for no reason other than their illusions of scarcity and security.

"It's all just made up, the way we've created society," he said. "But no one can see that. People think things are just the they way they are. There's no objectivity; no one believes things can be fundamentally different. But not so with your parents. Even if they couldn't change the whole world in one day, they at least had the guts to go be free and live the life they wanted."

But what about what *I* wanted?

That night in the tent we got what we had both been wanting, probably what drove us to take this little excursion in the first place. Laying there in our little nest of blankets, our naked bodies touching, sharing warmth, was the closest we had ever been to each other. It felt so comfortable. Sublime. His body existed inside my knowing; how it moved, how it felt. Jared existed inside me and I in him. My body, my movements,

109

my feelings, all there inside his awareness. We kissed each other, stroked each other. He brought my hand to his mouth several times so he could press his soft lips into it.

He put his hand on my waist, my thigh, my breast as we kissed deeply. I explored his torso, his back, his furry, strong legs. A sweet heat was building. It was dark there in the tent, but I was seeing blue lights, like flame, in my mind's eye. He put his hand between my legs and began to rub. A big space opened up in my belly. Everything, an unborn universe, my whole life ahead of me just dark mystery, got stirred and swam around in that space. I thought about touching his penis several times before I had the courage to let my hand find it. I wrapped my hand around the hard shaft and grasped tightly. It throbbed in my hold. Heat radiated from it. My spine went supple, my whole body moved like water, arching in waves. One of Jared's fingers felt the invitation and slowly entered me. I gasped.

He responded with an encouraging "*mmmmmmm*."

He went deeper and the sweet feeling spread. I moaned. He kissed me affectionately.

We continued like that for a little while until the urge to fuck became too strong to resist. It hurt at first, of course, and in retrospect it was novice, a bit sloppy and short. But to me it was perfect. It was blissful. Afterwards I had a calm sense of fulfillment. We laid wrapped around each other and he brought my hand to his lips again before he ended up falling asleep.

I did not fall asleep until after sunrise. I lay there in my contentment, in that delicious feeling, afraid that sleep would wash it away. I breathed and listened to the sounds of night: crickets chirping, the rustling of nocturnals ambling about the forest floor, the distant creek. What I thought was most beautiful was the sound of the birds, singing early in the morning. I lay there as dawn neared, Jared's arm flung over my chest, his face buried in my shoulder, breathing on me. The light was a hazy blue, pierced with yellows towards the East. I had heard the birds singing before, like that morning after our first kiss, but this was something more. I felt like I was being transported, invited into the magical realm of nature. Everything was alive: the cool morning air, the blue light, the sun I could sense rising beyond the trees. I wanted to join the birds in singing to it, heralding a new day, life reborn again. Their songs were sweet, fluid like liquid silver streams, gleaming. In that moment I knew life itself to be holy. And I felt fundamentally changed. Instead of feeling separate from everyone and everything, it was as if the whole world existed inside my very heart, intimate and familiar.

We stayed one more day and one more night. In that time all I saw, everything I felt was the Divine, and it was as if It was conscious of me as well. It knew me and It knew that I was awake to it. There was almost a conversation happening. I certainly didn't grow up religious in any sense of the word, but my parents had a reverence for life. I had the thought that this experience was probably what my parents had been after with all their LSD explorations. Maybe they had even touched it. I had never before and never again afterwards been this happy, this fulfilled. Sometimes I've even had the thought that this experience ruined me because nothing else was this. Even the good times paled in comparison.

On the ride home I began to get apprehensive. What was I going to do with this feeling? What were people going to think of me? As my fear grew, the feeling, the awareness of the aliveness of Life, began to dim. A sweet spark of it stayed with me for several weeks causing a lingering smile, but the absolute openness, the complete peace, the sense that I was seeing life in its true nature, slowly receded. The memory of this time has both given me hope and drained me of it.

17

Ethan and I stayed in touch on and off over the years. I visited San Francisco a few times to see him and my mom and the city that smelled of home, even though I refused to acknowledge it. And he visited me a handful of times. A few times in New York and a couple times in Philly and once in Baltimore. I didn't try to contact him or my mom when I was on the streets. I had enough wits to do it, but my pride wouldn't let me.

One Saturday in Richmond when I was bored out of my mind and Donny was at a softball game, I decided to give Ethan a call. He has lived in the same house with his wife Matilda for over ten years. I knew he would be at home when I called. He was surprised to hear from me; it had been almost a year since we last talked, when I saw him last in San Francisco. I told him that I had moved to Richmond, Virginia. He asked why and I said I moved away from Poolesville because it was too small, but I'm not sure why I moved to Richmond. I told him that I was living with a man and he got really excited for me. I did not share his excitement. He said he wanted to come visit. I let him know that it wasn't a good idea, that things were 'chaotic,' but he insisted. So three weeks later my brother, my little buddy, was arriving at Dulles Airport and I drove the truck to go get him.

I stood by the baggage carrousel where his flight's luggage was assigned. I fidgeted, crossing my arms, uncrossing my arms, looking around everywhere, pacing, wringing my hands. What a dreadful place, an airport, all the people milling about like apparitions, either too slowly or too quickly, wheeling bags under florescent lights, seemingly unaware of all the other people. How do people ignore everyone else's presence so easily? That has always baffled me. Finally, ten minutes after Ethan's flight had landed, when I had just about rubbed the skin off my forearms, I saw him coming from the far end of baggage claim, along with a small herd of fellow travelers. He always looked the same to me, his round face, his turtle-beak nose, his strawberry-blonde hair, although it was a bit darker after he turned thirty. He saw me too and smiled and did a little wave with his hand like only a little brother would do. He came at me like a train and hugged me with the one arm that wasn't holding his wheeled carry-on bag (the type that everyone seems to use these days). I put my hands on his wide back, but was overwhelmed by the strength of his embrace and his shoulder was digging into my neck, almost choking me. Then he grabbed me by the arms and held me out in front of him so he could take a good look at me.

"You look good, Mimi," he said. I doubt it. But he looked good, wearing his fitted jeans, lime green button up shirt perfectly complementing the color of his hair, which was nicely cut in a side part.

"Thanks. You too." I stood there speechless, not knowing what to say.

"Ready to go?" he asked.

"You didn't check any luggage?"

"Nope. I got it all in here," he said giving his wheelie luggage a little tug. "So, where are you parked?"

"This way." I pointed with a limp hand. We turned and began heading off in the direction of the parking lot. It always feels a bit surreal seeing someone for the first time in a long time.

On the ride home I wanted to say so much. I wanted to tell him that I was miserable. I wanted to tell him about my newest paintings. I wanted to tell him that Donny was a jerk. I wanted to warn him that Donny was not a San Francisco liberal computerhead like he was and that he needed to be careful. But I didn't say any of that. Instead I let Ethan ramble on, telling me all about his life. He was developing new software, whatever that entails. Matilda threw the raddest birthday party for him, the house full of their friends dressed up as super heroes from the 80s, drinking cocktails, smoking joints on the back deck, everyone having a ball. Leo was doing great in school. Mom had taken up crocheting and she was obsessed! I listened and nodded and said things like "Oh wow," and "That's great." He also asked me questions about my job and what I'd "been up to." I told him the basics.

When we got home Donny was on the couch watching a baseball game. He stood up when we came in and introduced himself and shook hands with Ethan. They both seemed delighted to be meeting each other. Donny was not intimidated by Ethan's Hugo Boss shirt or obvious metropolitan sophistication. This was his turf. And Ethan was not intimidated by Donny's primitive masculinity or his large frame. He has always been able to befriend anybody. So the two of them hit it off talking guy talk. Ethan follows the Giants well enough to make a show of his exasperation over some trade that happened recently, as would be expected of a true fan. Donny shared with Ethan some of his plans for around the house. When he said he was thinking of knocking down the 'old shed,' I knew it was just to spite me. The chatting subsided and Donny decided it was time for bed. I was glad about it. I had taken off work so I could pick Ethan up. I'm never tired at that hour and I was looking forward to having Ethan to myself.

"Are you hungry or thirsty?" I asked, settling into Ethan's presence.

"Can I have some water?" I got up and came back with a glass of water for each of us. He was looking at me. Observing me. "Are you happy, Mimi?" he asked as I sat down next to him on the couch, setting our glasses down on the coffee table.

"I'm okay," I tell him.

He pursed his lips and evaluated me. "Are you painting?"

A little light went on. "Yeah."

"Cool. I'd love to see your recent stuff."

"Alright. I'll show you around my studio in the morning." I had never called it that, *my studio*. But that's what it was. It was my own little painting studio. I smiled.

"Sounds good."

We didn't talk much more after that. We watched Conan O' Brian and laughed together drinking our water. We both

114

laughed real hard a couple times, like you can only do when someone else is there laughing too. It was the most fun I'd had in a very long time. After the show he was tired. We converted the sofa bed and I pulled down some sheets and a blanket and a pillow from the linen closet and we said our goodnights. I crawled into bed next to Donny, who was already snoring his head off, and I got a little sad that Ethan would only be in town for a few days.

The following day was Friday and Ethan and I hung out around the house. Since Donny had the truck, we couldn't really go anywhere. We had woken up late, so we didn't have much time before I needed to go to work. I cooked us breakfast that we ate at the kitchen table with its new red checked plastic tablecloth I bought at Walmart. Afterwards I showed him my paintings, which he made a big fuss over. Then we played cards out on the patio. I was kicking his butt. He said we needed to get out of the house on the weekend or he would go mad.

"Donny might need the truck," I told him.

"Well then we'll take a cab or a bus or something."

I prepared dinner for Donny and Ethan. Salad and burgers. The burgers were made into 4 patties, two for each, which Donny could cook in the big pan. The fixins were laid out on a little platter. I wanted to say something, to protect him from Donny, but didn't know what to say.

"You can hang out in the shed if you want, you know if you want to doodle with the paints."

"Hang out in the shed?"

"Well, if you get bored or something…"

He chuckled. "Mimi, that's nuts. You and I need to get out of this house…and I'm talking further than the shed."

"Okay. I'll ask Donny if I can take the truck to work tonight and work super fast so I can get home early."

That night at work Kim saw me cleaning like a whirlwind. I tried to explain it to her, but she just nodded, confusion in her little brown eyes. She understood at least that I had a need to get done quick. Or that I was on drugs. She worked at my pace, her forehead gleaming with sweat when we were done. I smiled and as a reflex returned her little bow. I got home almost three hours earlier than usual and crawled into bed, setting the alarm for eight a.m., five hours away. So the following day Ethan and I took the bus downtown.

* * * * * * * * * * * *

We had a good ol' time out on the town, walking around the historic district, visiting the Edgar Allen Poe museum and having a nice lunch: Ethan's first taste of Maryland blue crabs. We got home sometime in the early evening.

"What's the plans for dinner?" Ethan asked.

"Don't know. Let's see what Donny wants to do."

Donny truck was in the driveway, but he was not in the house when we went inside. Ethan and I walked out the sliding glass back door. Donny was sitting there with a Budweiser in his one hand and a Marlboro in his other.

"Howdy," Donny greeted us.

"Howdy," Ethan returned buoyantly.

"How was the museum?" Donny asked.

"It was okay," said Ethan, "Underwhelming, actually."

"Well, that's museums for you," Donny informed us.

The neighbor lady was outback hanging laundry. She saw me and paused in her task of pinning up a pair of big-hipped jeans.

"Hi, Mimi." She said loudly from across the fence.

"Hi, Sharon," I replied with my good neighbor smile.

"What was the guy's name again?" Donny asked.

"Edgar Allen Poe," Ethan informed him, "He was reared in Richmond."

"Pull up a seat," Donny said waiving his cigarette around in the direction of the empty lawn chairs. It was a humid

116

afternoon and I worried that Ethan wouldn't be able to stand it for very long. We sat in our chairs and waited quietly for someone to speak. Of course it was Donny who spoke first.

"You enjoying your visit?"

"Yeah it's nice. It's good to see my sister."

"And how do you like our little city?"

"It's nice. I like the old buildings downtown. So beautiful. All that brick. You don't see that type of architecture in San Francisco. Very stately."

Donny nodded proudly. "Yep. We got history here, way back to Jamestown. This is original America."

"Yeah, it's great." I was surprised to here Ethan agree. This was everything *his* west coast tried to distance itself from, to create something constantly novel and daring and kinetic. Donny took a long drag off his cigarette, his eyes squinting against the bright afternoon sun.

"You want a smoke?" Donny offered, extending the pack to my brother.

Ethan reached for the box. "Sure." He took out a cigarette and then grabbed the lighter Donny was passing him.

"You don't smoke," I said, bewildered.

Ethan finished lighting the cigarette, passed the lighter back to Donny then after an exhale said, "I do occasionally." I couldn't help but see Ethan like he was trying to impress Donny, like Donny was some cool older kid.

"Gross," I said.

"Mimi, let your brother enjoy his smoke," Donny grunted, his brow crinkled.

"Yeah, Mimi," Ethan smirked.

I couldn't believe it. Here was my brother, my little brother who I took such good care of when my parents were stoned out of their minds, and he was palling up with Donny, the asshole who was a big, loud, overbearing thorn in my face. The Virginia sun was beating down hard and the moisture in the air was starting to collect on the back of my neck and above my lip.

"Wanna watch the Orioles game in a few?" Donny asked Ethan.

"Sure." Ethan put his legs up on the vacant lawn chair, sliding to a reclined position. They sure were getting chummy. Why would Ethan want to spend those hours watching a game with Donny when he was only here for such a brief time to see me?

"Mimi, go fetch your brother and me some beer." Something sank. My head began to buzz. I wanted to bash that jerk's face. How dare he tell me what to do! *Go fetch him a beer? What am I, your goddamn golden retriever? Fuck you!* I turned to Ethan, expecting to see something sympathetic, but he sat there grinning, happy to let the Mongoloid treat me like a piece of crap! I was dumbstruck. My stomach turned upside-down. I was alone again. The buzzing in my ears got louder. I stumbled out of my chair and into the house, where I leaned on the kitchen counter and whimpered and felt the sour burn of this life once again wanting to eat away at me. I poured myself a glass of water and tried to catch my breath. It was so damn hot and muggy. I was going to melt, I was sure of it, turn into a puddle of acrid liquid in the middle of Donny's kitchen floor and no one would care. Donny and Ethan would walk in and see the puddle, rank fumes filling their nostrils, and it would be no surprise to them to see me that way. That was how my existence here on Earth was bound to end. I almost choked on stomach acid coming up my throat. I drank more water, trying to stop panting. When I collected myself enough I grabbed two cans of beer from the fridge and rushed outside to give them to the guys.

"Thanks," Ethan said. Donny didn't say anything, except after a while when I was standing there.

"Will you sit down! You're making me nervous just hovering there like a wasp."

Ethan giggled.

My throat started to feel like it was closing. "I'm going to bed," I gasped.

"What? It's the middle of the day," Ethan's face opened up, looking like the pouting, needy little boy I remember.

"I'm exhausted."

"Mimi, your brother leaves town tomorrow. You don't want to waste the day sleeping."

"I can barely keep my eyes open," I said. And it was true. I couldn't even look at them.

"Are you okay?" Ethan asked.

"Yes," I stated, then turned to go inside and into the bedroom where I shoved my face in the pillow. I couldn't cry then. All the sadness went to my head and my belly as food for the ghost. I groaned and moaned. I sniffled and choked and coughed. It must have lasted an hour. Afterwards I heard Ethan and Donny inside watching the baseball game, cheering and shouting and having a good old time. I never hated Ethan before that day. He never even tried to rouse me, to check in.

I didn't really sleep. But I couldn't get up either. I couldn't face Ethan, joining Donny, treating me so badly. I was a prisoner in that bed for twelve hours.

I got up early in the morning with first light and made myself some coffee. Ethan staggered into the kitchen, sleepy eyed.

"What time is it?" he asked.

"After six."

"You feeling better?" His eyes were closed, occasionally opening slits, still unable to receive the new day's light.

"I'm fine."

He pulled out a chair, sat down and ran a hand through his strawberries and oranges hair.

"I gotta tell you Mimi, you worry me sometimes." Now he opened his eyes to look at me.

I laughed dismissively. "You don't need to worry about me. I am the big sister after all."

If he was so worried, then why did he treat me like shit the day before?

He took a breath. "Mimi, I mean it." He reached across the table to take my hand. I took it back and let it hang at my side. "Mimi. I don't know how to say this…"

"Ethan, I told you, you don't need to worry. Stop patronizing me."

The room was a cinder block. Unmoving. Stale. Gray.

"Do you want some coffee?" He didn't speak, but of course he wanted coffee. Out of obligation and to get away from the table, I stood up to put on a pot of coffee. Donny would want some too when he woke. I wished I was strong enough to not do things for people when I didn't want to, just to keep things smooth. Sometimes I wished to tell Donny to go fuck himself when he asked when dinner would be ready, or I'd want to tell him that it was his fucking turn to make *me* dinner. But I knew that that would not have gone well. I was scared of him. Sometimes I try to understand my decisions around Donny, and find myself getting nowhere. There was the sex. Which I craved. And it was *some* human connection. But I knew all along that it was going to be trouble. Maybe at a subconscious level or something I believed at times the relationship would actually work.

I made Ethan his coffee, set milk and sugar out, 'cause that's how he takes it, and went to the couch to read. He came out of the kitchen about 10 minutes later and put his clothes from the previous day and his toiletries in his duffle bag. Donny came out of the bedroom and went to the kitchen.

He shouted, "Any breakfast?"

"No! I have to drive Ethan to the airport."

He grunted.

"Okay, well I guess I'm ready." Ethan declared.

"Are you taking the truck?" Donny yelled from the kitchen.

"Yes. I told you I would need it today."

"What time you gonna be back?"

"I'm coming right home. Four or five hours, depending on traffic."

"Alright. Don't make me wait all day. I wanna go to the pub to watch the game."

I grabbed my bag and opened the front door. "Come on," I said to Ethan.

We didn't talk most of the way. Maybe he wanted to. But he never said sorry. I can't understand why he was being such a dick. It was like he was more concerned with getting along with Donny than treating me with dignity. How fucked up is that?

18

It's been Indian Summer, early October and hotter than August was. Flowers are still in bloom. But it's definitely October, with the light being all slanted and amber and rich. The flatness and hazy edges of things under summer's bright light starts to take focus; depth and density come into being. Autumn is the dusk of seasons, the closing, turning everything gold and brown and ready to harvest. When it does get colder, a whirling wind will blow the browned fallen leaves in aimless circles and shake the yellow and red waving hands that still hold on to their tree's branchy arms. It is the most beautiful season, with its stunning sadness, the wisdom of just letting everything go. But it also harkens the cold winter, when all is frozen silhouette and as dead as things can get while they're still alive.

We are out on the lawn, some people running like children, some walking like the dead among the perfect hedges and purple asters. It rained yesterday morning and the earth is still soft under my sneakers. It would be easy to escape, I imagine. The wrought iron door next to the front gate where the cars come in seems unlocked. I've seen people open it without a key.

Daryl is making a crown out of the persistent dandelions; they would bloom forever if they could. Ann is sitting on a bench smoking, looking smug with her sunglasses on, two benches down from the other smokers huddled together wheezing and ranting. Nigel is tossing a red rubber ball with Joan and the new redhead lady whose name I can't remember.

"Wanna play, Mimi?" he shouts.

I shake my head.

The sun today is not as hot as it has been, only warm and humid, but still too much for my friend from the underworld, who is sitting under the magnolia tree. I walk over to her. She watches me approach, smoking her cigarette.

"Hi, Mimi."

"Hi, Val."

She looks different today. There is the slightest light reflecting off her dark eyes. Her perfectly pale skin doesn't have its usual grey-green hue. One side of her mouth curls up a bit. A smile.

"Well, are you going to sit?" she asks, sarcastically. I bend down, put my hands on the soft earth, and let myself fall back the six inches onto my rump. It's a bit of a strain. I'm not young anymore. Val is sitting more erect than usual, more erect than me. Usually I feel like I'm in the company of a corpse, trying to find signs of life. Today she is stronger than me. Cigarette smoke surrounds me like a blanket. Its smell invades my nose and it causes my eyes to blink. I swish it away from my face with my hand, and let out a little cough. Val stretches her arm out to her other side, putting as much distance between me and her cigarette as possible. She looks at me tenderly.

"What's going on?" I ask.

She looks down at the grass, brushing her free hand over the blades in front of her.

"I talked to Sandra today. She…"

"Sandra?"

"My social worker."

"Ah."

"Anyways. She told me that things went well with my meeting with Jensen and it looks like I'll be leaving here in a couple days. She says she just needs to make all the arrangements so I have a place to go and all that."

"What?" I say, obviously surprised and upset.

"I guess the nurses and Westland think I'm ready."

Unbelievable! Is my lip twitching?

"I thought you'd be happy for me," she says deflated.

"What about me? You're more fucked up than I am!"

She looks hurt, her body losing its new strength, slouching over. "I thought you'd be happy for me, Mimi." Sadness in her voice. Is this the first time I have witnessed actual emotion from her?

I push myself up with a grunt and start stomping through the lawn. What about me? What the fuck about me? When the fuck do I get out? One fucking thing after another. My whole life, just one goddamn fucked up thing after another. Fuck, fuck, fuck it all. I hate it. I hate you, do you hear me? Fucking all of it!

I run up to Nigel holding his red ball, eyes widening as I approach. I punch the ball from underneath, it hitting him in the chin.

"When the fuck do I get a chance?" I scream in his face.

He grabs me hard by the arms. "Mimi, calm down!" he shouts.

"I hate this place! I hate it! I'm not going to hurt anyone!" My throat stings.

"Mimi!" he shouts, shaking me, "do you need an injection?" Blood is leaking out his mouth, down his bottom lip and chin.

"I didn't mean to!" I yell, "It was an accident! I can control myself. I was trapped!" Fire and buzzing. Nausea from everything spinning. It's too hard. I go limp. Nigel tries to keep me standing, but can't and I melt to the ground.

He kneels beside me. "Mimi!"

I cry.

"Mimi, relax."

Why am I still here? I didn't mean to do it. I had no choice. I can take care of myself. Can't I just have my shitty fucking life back?

This crying is a river. Things from deep inside my belly getting washed up on the shore. My hands grip the earth, my cheek pressed into its warm softness. I could live like this. I could live in the woods with the earth. I could be the girl I once was with my hair all long and tangled and I'd live among the trees. I spring up to my feet and dash for the front gate. Nigel's hand brushes my calf, trying to grab me. I run, my face wet with earth and tears, my arms bent and chugging beside me. I am a locomotive. No one can catch me. I will just keep running like this down Morison Drive and off into the first wooded area I see. I'll eat berries and acorns and road kill and robin's eggs. It will be hard at first, but I'll get used to it and it will be easier than living with all these fucking people.

Freedom. The door. I put my hands out, slowing down, grab two iron bars and *yank*. A searing pain like knives deep inside my shoulders. I scream. I back away, screaming, the pain shooting down my arms, muscles tearing. I'm on my butt, trying to hold my shoulders with each opposite hand, but the stretching hurts. The door was locked.

Screaming turns to crying. My face on fire. Throat stinging. My shoulders throb.

I lay back. I am always burning.

Someone kneels beside me. They rub my arm tenderly. They put my head in their lap.

My cheek is being stroked. My arm is being stroked. I am a cat. I make purring sounds between sobs.

Commotion. Distressed talking. I turn my head to look up. Nigel is standing over me, with Hillary just behind him. I can't make out the face of the person holding me, the bright sun just behind their head, a halo, is blinding. It is an angel, head turned up facing Nigel and Hillary.

"She's okay," my angel says with a familiar voice, "She's fine." Then the angel looks back down at me and continues the petting. I squint my eyes against the light, staring at the face.

Slowly the form within the shadow reveals itself. A pointed nose. Pouting pink lips. Dark and distant eyes. It's Val. Holding me. Val…who I can't imagine holding anything mammalian. How strange. Whatever. I bury my face into her belly, releasing these lingering sobs, little bursts like a bubble machine in my sternum. An autumn breeze blows. Val continues to rub my arm delicately.

Are Nigel and Hillary still here? I turn my head to see. No. They're gone. I turn back, burying my face into the nook where Val's leg meets her hip.

I rest in the stillness that always follows crying. The smell of earth under Val. The smell of Val, something synthetic and caustic like nail-polish remover. When was the last time I was held after crying? I can't remember. Did Jared? Did I ever cry in front of Jared? I must have.

Why bother myself with thoughts like these? I take a breath and nuzzle against Val's thigh. Val's petting becomes rhythmic and so light and not as soothing. She must be away somewhere, off in her own thoughts. Oh well.

After a while I look up. Val turns to meet my gaze.

"Hey," she says nonchalantly like the depressed young woman I have come to know.

"I'm sorry," I say.

"No problem," she says, cool as a cat.

"Thank you."

"No problem." She looks down at me, trying to figure something out. Maybe like how weird it is that this older lady that once looked after her suddenly turned away from her in her moment of triumph. Or maybe that is just my thought.

"Let's get out of the sun," she says.

I slowly rise to a sitting position. Val stands up and I follow. We walk back to the magnolia tree and crawl into her shade.

I feel uncomfortable. I almost want to bury myself in her skinny body again. She is giving me no signals to proceed with that idea. She lights up a cigarette and exhales over her right shoulder, away from me. I watch her. Her skeleton hand holding the little white stick. Suicide. She tried to kill herself. Her stepfather molested her. She was raped. Abusive boyfriends. All torn up. What is she gonna do in the world?

"I'm sorry," I say.

She exhales smoke away from me, then without turning to face me says, "I said 'no problem.' I mean it, Mimi. No big deal." She is looking off into the distance. I follow her gaze. Squares everywhere. The building. The green yard. The hedges. The wall. Joan and the redhead are still playing with the ball, bouncing it now. Nigel is standing next to the building with arms crossed, talking to Hillary. It looks like they are both looking at me. Are they? Probably.

"You'll get out soon enough," Val says.

I sigh. "I'm not so sure. They think I'm a danger."

"Well, you certainly didn't help your case today." She takes a drag off her cigarette, still looking into the distance, over the wall maybe, where some future awaits. "You know, everyone is crazy," she says in her breathy drawl. My eyebrows rise. "It's true," she says as if she could sense my reaction. "The whole world is psychotic. Everyone is O.C.D. or bi-polar or depressed or has an anxiety disorder." She takes a drag off her cigarette, then instead of exhaling, lets the smoke slowly escape from her open mouth, rising over her face shrouding it like a veil. "I keep having these dreams, these same dreams, where this black pus is covering the earth. Its noxious and poisonous and killing everything. People are in pain."

"It represents evil." I shudder.

"Well...I guess so. But it's pollution." Her face crinkles. "See, that's what I don't get. They call *me* crazy and locked me up because I tried to kill myself. I'm not the one destroying the earth. It's basically mass suicide. And murder, if you include the animals. That's crazy. And everyone is just watching TV, and buying shit they don't need. All because they're afraid, Mimi."

I nod.

"I'm not afraid." She takes a drag off her cigarette. I've never heard her talk so much. She exhales and shakes her head, the smoke fanning out side to side. "Black pus. All the killing.

Wars and pollution. And they call *me* crazy and locked *me* up."

She coughs a little, reminding me that my own throat hurts. "Most of the religions even promote paranoia. 'Ooh, you better be real good or God is gonna get you.' That's fucked up stuff."

I have never heard her talk *about* things. Other than just our day to day.

"You know," she says eagle eyeing me now, "when I get out of here, Mimi, I think I'm gonna become a Buddhist. I'm gonna join a monastery."

"You know anything about Buddhism?" I ask.

"Not really. But it seems simple. That's what I want; simple."

I nod. Makes sense. But there's more to it than that, I'm sure.

Val goes back to her distant land and her cigarette. I feel like I should say something. But what? I agree that the world has always seemed twisted to me, that people have always seemed cold and out of reach. But I was never sure what was twisted, the world or me. In either case, I've always felt separate from it all. Severed. On the outside of the glass bubble.

"The question is, 'Is there hope?' That is the only real question for me right now," Val says to the sky stretching out beyond the wall. "Usually I don't think so. But moments like this, sitting under the magnolia tree with you…I think there is."

I inhale the clear, faintly sweet air. I love Val. "Maybe we just need more moments like this," I say, "Maybe we need to stop being scared of each other and just start playing nice with each other." I look around and see people playing with a ball, Holly and Eric running around, chasing each other, Daryl wearing his crown of dandelion flowers. "Maybe *this* place is heaven," I say laughing, with a sweeping motion of my arm presenting the heavenly world of mania in front of us. Val laughs too. We both lose it, snortin' and shrieking with laughter. Cracking up.

127

We end up on our backs, looking up through the boughs of the magnolia tree, magnolias floating like tea cups on saucers made of leaves. Our arms are intertwined. She takes my hand in hers.

"I don't think I've ever heard you laugh before," I say.

"It feels good," she says still rumbling with aftershocks.

A whistle blows. Its time to go back inside.

"Mimi," she turns to me, "Will you tell me what you did to that person?"

* * * * * * * * * * * *

Screaming. It's loud. I open my eyes and face the digital clock. Two thirty in the morning. Sometimes the screaming here angers me, sometimes it breaks my heart. Tonight it does both. I pull the covers over my shoulders and turn to face the wall. I lie for several minutes, expecting to fall back asleep, but it's no use. I am wide-awake. I turn on my back again and my eyes adjust to the darkness. I can see my crayon pictures on the far wall, little snippets of my inner worlds put on paper. Tomorrow we start art therapy, Nigel has been telling me. I don't know what that will entail, but it can't be all bad. Art is always therapeutic. I'm not sure I need someone telling me how to do that.

I can't believe Val is leaving. I will miss her, my strange, young companion. I will make a picture; an almost motionless grey-green sea under low, dark clouds.

I need to pee.

I get up and put on my fluffy blue slippers. I walk to the door, open it, and head down the corridor. Someone is in front of me. I stop. The figure is slumping a little to one side. The small nightlights, the exit sign, light coming in through the window of the door to the stairwell cast just enough light to see. I let out the breath I didn't realize I was holding.

"Hi, Joan," I say. She doesn't respond. I approach her. Her eyes are off somewhere else. Her jaw is trembling.

"Hi, Joan," I say again, louder to penetrate deeper. But she isn't there.

"It's the yellow light," she mumbles. I nod. "Yellow light means hide," she says. I put my hand on her shoulder. Her body responds only minutely. She is cold under her nightshirt, and her muscles are stiff. "Circle means it all happens again, the same." I look at her face, into her eyes, hoping she'll see me. I need to pee bad.

"Hold on," I say, "I have to pee." I walk around her and down to the ladies room. I don't turn on the lights. I sit on the toilet. It is cold. Toilets are always cold. Pee comes gushing out. I should know better not to drink a glass of water that close to bedtime. Dr. Westland says that if I give up coffee or cut down a lot, it might keep me from needing to pee in the middle of the night, but fat chance of that happening. I wipe, flush, walk out the stall and out of the ladies room. To my left, Joan hasn't moved. I walk around to face her again.

"Joan, you have to go to bed," I just about shout, hoping to pierce through the fog, the worlds that separate us. But she doesn't flinch. I take hold of her forearm to lead her back to her room. She won't budge. I don't want to make her fall. I'll go get the tech on duty. I walk down the corridor, turn left at the common room and walk up to the nurse's lounge. Julie, the night tech, is in there watching TV. *Three's Company* rerun. She sees me and gasps, putting her hand to her chest.

"Mimi, you scared me."

"Joan is standing in the middle of the hallway."

"Is she okay?"

"Yeah. She's not really, um…there. You know?"

"She's not lucid?"

"No." Julie gets up and we start walking, through the common room and down the corridor. "She was saying some really weird things."

"Okay. Go to bed now, Mimi."

"Do you need my help?"

129

"No, I'll manage. Go to bed."

"Will she be okay?" I say in a hushed tone because we are approaching Joan and I don't want to be rude talking about her in front of her.

"She'll be fine. Goodnight, Mimi."

"Goodnight." I walk past Joan, "Goodnight, Joan," and back to my room. I turn back around to see what's going on. It is dark, but it looks like Julie is holding Joan's arm and hand, leaning towards her, talking into her ear. I go back into my room, and sit on my bed. I look towards the window. Through the blinds I can see a pale yellow three-quarter moon. She is the empress of night, her presence unchallenged in the sky. I lay down in bed and slide under the covers. Sleep won't come for a long time, but it will come.

19 ➤

My life was, I imagine, the typical picture of a teenage girl in love. The routines stayed the same as before; I went to school and did my homework, I painted, I helped out around the house. The rest of the time was spent with Jared. The two of us went to the movies, went out for food or coffee to play cards or read, hung out in the park. The big game, of course, was when and where were we going to have sex. It was safer at my house than his, because even if my family came home it wouldn't have been such a big deal to them, although it certainly would have been embarrassing and uncomfortable for me. We had a few close calls, but nothing to turn my face red and give my parents serious teasing ammunition.

We tried in Golden Gate Park but people kept coming by, no matter where we were. One night we brought a blanket and tried to find a hidden spot in the trees, but we kept hearing noises and got spooked. Our "secret spot" on Bernal Hill was a good bet, and we would go camping as often as we could. My parents definitely liked to joke about how much I loved camping, 'a real nature girl,' they would say and chortle together.

But sex wasn't our only agenda or even what drove our relationship. We truly enjoyed each other and cared about one another. I know he cared about me too.

I decided to do a painting of Jared, but not one that anyone would recognize. More symbolic, capturing his essence, not his form. I painted a very handsome middle-aged man wearing white, flowing clothing. He has dropped a heart on the ground, not a heart like Valentine's Day, but the actual organ, and the ground is a mess of poverty and destruction. The heart has broken open. Out of the cracks a soft light emanates, butterflies and spring flowers emerge. I tell people that it is a Creation Myth, and don't explain further. I called the piece *The Heart That Continually Breaks Open*. That was Jared, always sad about nuclear weapons or the Middle East or whales. But sad like only love can be sad. He cried in front of me. He cried not just for sad things, but for beauty too. He cried one time when we were watching the sunset over the Pacific. He cried holding a little puppy he found on the street. He cried at sad parts during movies and redemptive parts. And one time he cried for me.

We were sitting in the front seat of his father's Buick. It was night and we were driving home from an amazing Fleetwood Mac show at the Great American. The moon was full and floated over the city like a beneficent angel casting a cool, like jazz cool, light. My hand was in his, resting on his lap. I was lost in some thoughts or perhaps just relishing in the night and the moon, when suddenly Jared was squeezing my hand harder. He released a little than gave it two more squeezes. Then he let out a sound that was almost like a cough.

Choked up. His body contracted fiercely with each released "cough." His mouth bowed down a bit, his face contorted and his eyes were not exactly looking at the road, but were seeing somewhere else. I got a bit concerned so I squeezed his hand. He turned to look at me and he had a stream of tear on his left cheek. His eyes glowed and I never felt the core of him more intensely.

"I see you, Mimi," he said, "I see you."

I wanted to say that I saw him too, that he was the heart that continuously breaks open and I've never known anyone as beautiful and wonderful as him. But instead I just looked into his eyes and squeezed his hand, my breath unmoving.

I don't think we talked the whole rest of the ride home. What would there have been to say? We rode with the moon, holding each other's hands tightly.

He dropped me off in front of my house. I wanted him to come up, but my family was home, including Ethan probably asleep in our room. We kissed slowly. His mouth was full of dew, blessed by the moon. I was lapping it, a doe at an enchanted forest pool. My whole body glowed pale blue. He cupped one side of my face and looked me earnestly in the eyes, his eyes shiny wet.

"I love you, Mimi."

"I love you too," I said more clearly than I've ever said anything.

We just looked at each other, bathing in each other's presence. This was perfect. *He* was perfect, sacred perfection itself, tender and glowing. Eventually I leaned in, pecked him on the lips, opened my door and got out. I ducked to look at him.

"Goodnight, Mister," I said.

"Goodnight, Mis'ess," he said smiling. I shut the door, walked up the steps to the stoop, went inside my house. Everything was dark. The quiet in there felt different. The air suddenly seemed stuffy, dusty. It was hard to breathe.

That night I couldn't fall asleep for a long time. I kept replaying the events of the night in my mind. Flashes of holding each other at the concert, the drive home. Jared had the most pure heart of anyone I've ever known. And I have never again been so connected with another person, although I have sought it out. I'm sure he also cried for his wife and each of his children in turn, probably over and over again. But that night he looked me right in the eyes, and he saw me and he cried. No one can ever take that away from me.

* * * * * * * * * * * * *

It's not like things were always blissful. We had our disagreements. Mostly Jared would get upset or frustrated with something I would say or not say. I never expressed any upset with him, although maybe I should have. Maybe I should have been a little bit more of a South American firecracker. The biggest thing was that Jared often thought I didn't understand him. I remember one time sitting together on the top of the hill in Dolores Park. We were sprawled out with a little picnic lunch on a blue checked blanket, talking and playing cards. Jared had just read *Silent Spring* and was really pissed about the environment.

"I mean, how can we stop any of this? This country is ignorant, trashing the only planet we have. It's fucking asinine."

"I don't know," I said, earnestly thinking I could help solve this problem. "Maybe we can have an event at school. Something like Earth Day."

"The people who would participate already care. How can we possibly effect the people who don't care or think the whole thing is bullshit?"

I cocked my head sideways, peering up at the wispy clouds being pulled apart like cotton candy in the blue sky.

"I think that light is intelligent. Or intelligence. Like it's God or something."

He looked at me through one eye.

"Mimi, what the fuck are you talking about?"

"Well, I mean look at how everything alive responds to light. Life needs light."

"What the hell does that have to do with what we're talking about?"

It felt like he punched me in the stomach, and I recoiled from the blow.

"Well, maybe if we can get people to see how magical life is, they would start caring for it better."

"You've been reading too much poetry. Poets have been saying that for years, Mimi. It hasn't gotten people to change a damn thing. They hear that shit, and then they just go about their business and forget it." He let out a big, restless sigh, "I just don't understand how people can be how they are. I don't get it. And I don't know how to do anything to change it. I need to get out of here. Get out into the world and join the fight." His eyes looked down at the grass as he went into thought.

"You are doing the best you can," I tried to assure him.

"Am I?" he said, his eyes half closed, glaring at me. I felt bound up and far away. I didn't know that the critical look was really for himself.

"Well, you're gonna do a lot. You're only eighteen. You have your whole life to help create change in the world." That calmed him down. He began mindlessly picking at the grass, scanning the cityscape that lay before us. I wanted to touch his hand, or wrap myself around him, but I was scared to.

He laughed a little to himself. "Sometimes I think you dose up on your parents' LSD, the things you say." He was smiling, but a smile that separated us, scrutinized me. It was stagnant air, the distance I felt in moments like these, and it made me shudder.

* * * * * * * * * * * * *

I guess it's strange to think I had pot dealers for parents and a stoner for a boyfriend but never touched the stuff myself. Not that Jared was off the handle with it or anything, like my folks were. He smoked with his friends and when we went to shows and out camping, but I think he appreciated the space we shared and that he didn't feel the need to get high.

My parents, on the other hand, still got high all the time. They smoked weed how most people smoke cigarettes. And I didn't like most of the characters that came into our house to get high with them or buy their stuff. Some of them were quite young and on a couple occasions they were people I recognized from school. When I walked in the door and saw a familiar face at the kitchen table sharing a joint with Mom, a newly purchased dime bag sitting in front of her, I'd hurry to my room pretending not to see.

My parents thought it was funny that I was such a "tight-ass." They believed it some sort of cosmic joke that they would have a daughter who was so uncomfortable with their loose ways and their childlike behavior.

Ethan was the great balancer. He loved Mom and Dad for being the big kids he enjoyed so thoroughly and who were so receptive to his affectionate ways. They all had a certain pack mentality. But Ethan also loved me on my own terms. I was his big sister and in many ways his best friend.

One evening at dinner, my parents confronted me about my dwindling presence in the house. I had just come home from painting late at school. I had been very involved in a piece of three birds singing on the branch of a redwood tree, inspired by the experience I had had that first time camping with Jared. Ms. Wilkinson was kind enough to stay until six or so, seeing how entrenched into the work I was.

I walked in the door, hung up my coat, put my bag down on the sofa and came into the kitchen where everyone was sitting, already eating.

"Well, well, well, look who decided to come home for dinner?" Mom jested.

I gave a contemptuous smirk.

They were silent for a while, as I served myself steamed peas and carrots, rice and teriyaki tofu. Mom had taken an Asian Vegetarian cooking class and for two months, that became the usual fare. It was a nice change at first, but a person can only eat so much tofu.

As I ate, the silence grew uncomfortable.

Dad spoke up, "You know, Mimi, we've become a bit concerned that you are hardly ever at home."

"What's the concern?" I asked, chewing on a mouthful of peas, not looking up to meet his gaze.

"Well," he paused for thought, "The concern is that we miss you."

"Well, I'm home when I can be. I do have a life, you know."

"And that life includes your family," Mom interjected.

"Yeah? When was the last time you saw your family?" I jabbed, suddenly looking up at her. She was hurt.

"That's different, Mimi," Her throat tight and scratchy, "My parents were awful. They were so strict and yelled at me for everything. I couldn't breathe around them. I had to escape. What are you escaping from?"

I shrugged, putting my attention back on my food.

Dad joined back in. "Mimi, we give you all the freedom you want. We love you and support you in whatever you want to do."

"This conversation doesn't feel like I'm being given all the freedom I want."

That shut them up. Ethan just watched, not saying a word, but I could sense that he wanted my parents to win. He wanted more of me too.

"I just don't like being around a house full of stoners," I declared. "And I hate being here when people are tripping. I just hope you aren't selling acid to any of my friends."

We all continued eating dinner quietly, looking only at our plates. We were a shopping cart with one wheel that wouldn't go the same way. It was challenging for them, I know. But it was more so for me. I was the wheel being dragged sideways.

20 ➤

After unwanted, messy quick sex with Donny, I lay in bed, feeling like my gut was full of worms. He went for work and I was his kill, left up in the tree for him to devour more of later. Energy raced in my head like frantic scribbling. I sat up, holding my head up with my hands. I lay back down, thinking I could sleep it off. But sleep didn't come. I sat up again. I got up and went to the kitchen to pour myself some orange juice and make coffee, bumping into doorframes and the kitchen table on my way.

I sat at the plastic kitchen table in the plastic chair. I wanted to be outside, but it was November and mornings were frigid. I couldn't drink the orange juice. Anything in my mouth made me want to gag. So I dumped it down the drain. I brought my coffee with me to the couch; I would sip it slowly while I read.

Assuming my usual position on the couch, lying down with my head on the far side so I could see the room and anyone walking in the door, I cracked open my little paperback novel about a witch living in Vermont, casting her spells on the townspeople and all the while looking for love. I don't usually read such pulp, but I had been needing something easy and entertaining. But I couldn't read either. My mind was a sand storm, my body a power plant. I put the book down and grabbed the remote, turning on game shows. My attention drifted back and forth from the TV and my racing thoughtless thoughts, about everything and nothing. I was a prisoner. Eventually I fell asleep.

I woke up just a couple hours later and immediately was pulled back into the agitated state. I wanted to cry. I sat up. The TV invaded my head like nagging relatives. I threw the remote at it. I decided to paint this out.

I got up, got dressed in some old jeans and a t-shirt and bundled up in layers. There was no heat in the shed.

I walked out the sliding glass door, hurried across the lawn and spun the combination on the lock. My hand was shaking, and I had to attempt it three times before the lock popped open.

I sat down at my easel, not knowing what would appear on the canvas. I felt like I was on a fast ride that I couldn't disembark. A familiar feeling. The ride jerks, this way and that way and this way and jerks and jerks and spins, shut up! shut up! shut up! and I want to drive this thing into a telephone pole and end it once and for all. Let there be some respite somewhere in this life!

The canvas I put in front of me was medium sized, 36" by 48". I filled my palate with reds and yellows and brown and cobalt blue. Turpentine sat in a shallow bowl, emanating its heady odor, like a pool on Venus. I dip my large square brush into the maroon red and start smearing it in large strokes across the bottom of the canvas. I continue up the canvas in this way, introducing other reds, oranges, browns, getting darker until the very top is a deep purple.

I dipped a size 10, medium sized, round brush into the black and watched as shapes emerge on the canvas. Cars? Machinery. Motion. Wreckage. I highlight and fill with oranges and reds, shading with browns and purple. Carnage. Destruction. Swirling motion around the top. This was one of the most abstract pieces I had ever done. It was flowing out from a place way down in my belly. My heart and mind did not have much to say about this. The gut is allowed to speak for itself, uncensored, unguided, to talk about all the twisting and contracting and acid it has known for so long. My arm dances fast, brush in hand, agreeing to be the voice of my belly.

138

After what was several hours (although it felt like no time at all) I heard a noise. The shed door opening. A part of me stayed in the painting, but another part of me knew that Donny was standing behind me, watching, breathing.

"What the hell is that shit?" he said.

I wanted to turn around and let my belly spill its acid all over him. To burn him. Instead, I kept on painting. He wanted a response. I wasn't going to give him one.

"You making dinner tonight?" he asked.

"No," is all I said as I painted fast black streaks, like fire coming from the center of the painting. He wanted to say more. Wanted to call me names. But he didn't. He turned around and left to curse in his own head about his crazy bitch woman.

I knew I needed to get out of there. But how? And where would I go?

21 ➤

She didn't even say goodbye. Coward. Or maybe she just never cared to begin with. Little bitch. Well, good riddance. She was nothing but dead weight anyways. What an idiot I am, thinking we were actually friends. Someone like that isn't a friend to anyone, selfish little bitch.

I lie in bed, on top of the covers, fully dressed in jeans and a t-shirt, my usual attire, hands clasped together over my belly, head propped up on my pillow. Val left early this morning when I was eating breakfast. I knew she would be leaving today. We even gave each other a little hug last night after playing poker. But I guess I didn't matter enough for her to find me in the dining hall today and say goodbye. She just wanted to get out of here and forget about all of it, including me. Tears coming, goddammit! I take the mug that holds my pens from my desk and throw it as hard as I can against the far wall making a loud 'thud,' the five or six pens scattering, the handle breaking off when it hits the floor. Goddammit!

Little shit.

Warm daylight reaches in through the window, mingling with the heavy air. The sound of an airplane high above, gliding atop the thick silence.

* * * * * * * * * * * * *

I know that my face is all red and under my eyes is all puffy, but I don't care. I want to be here for this. Art therapy. I'm here for the *art* part. Me and about eight others sit at round tables in the Activity Room. The woman at the front of the room has big black and silver frizzy hair surrounding an oval face and oval nose of olive skin. Bubblegum pink lipstick, purple eye shadow. Her name is Shelly. Sitting here at this table, paintbrushes splayed out in front of me, this smiling exuberant woman talking about feelings, I can't help but be transported to Ms. Wilkinson's class in high school. I turn to my left, but of course Jared is not there. Just Joan, looking intently at Shelly, trying to absorb what she's saying. I crack a little smile. I want to ask her about last night, but I probably shouldn't.

We begin painting. Watercolors. Not my forte or my favorite medium, but they are fun in their own right, the hazy pictures they create, full of emotion. Dreamy optimism. Melancholy.

Shelly said the assignment today is merely to paint how we are feeling right now. I am painting an oak tree where the land is just beginning to gather and roll up from the plains, eastern Colorado maybe, under a low blanket of clouds spread out over the land, dulling its reds and greens. It is strange, the beauty found in all the stark and dismal places a human soul will go. Why is that beautiful?

Shelly comes around and talks with each of us.

"Ah, Mimi, I've heard that you're quite the artist. This is lovely. Did you study art in college?"

"No."

She crosses her arms and purses her pink lips. "What's going on with this tree?"

I stare at it. Must I say more? "I don't know."

"Hmmm. Are there birds in the tree?"

"No."

"Do birds ever come and land in this tree?"

"No. Not any more." I know what she is doing. She is analyzing me. "I think the picture speaks for itself," I say.

Shelly swallows. "I see. Well, fair enough." She is about to move on.

"Do you think we could use oils next week?"

"Oils? Oh no. Far too messy."

"How about acrylics?"

She looks at me with measured distance. "I'll see what I can do," she says coolly, and then she moves on to Joan and talks with her about the purple and green explosion on the paper in front of her. I stare down at my tree again, of decent size and nice shape, with a few leaves hanging on. A grey silhouette among the sleeping old, green hills. And those damn clouds. They have showed up in so many pictures and paintings over the years, a cottony film over who-knows-what would show up in that place they occupy on the top half.

* * * * * * * * * * * * *

I sit at the little table playing solitaire. Primetime sitcoms blast from the TV. If I could get away with throwing a rock and breaking that wretched thing, I would do it. Back in my bedroom a dent in the wall, where the mug hit it, waits loudly to be discovered. More evidence, they will see, of my inability to control myself. I wanted to do that. I wanted to throw it. But now I'm regretting it. My heart isn't in this solitaire game. The laugh track from the TV is the most asinine thing I have ever experienced and it rakes on my eardrum and my sensibilities. Talk about crazy. A laugh track? To coax people into laughing? So they don't catch themselves laughing alone? Now that's fucking crazy.

I meet with Dr. Westland tomorrow. Last session he told me that I am definitely making progress. I guess that's true. I could hardly talk when I first got here. I forget that sometimes. How long ago was that? How long was I on the third floor? I have been here on the second floor for about eight months. I should ask Dr. Westland how long I was on the third floor.

Nigel approaches. He sits in the chair next to mine. "How's it going, Mimi?"

I wonder if he knows about the dent in the wall. "Fine." Three of clubs. I can put that on the four of hearts. He puts his head low, near the table and turns to look up at me, trying to get me to look at his face. I don't.

"Your brother called. When you were in art."

"Okay."

"He wants you to call him back." Nigel pauses. He is getting frustrated. "He really wants to speak with you, Mimi."

"Okay. Thank you," I say snidely. What does *he* want? I wonder if mom is sick. Shit. I should call. "I'll call him after dinner."

Five of diamonds? Nothing. One, two, three. Eight of spades? Nope. One, two, three.

"Are you okay, Mimi? You seem agitated."

I almost cry, but I stuff it. "I'm fine. Long day."

He looks at me sympathetically. I'll tell him how I feel later. I don't feel like getting all upset right now.

"Alright." He gets up. "Well, just holler if you need anything. Actually, take that back. We got enough hollering going on here." He smiles at his own wittiness. I smile too.

One, two, three. Queen of hearts, yes! That's what I need.

* * * * * * * * * * * * *

"Hi, Mimi!" he says sweetly. And I believe it. But I don't trust it. He has demonstrated that his caring can recede, if that is what is convenient for him. Who loves true in this world? Can anyone? Or are we all so selfish?

"Hi, Ethan." The receiver is warm against my ear; someone was in here just before me on a long call. Gail sits in the chair opposite of me in this little room, looking at the floor, investigating her little old hand, but listening in on me. "I'm fine. You know, same old same old."

A pause. "You know, I'm thinking about coming out for a visit."

"Oh. I don't think that will be a good idea." Another silence. "Yeah, I'm really not in a state to entertain anyone right now. It's not like you could stay here or anything." Gail looks up at me, mouth open like she wants to say something.

"Oh, I know that, Mimi. I would stay at a motel in town, just for a few nights, and come and spend a couple days with you. Gail says you've been painting again. I'd love to see what you're making."

"I don't think you'd like it. It's all very abstract."

"Mimi, there hasn't been a single painting of yours that I haven't liked."

"That's not true. What about the ones I did of you as a turtle?"

He laughs. I can't help but break a smile. "Well…I like the paintings…just not the subject matter. It's not nice to immortalize your little brother as a reptile."

"I thought I was capturing your charming inner essence."

"My charming inner essence is a turtle?"

I don't like where this is going. "It was."

Silence. "So, how about Thanksgiving? Does that work for you?"

"No. I told you, Ethan, I don't think it's a good idea for me to have guests right now."

Gail crinkles her forehead and shakes her head, disappointed.

I hear Ethan breathing. I wait.

"So, when are we going to be able to see you?"

"I don't know. Maybe when I get out of here, I'll come by for a visit. After I've settled down and made some money." God, how am I going to do that?

"Alright, Mimi." He's upset. Good. "Well…I guess that's it for now. I wanted to talk some, it's been so long, but you don't seem to want to."

"Okay. Well. Maybe some other time."

"Yeah," he exhales with sarcasm, like saying 'yeah, sure, whatever.'

"Alright. Take care, Ethan."

"Yeah. You too," he says, all sarcasm replaced with resignation, disappointment. I take the receiver away from my ear and put it down on the base.

"Well, what does he expect? I am in no position to have visitors." Gail looks at me with disapproval and a big helping of pity. "Don't look at me like that."

"Mimi, I think you are embarrassed to have your family see you here." She sits up straight in her chair, the giant Minnie Mouse head on her sweatshirt inflates itself, smiling at me. What a stupid thing. "It's not like they don't know you're here. And your brother has already been here once." Don't remind me. "You don't remember, but he was here and so sweet with you."

"I don't know what the point would be."

"Don't you want to see your family?"

"No. They don't really care about me. They do, but they love themselves first. I am not interested in people whose affection is like a light switch."

"Now I don't think it's like that, Mimi. Your brother calls you about once a week the technicians tell me. He obviously cares about you."

"Well, its like I said, he does and he doesn't."

Gail sticks out her bottom lip, her eyebrows dive down into one another. "Well who *are* you interested in Mimi? You gotta have people around. We all need people in our lives."

"Right now I have you and Dr. Westland and Nigel. When I get out I'll make some friends."

"And these friends will care about you more than your brother and your mother do?"

I sigh. "I sure hope so."

"Mimi, you have the emotional maturity of an eleven-year-old."

Bite me.

22 →

High school ended. Like many of my peers, I was relieved, excited and nervous. But unlike them, most of whom were going off to four year colleges with some idea of what their future might look like, I was unsure of how to step into the future, how to take that cauldron of chaos and make of it what I wanted. Although my overall grades were decent my last two years of school, I scored low on the SATs. People told me to retake them, but I felt incompetent and defeated. I applied to SF State and USF, but wasn't accepted to either of them. I decided to go to City College and thought I would transfer out from there.

Jared was accepted to most of the schools he applied to, but decided not to attend any of them. He thought it was stupid to just follow the herd and go off to get some expensive "education" only to get further indoctrinated into the system. He said that if he saw it as a means to an end that he was actually passionate about, he would consider college. His

145

parents were pissed. He ended up getting a job at the Sierra Club doing menial administrative work. He also fell in with a group of anarchists that I felt were weird and secretive. Paranoia loomed around them like a cloud of gnats (which they probably didn't know about; gnats seem to be an east coast phenomenon). I stayed away from this bunch.

I got a job at a bookstore on Divisadero. Jared and I hung out on the weekends, doing our usual, but also now that both of us were making some money, we explored restaurants and found a couple bars that would serve us alcohol. I was never a lush by any means, but being young we both enjoyed the buzz and the lowered inhibitions that came with a few drinks. And exploring the city at night was the thrill of discovering a strange unknown universe. One time bumbling through the Castro, pretty drunk, we found ourselves in an alley and suddenly saw movement in the darkness. My vision focused and I saw a man kneeling next to a garbage can, giving another man a blowjob. I shrieked, clasped Jared's hand and started running. We saw several other men engaged in scandalous activity, or leaning against the wall waiting and we ran and giggled and I shrieked through the whole alley until we ended up on Sanchez St. thrilled with shock.

One of the last good memories I have of Jared is what would be our final hike up Bernal Hill. It was October. I had already started classes at City College and was seeing less of him than I wanted. He never mentioned it, so neither did I. The omnipresent sense that he might be slipping away filled me with unease. This hike up Bernal alleviated it for a time.

The afternoon light was that rich honey color that only happens in autumn. Beige dry grass and weeds swayed rhythmically in the breeze, bending and shaking, ecstatic rattles gesturing toward the top of the hill, ushering Jared and me. We walked leisurely, hardly speaking. Everything felt so quiet around us. The breeze, alive in all that emptiness, was the movement of nature spirits. Jared's fair skin glowed amber in the sun's warm light, and his lips glistened like a maraschino cherry. His blue eyes took on a new life that day sparkling in the sun like a bright, warm sea, touching far away lands. He was older, I realized, not the high school freshman I met four years ago. And his face had become even more handsome as it had filled out. I noticed. And I noticed how so many other girls noticed too.

We found a flat clearing near the top. He put his jacket down on the ground for me to sit on. The city in front of us was all silver and gold in that light. The fog doesn't come 'round this time of year. This is San Francisco summer, fashionably late and with its own spirit and agenda. Jared leaned back, supporting himself with his forearms. I hugged my legs and rested my chin on my knees. "You recline at every chance you get. If you aren't standing, you're reclining," I quipped.

He looked at me with a crinkled face, "What are you talking about?"

"It's true. When we sit in booths at restaurants you slouch down so far I can barely see your mouth. Sometimes I think you're gonna slide right under the table."

"Whatever," he said with a grin and we both laughed. He slapped my thigh. "You're full of shit," he said, still laughing.

I was still laughing too. "Nah ah. It's true. And you can barely see over the steering wheel when you drive because you recline the seat so far back." I laughed so loud. He was laughing at me, how hard I was laughing at him. He sat up quick, and was suddenly on top of me, holding my wrists down on the dirt, a wicked smirk on his face like he was going to bite me or say something real sarcastic. Then I saw it again…in his eyes…that warm sea, somewhere far away.

"Mimi, I love you." That's what he said. And all the energy drained out of my body. I wanted to cry. Some feeling that was bliss and an awful, empty sadness at the same time. Concern spread across his face. "Are you okay?" he asked.

I sniffled a bit. "Yes."

He looked at me, surveying, trying to figure out what was going on and what to do. He released my wrists, but was still straddled on top of me. It felt good to have him right there. I gave him a little smile. "I'm sorry," I said.

"For what?"

"For being so weird."

"Well, you *are* weird." He looked at me. "And you're really sweet too. And smart. And fun." It was how he used to talked to me when we were first falling.

Energy started coming back into me. His smiling face looked down at me, against the gold sky. Never had I seen a person the way I was seeing Jared in that moment. An angel. The beauty and wonder of humanity, some indescribable miracle…right there in that warm smiling face, those eyes of countless seas, life itself, reaching all the way from the big bang to this glowing moment, smiling at me.

"I love you too." I said.

"I know," he said, followed by one of his sly smirks. "You're fucking crazy about me."

I smiled back. "Now get the hell off me." I lifted my hips, giving him a push.

He rolled off and settled in next to me, closer now, reclining on his forearms again. I was still lying on my back, looking at him, looking at the clouds of liquid gold, moving, changing their shape. Storytellers.

"Mimi," Jared said suddenly.

"Yeah."

"I'm thinking about leaving."

"Where you wanna go?" I asked a little disheartened. Not that he hadn't mentioned traveling and moving before.

"I don't know. I think south. Argentina maybe."

"Oh."

He turns to look at me. "Wanna come?" He was afraid I'd say yes. I could feel it. And it made me so utterly sad.

I just lay there for a moment. "I don't know. I'm doing the college thing. I think maybe I'll become a librarian or editor or something."

He turned back to look at the skyline. "Oh. Okay."

"But maybe."

"Well you got time to think about it. I'm not leaving any time soon."

Liar.

He left sooner than anyone thought he would. He felt like he was at a dead end and if he didn't get out he was gonna fail in life or die or something. Trapped animal. And I did think about it…all the time. I thought that moving to another country sounded scary. I thought about how losing Jared would be even scarier. I thought about what I wanted out of life. I wasn't sure.

23 ➝

East Coast winters and I could never belong to each other. I always found myself awed by each year's first falling of snow, absorbed into its holy quiet. But besides those few moments with my face pressed to whatever window I happened to be nearest, I always felt assaulted by the frigid temperatures of the cold months. Donny said I was a wuss. The winter the two of us lived together I would hardly leave the house except for work. Even to go out with Donny, I made him warm up the car and have the heat blasting before I would get in. I spent my days on the couch with a blanket over my knees.

"You're too young to act like such an old lady," he grunted one day after coming home from work, finding me in my usual position. "You know we have heat in here. If you're cold you can turn up the thermostat. This isn't some shack out in the boonies."

"It doesn't matter how hot I make it. When it's this cold outside, I'm cold no matter what."

"Well, that doesn't make any sense," he snorted. "You don't make any sense," he mumbled to himself, loud enough for me to hear.

I let the wave of hurt pass through me, and mindlessly turned a page in my book even though I wasn't really ready to. When he walked into the kitchen to get himself a beer, I turned the page back to where I was. All I needed was for him to see me flipping the pages of my book backwards.

Donny came back into the living room, came around the couch and slapped my shins with the back of his hand, indicating that he wanted room to sit. He couldn't sit in the La-Z Boy? I pulled my legs in. He sat down heavy, causing me to bounce, cracked open his beer, and used the remote to turn on the news. It was blasting loud and I was losing Dinah, the main character in my book.

"Can you turn that down a bit?"

He exhaled loudly and pointed the remote with a straight arm, twisted sideways, and pushed the "volume down" button like he was shooting a pistol.

I kept on reading. He put his hand back to push himself deeper into the couch, but his hand pressed right on my foot and it hurt so bad with his full weight on it. I kept myself from yelling out, not wanting to give him the pleasure.

After another twenty minutes of stony quiet, occupied only by his breathing and the gauzy sounds of the TV, I got up to get ready for work.

"What's for dinner?" he asked, still looking at the TV.

"I was too tired today. You can order a pizza or make a frozen dinner." I could feel him turning red as I walked into the bedroom to put on my work shirt and a sweater. I came back out into the living room and fetched my coat, hat, scarf and gloves from the closet.

"This is the second time this week, Mimi. Goddammit!"

"I'm sorry," I said as I wrapped the Washington Redskins scarf around my neck. "I'll see you later."

"Uh huh."

I walked out the door and trudged through the wall of cold a mile long that brought me to the bus stop. My eyes always tear from the cold.

The bus dropped me off on the corner of West Main and Meadow Avenue and I walked another half mile or so to the office building I cleaned. Kim, the Korean lady, was always there before me, sitting on an armchair in the entrance room reading her Korean newspaper.

"Hi," I said.

She nodded her little bow of greeting, smiling, then stood up and we walked to the janitorial closet together. She usually wiped down surfaces while I vacuumed and emptied wastebaskets. We alternated mopping and cleaning the bathrooms. That was my idea. During my first couple weeks of working there, I grew uneasy knowing she was the one always scrubbing the toilets.

This night was a struggle. The ghost was active, ranting on and on in my head, cursing about everybody and everything, but mostly about Donny. He was a beast of fire, an old angry boar and I hated him and he lived so close to me, he was under my skin. I couldn't get him out. Mopping the hallway floor, the familiar smell of ammonia filled my head and I thought I might need to run outside, run in front of a car...or jump out a window just to get the damn ranting to shut up. I noticed my body was shaking. I had to stop mopping and put my weight on the mop resting in the wheeled, yellow bucket.

Kim came out of the bathroom with her pink rubber gloves up to her elbows, holding the plastic pale with rags slung over the rim. She stopped and looked at me.

Her little, dark eyes examined me.

"You," she said, pointing at me, then she drew a line from her eye, down her cheek and made a frown.

I nodded.

She nodded in sympathy, looked at me with those little, dark eyes, wishing she could say something that I would understand. Instead she pulled off one of her gloves, patted me on the arm and said something in Korean. I smiled. But the ghost wanted to rip her up. That fucking ghost robs me of any moment that might be worth something. I hung my head down as Kim continued to pat me lightly, like the fluttering wing of a little bird. Then she put her glove back on and walked into another bathroom, suddenly gone.

I gathered myself together, stood up straight, exhaling slowly through ring shaped lips. This body would have to finish its job tonight. I lifted the mop out of the soapy water, put it in the top compartment, pulled on the handle that squeezes the water out, and plopped it on the linoleum floor. I resumed the back and forth motion. Just two more floors.

When the offices were clean we put everything back into the closet, cleaning off the mop-head, the buckets and the rags in the large floor sink in there.

We bundled up and walked outside with the large garbage bags full of trash, Kim locking the door behind us. We threw the trash bags into the dumpster on the side of the building.

I looked at her and she smiled.

"Bye," I said.

She nodded her head, cheerily.

"Thank you."

More nodding, and then a dismissive wave that was meant to be friendlier than it looked. And with that, she was off. As far as I could tell, she walked home.

It was usually about four in the morning when we finished our shift. I would wait at the twenty-four hour diner for the first bus of the morning, which was at five fifteen, drinking decaf coffee, reading my book. This morning, the bus was ten minutes late. Walking home, after getting dropped off, I thought freezing to death might not be the worst way to go. I felt both relief and dread as Donny's house came into view.

I walked in, hung up my coat, put away my gloves and hat and scarf. I entered the bedroom quiet as a fly, but it didn't matter 'cause Donny was awake. He turned over loudly, making sure his presence was known. I undressed, put my clothes in the hamper and slipped into my nightgown and slid into bed, just the very edge of my side, and turned with my back to Donny. He put his hand on my waist and started stroking up and down. He brought his hand up and cupped my breast.

"I don't feel like it," I said sheepishly.

"Goddammit!" he growled and sat up suddenly, swung his legs over his side of the bed. He rubbed his face with his hands and exhaled. Him just sitting there I was afraid of what he might say or do. But he did nothing. He got up and headed to the bathroom. I relaxed, not knowing how long I had been holding my breath for.

Donny got dressed and left. Lying there, thinking, and unable to sleep, I determined I would wake up "early" and scan the paper for apartments for rent. I had lived on my own before I met Donny and I could do it again. This was not better than loneliness. I set the alarm for ten thirty.

The alarm rang loudly and I smacked the off button and sat up, feeling as if I had only been hovering in the limbo that separates sleep and wakefulness for the past four hours. I crawled out of bed, shuffled to the kitchen, put on coffee and poured myself a glass of orange juice. Donny left the paper on the table, as usual, and I sat down and found the classifieds. There weren't a lot of listings, mostly just advertisements by property management places, who always do credit checks. The Sunday paper would have more. I circled a few things that looked good: close to a bus line, had laundry facilities in the building, and cheap. I didn't call any of the places. I wasn't ready for that.

I washed up, made myself a sandwich and curled up on the couch with my book.

I must have dozed off, but I woke when I heard the door close.

"Hello?" Donny called out.

I stretched and made a little noise. "Hello," I answered.

"Anything exciting to tell me?" he asked as he hung his coat up.

I tried to think of an answer.

153

"Didn't think so." He walked into the kitchen for a beer. I sat up and rubbed my eyes.

Then I heard a loud noise. Donny came storming out of the kitchen shaking the newspaper in his fist. "What is this?" he yelled, his face red, pointing to the little circles I had made with a pen. As he walked around to the front of the couch I instinctually stood up. He grabbed my face with his hand, his fingers digging in, one going in my eye, and pushed me back down on the couch.

"Are you leaving me?" he spat, his neck muscles bulging.

"I..."

"What?" He slapped me hard across the face. "After all I do for you? Given you a home and a life!" His screaming shook my bones.

Then he stormed out.

I was dead. What could I do? I couldn't move or even cry or breathe. I wasn't there.

The ghost, for the first time since DC, fully inhabited my body. My vision returned, but it was the ghost looking out from my eyes. She stood up in my body. She saw that fucking baseball trophy and grabbed it by the little brass man. She walked resolute into the bedroom. Donny was turned the other way, unbuttoning his shirt. She swung and the marble base cracked him in the side of the head. He fell to his knees.

One. Two. Three. That's how my arm went down, how the trophy hit his head, like a beat, the impact ringing up my arm with each strike. I was only witnessing. The ghost was doing it and with a sense of pleasure. It was something she had wanted to do, to act in this world, to make herself more real. I was in shock, seeing Donny like a puddle on the floor, crimson moving out onto the beige carpet, maybe dead. The smell of sulfur and something acrid filled my head as I helplessly watched what was happening right in front of me. To me! 'This is bad.' The brass man slowly slipped from my fingers and hit the floor with a thud. I got woozy, everything turning grey-green. I fell to my knees.

154

The next several weeks and months are just a blur. My memories are drained of color, except a red hue. Red over grey. I remember jail. I remember the trial a little bit, but I didn't speak. It was apparent to everyone in that little room that I wasn't really there. And that's what was scariest of all. I lost my sense of myself. I didn't know who or what I was. A terrible hell creature with relentless thoughts of death and the awfulness of this living. The world bent and stretched in unfamiliar ways so that I had trouble moving and walking at times. People wanted to hurt me. I saw only hate in them; I felt only pain and malice when they grabbed me by the arm to move me where they wanted me to go. I screamed out. I think I screamed all the time. I was drowning in a sea of venom. I saw no light in there, none, in all that time in jail and the third floor of the hospital for patients who are way gone or dangerous.

I am not a religious person, but I do believe in some sort of afterlife. There has to be something more for me than all of this, or this living is just in vain. I cannot accept life being in vain, 'cause it sends me back to terrible places. And I have seen beauty. I have known it. The camping trip with Jared, the times we knew love together and even in snippets since my youth like in landscapes I have found myself in and truly inspired art and the goodwill of people that I have encountered. I heard a story of these two men, I think the governor and the priest, on this Greek island who were told by the Nazis to hand over a list of all their Jewish people. The Jews, numbering a few hundred, were hidden out in rural areas and when the Nazis came for them, these two men gave the Nazis a list that had only two names on it: their own.

These thoughts and memories are an anchor that has kept me at least close to land, if not fully on it. They keep me from being torn away and cast out fully upon those violent seas. The unresting mind. The terrified soul.

24 ➤

Sitting around the tables in the activities room again for art. It must be Thursday. Shelly walks around the tables passing out watercolor paper, her black sweater dress and black tights a perfect canvas for orange-red lipstick, the silver streaking her hair, silver hoop earrings, shiny olive-tan skin, a warm fruity smile. She must be Italian or Jewish, with that skin color and her whole look. She could be a resident of New York. What is she doing here?

She tries to remember everyone's name, saying it as she puts the paper down in front of them. "Ann. Hi, Ann. Daryl. Hi Daryl."

"He can't hear you." Ann yelps.

"Oh, that's right." She pats Daryl on the shoulder like an affectionate auntie and when he turns around she smiles at him. "Teddy. Hi, Teddy. Joan. Hi, Joan. Mimi. Hi, Mimi."

"Hi."

"Karen. Hi, Karen."

Hey! She didn't give me a paper. "Shelly?"

"Yes, Mimi?"

"You didn't give me a paper."

"I know."

What? What is going on? Is she fucking around? Was I too curt last week?

She finishes passing out the watercolor paper, goes over to her black briefcase with a blue ribbon tied to one of the handles and pulls out some white thing. She starts walking through the room. "Now everyone…today I want you to think about your youngest memory. What memory stands out from your childhood?" She puts the white thing down in front of me. A canvas. Square, twelve by twelve, glistening with gesso, like an old friend, happy to see me. "And when you think about this memory," Shelly goes on, walking back up to the front of the class, "you can paint a picture from the memory itself, like you took a photograph, or you can just paint anything while you are keeping the memory in mind." She reaches back into her big briefcase and pulls out a red cloth bag and a plastic box. She makes her way over to me again. "Think about colors, when you think of this memory. Think shapes. Think movement. Is there a lot going on? Is it quiet? Is it scary?" She places the plastic box down in front of me. In sharpie it says *Mimi Rizner*. Paintbrushes. For me. She places the cloth bag down. I peer inside. Acrylic paints. I reach my hand down into the bag and pull out a handful of tubes. Cobalt blue. Raw Sienna. Red Cadmium. Some of them are quite empty. The red cloth bag also has writing on it. Shelly Mandel. Hers. These are her paints. "On the table there are paper cups with water and paper plates for your palette." Wow! Acrylics. A canvas.

I look up and Daryl is smiling at me. I smile back at the crazy old bat. I reach to the middle of the table and grab one of the Dixie cups and pull a paper plate off the top of the stack.

I squeeze the tubes of paint, little slugs of color making their place on the paper plate palette. But what now to paint? What is my earliest memory? I don't remember too many details anymore. I see myself at some concert parking lot, full of bearded men and smoke, mom with a belly full of my brother-to-be and orange Bertha enjoying her rest, smiling benevolently at me, her side door open in case I want to crawl in for a nap or to raid the cooler for some chocolate chips. I mix the cobalt blue with titanium white. I'll start with the blue sky. Then I'll paint sweet Bertha.

I look up. Everyone is already painting. Joan's paper is almost completely covered, a black and brown storm, a young child's rendering of anything from a horse to a secret world under the bed, an ether without ground, inhabited by all energies and creatures.

"Dammit!" Ann shouts, "I can't get anything to look right."

I smile. Ah, yes, my own personal heaven. I really saw that, under the magnolia tree with Val. I shake my head. With a larger square brush I start coating the top of the canvas sky blue, leaving in streaks of cobalt to add some magic.

By the end of "art time" I have only just begun with Bertha. I have her orange shape and her black tires, chrome bumper and hubcaps, but no details yet, and no shading, not to mention the surrounding carnival of stoned and barefoot people, leaning on their vehicles with their cans of beer and their joints, their brightly colored outfits, the teeth-grinding tension of waiting for the acid to kick in. How strong would it be this time? Brightened colors and laughter and breathing clouds or knocked into another universe completely?

* * * * * * * * * * * * * *

The smell in here is becoming familiar. Does this same sweet musky scent, like ginger and old carpet, float around his own house, surround the furniture, the vases on end tables, the people, the family who live there, unable to recognize something specific about the odor of their own home, *their* odor?

Dr. Westland sits back in his seat, grinning.

"I don't know, Doc," I say breezily, "Maybe I'm just fucked up. I can't seem to shake the ghost."

"I have seen great improvement since you've been here, Mimi."

"Well, the ghost has been more dormant. More under control. But all my life she goes back and forth, being more or less active. But she never actually goes away. Not for good. That's the problem."

Dr. Westland exhales. "Mimi…sometimes our habits, our wounds have a certain inertia. They perpetuate themselves almost like they have a mind of their own." He pauses. Looks uncertain. "What I think you're doing is personifying your fears, your anger. These can be very big feelings and hard to accept." He looks at me earnestly. "I believe the ghost is just your wound, personified."

I shake my head. "But I remember her coming into my body. I remember exactly. It was at Woodstock…"

"Mimi," he leans forward in his chair, "I don't want to invalidate your experience or tell you what to believe, but I'm not sure it's really going to be helpful to work with your emotions in this way. The way you describe this experience sounds more like your own thoughts, *your* anger. You told me yourself that it doesn't feel like an outside voice, something audible you hear with your ear." He pauses. Looking at me. "You know, sometimes it's recommended that people actually work with their psychological or emotional habits by naming them…distancing themselves. But I think you're stuck. I think what would be good for you would be to take some responsibility for your emotions and your behavior."

I sit up rigid like cold stone.

"What would happen if we said there was no ghost, that you just have harbored fears, confusion and anger for a long time and there's a lot of build-up there? And that we could release this build-up, over time. And we could say that it's okay to be angry. That it's okay to be afraid. We could let these emotions just pass through us when they come up." He waits for me, energy coming from him, filling the room.

"That sounds good," I say like a dead person. I'm still. But inside there are a thousand fast moving centipedes zipping along channels.

"Good."

But. "The only thing is I'm not sure I believe it."

"Well…let's suspend belief for a while. Let's just say we are trying on a new perspective to see how it feels, just like trying on new clothes."

We?

I sigh.

I suppose I can…
"I can try it."
He smiles big. "Good, Mimi."

* * * * * * * * * * * * *

I'm in a tunnel. Lots of colors. Everything is light. Warmth. What sweetness!

A faint humming.

Light is getting brighter. Whiter. Something is happening there, in front of me. I am not alone. Who is that?

A man.
I know him.
No I don't.
He is made of light, eyes of light. He exists here.
I am visiting.
But I am from here too.
He has robes of white light, iridescent pink and blue. Red-orange light, his beard. His eyes are spiral galaxies. Forever.
He smiles at me.
Everything is warm. And so sweet.
Do I know him?

Getting darker.

Darker. What's happening?

Darkness.

Silence.

Does light make sound?

I feel my face against the pillow, the weight of my blanket on top of me. I take a breath. I move my fingers.

I'm awake. In my bed.

I was dreaming. Or was it a vision, something real? It still feels so close. That sweetness, bliss, all inside my body. A smile curls up on my face.

What was that?

Who was that? An angel. I gasp. An angel? I was visited by an angel. A sweet buzzing up my chest into my face. Wow!

I sigh as I cuddle myself up in my blanket, pointing and flexing my feet in rhythm with this delicious feeling.

But he didn't have wings. Don't angels have wings?

Do they? Always?

Maybe he is something else. A saint. A saintly disembodied soul.

I take the blanket in my clasped hands and raise it to my chin, cozy with this feeling. That was amazing. I was visited by a saint.

I smile alone in the darkness.

25 →

"I don't think you should come."

We were on a bench in the Panhandle, eating sandwiches. He looked at me tenderly. I couldn't believe what I was hearing. My face caught fire. My belly churned like the depths of the underworld. I wanted to simultaneously crawl under the roots of one of the eucalyptus standing nearby, and explode like a volcano.

"Are you going to say anything?"

What did he expect from me? What was I supposed to say?

"Mimi, you know I care about you. You're my best friend in the entire world. I just feel like I need to go do this by myself." He took a breath. "Besides, it's too dangerous. I don't want you getting hurt."

"I'm not afraid."

He was silent. Looking at me. I searched his eyes. There he was. Loving me. But from a distance. And he knew I could see it. "There is this nagging feeling I carry around with me like I don't know what my purpose is. I need to figure it out. I need to discover some…things."

"And you need to do it alone?"

"I think so. Yes. At least for a while."

"And what do you expect to discover?" I prodded.

"I don't know. Peace?"

I couldn't look at him anymore. My attention turned to the crows sitting high in the branches of the Eucalyptuses, watching us, having their council about all they were surveying, shaking their heads saying 'Isn't it a shame? Isn't it a pity?'

I watched people walking by, couples, families, old men, people on bikes cruising exuberantly through the cool air, two girls on roller skates, giggling, clutching each other with little shrieks every time one of them thought she was about to lose her balance and spill.

"I need to go," I said.

"Where?"

"Home." I still couldn't look at him.

"Why?"

"Because I do."

"So that's it?"

"What do you want me to say, Jared?" The ghost was getting active in me, getting stirred by the despair I had come to know, the feeling that would haunt me, that would be the undertone of all of my days, the good and the bad, only

162

undetectable in moments during sex or painting or visiting with Ethan, and a few others here and there, little gems sparkling in the tar pit.

"I don't know. Say it's okay," he implored. "Say you understand."

"It's okay," I said with a hot throat as I stood up. The sandwich I had forgotten about rolled off my lap, hit the ground and scattered: broken bread, shredded lettuce everywhere. "I'm going home." I walked off, hearing him call my name behind me twice. But he didn't come after me. I stomped up Buchanan Street, a cauldron of bubbling, gassing molten ore. I couldn't cry anymore. I stopped crying in tenth grade after two years of crying every single day after school. And in the following two years the ghost had been mostly dormant, unable to exist in the light of Jared's love. As I marched on through the pushing wind I was becoming reacquainted with fire and acid. My curse. That which possesses me.

* * * * * * * * * * * * *

I was silent for three days. Anything that would have come out of my mouth would have only been the shrieks of a banshee. I stayed in my room, only coming out to eat late at night when everyone else was asleep. I locked the door. Ethan slept on the couch. Jared tried calling and visiting, but I would not leave my room.

Mom and Dad tapped on my door several times over those days, obviously concerned, but they also knew it was just the broken heart of a teenage girl: a force in the universe to reckon with for sure, intense and valid, but in the scheme of things, through the good and bad, elation and gloom, time keeps rolling on and a broken teenage heart is not the worst of things. So I was basically allowed my three days of personal Siberia, a settled grey punctured with biting winds, the universe, this life, seeming the most terrible invention, the blood of my young heart fathoming the meaninglessness of its coursing.

In the pre-dawn hours of the fourth day I had a strange vivid dream. I dreamt that a silver-blue lady handed me a large drop of dew, prismatic with light and clear, sweet sadness. I woke up and lay there in the hazy grey-blue first light of day, calm. I fell back asleep. I had the same dream and again awoke, feeling a little better. This happened two or three more times. When I woke for the final time, it was fully day, about nine in the morning. And I felt empty. But a good empty. Empty of even despair. Everything was quiet. I could hear the birds singing. They did not bring the bliss they did before during that first camping trip, but it felt good that I was empty enough to notice them. I breathed in the clear nothing. In hindsight I realized that the lady was giving me my tears, the ones I could not produce myself.

I got out of bed and went to the kitchen. Ethan and Mom were surprised to see me there. And happy. Dad was at work.

"Sweetie, do you need anything?" Mom asked.

"Granola."

"Sure." She began fixing me a bowl of granola. Ethan looked at me with wide, dewy eyes, unsure of what to do with a teenage girl with a broken heart. At his age, romantic love was just something in the movies, something that people talked about and sung songs about. He stood up and wrapped his arms around my neck. I inhaled and almost cried, but didn't. I wrapped him lightly with one arm, like a sheer fabric. He squeezed a little tighter, then let go. Mom set my granola down in front of me, and hovered there for a moment. I gave a weak smile. They both sat back down at the table and watched me eat in silence. I was suddenly an animal at the zoo. But I didn't care.

After eating what I could, I put on some jeans and left the house. I walked over to Church Street where I sat in a café on for a long time, not reading, not really thinking much, just sitting, watching everything going on around me. I eventually got up and walked to Bernal Heights. I climbed the hill and sat up there, just staring at the city. I laid down in the dry grass and dozed off under the warm sun, and dreamt of a circus.

Cold air, the signature of a San Francisco summer afternoon, enveloped my body and pulled me out of my slumber. I sat up quickly rubbing my arms, but it wasn't helping. The fog is more than formidable. So I went home.

At home, Dad was delighted to see his little cat. We had dinner, which was quieter than usual with a slight air of discomfort. I didn't have anything to say.

After dinner I called Jared and informed him that we should meet for lunch the following day. "Sandwiches?" he asked. No, pizza.

* * * * * * * * * * * *

Our rendezvous was brief and formal. He kept apologizing and telling me that he loved me, but nothing penetrated the wall I had erected. I just said that he should do what he needs to do and that I supported him. He said he would be back and that he would keep in touch. And he told me to take good care of myself. I guess I fucked that one up.

Jared left a month later to go rescue Argentina from the political mess it was in. He said that the opposition were being disappeared; students, union leaders. He had grown more and more distressed, almost obsessed, in the months leading up to his departure, as if Argentina was the very fulcrum of human injustice.

He would be in Argentina for two years before I would see him again. I attended City College, taking core classes with the goal of eventually studying literature. I quit my job at the bookstore and began working at the school's library, checking people's books out and returning books to their places on the shelves. My free time was spent sitting in cafés drinking coffee, eating pastries, reading a book. I liked Café Trieste the most, and it was worth the trip to North Beach. Ethan would come along on the weekends, and when we weren't reading, we'd talk. We'd talk about Mom and Dad, or his life: girls and school, stories about what he and his friends did on a particular day. Sometimes we reminisced about the old days cruising around in Bertha under an open blue sky and all the crazy things we saw and did. We never talked about my life. My life was my studies, books and painting. Not much to talk about there. I began to fantasize about travel. I often thought about dropping everything and buying a one-way ticket to Buenos Aires and surprising Jared.

During those two years, communication between Jared and me was what I feared it might be. I got the occasional letter and we only talked on the phone five times: his birthdays, my birthdays and when he called to tell me he'd be coming home in a month for a visit.

It was his parents' insistence that brought him home, not a sense of longing for or loyalty towards me. On that final phone call he told me he had some news and that I wasn't going to like it. He was engaged. Hard swallow. Silence. That's great.

When Jared was home we arranged to meet for coffee. I was already practiced at being quiet to the world, aloof, so including Jared in that treatment wouldn't be difficult. I was there at the café reading *Of Mice and Men* when he and Beatriz arrived. He was smiling big. I stood up, didn't take off my sunglasses, and put out my hand. He grabbed me in a warm hug. I was a wood statue. He let go and looked me up and down, still smiling.

"You look great," he said.

"Thanks. You too."

He stood there, seemingly so much older now, a young man wearing a button down shirt, shorter hair, his body filled out, fists on his hips. An engaged man who worked with labor unions in Buenos Aires. He couldn't have done that in San Francisco? He pulls his fiancé to his side. She is docile, shy, beautiful with caramel skin, raven black hair, thin but strong limbs emerging from a bright red dress.

"Mimi, this is Beatriz," he said pronouncing her name in an Argentine accent.

I was surprised when Beatriz leaned in to kiss me on each cheek. I gave her a tight smile. Her face froze, her eyes orbs of fright as she pulled back. She knew who I was.

"And this is Junior," Jared continued, putting his hand on Beatriz's abdomen. It took me a second to register what he was saying, then I noticed the slight curve of her belly under his hand. Congratulations.

They ordered espresso and told me all about their life in Argentina, how they met in Cordoba and lived on a small farm that was owned by her grandmother for about a year before moving to Buenos Aires where Jared could work with the unions. He wasn't ready for farm life yet. And they laughed how she wasn't made for farm life at all.

"I like to sleep," she whispered, leaning in, smiling like she was telling me some dirty secret.

He asked me about my life, my family. I gave him the cursory state of affairs, everyone was fine, painting was good. She spoke fine English, but didn't speak much. I suppose I had no right asking for an explanation, for answers from him. Jared and I hadn't really been together since he left. Or maybe even before.

After about a half hour I told them I had a study date and I excused myself. Jared stood up after me and gave me a hug and looked at me in the eyes, wanting me to see him, to see him seeing me, as if to say 'I love you.' I turned to Beatriz. We said goodbye giving each other polite nods and I left that café like a sudden gust, napkins lifting at their corners.

26 ⟶

I haven't been taking my meds. I haven't needed them. Maybe today I do. Everything is chattering, swirling. Chaos in everything. The world cannot stop spinning. It's what it does. But constant motion makes me nauseous.

I miss New York. No I don't; that was more movement than anywhere. But I was happy there. In the beginning. Or maybe I just thought I was. My first taste of independence. Freedom. The life I was building for myself. I was becoming…an artist. Or at least someone inside the world of art. The world of art; the only place where humanity looks at, explores, the profound and profane nature of this living. Why did I move away? I was looking for something. Someone? Peace, Jared, an escape from the fucking ghost that haunts me, haunts us all. Oh, yeah, not supposed to believe in the ghost. Well this *wound*, then. I see it everywhere. This whole world is upside down, bleeding, all the blood draining out, like a killed deer. How is it, then, that people, fathers at the park with their children, audacious young teenagers yapping and howling with delight, these people seem so settled, so okay in themselves, in this life? How are they doing that? Those smiles that seem so real; genuine happiness. Do I ever smile like that? Big, warm grins. If I'm thinking about it, it goes away. This critical mind. Reason. Or is it the ghost? Or is what we call reason the ghost, killing every grin? Maybe Dad and Mom were right trying to keep us wild.

I lay here in bed fidgeting. Some body part is moving whether it be my rolling ankles, my tapping hands, my whole body turning to one side, then the other, then on my back again, then legs pumping, hands tapping, ankles rolling, sighing and groaning, this torture of constant motion.

I tried going to watch TV, but its images moved faster than I am, sped me up even more. I almost puked. I tried playing cards twice, but I couldn't focus. So I'm back here in my bed. Maybe I should tell a tech that I need more meds. But then they'll know I'm not always taking them, that I hide them under my tongue and flush them down the toilet. Then I'll never get out of here. Everything's been going so well. Dr.

Westland even tells me that I'm doing better all the time. What if he's lying just to encourage me? Or get me to behave? No. He wouldn't do that.

But why did I move to Philly? That was the beginning of the end. I was so alone.

I've always been alone. Even with Donny, I was really alone. He didn't see me.

Maybe they won't let me out. Maybe they shouldn't. What I did.

Maybe I'll be in here forever like Joan.

I saw Donny at the trial. I don't remember much about that time. But I do remember seeing Donny. He was scowling at me. But once we locked eyes. And his scowl melted away. And we both felt the same thing for each other. Pity. Compassion.

But what if they don't let me out?

A knock at the door.

"Hello?" I call out feeble, shaky.

"Mimi?"

It's Nigel.

"Yes?" I sound like a terrified child.

"Can I come in?"

"Yes."

Nigel opens the door. He looks concerned. "You alright?"

"Yeah." I prop myself up on my elbows.

"Whatcha doin'?"

"Just lying here. Thinking."

He nods slowly, studies me. I can't seem to look into his eyes; he is out of focus, like background.

"You've been in here all day." He walks in and sits on the corner of my bed. "You weren't at lunch."

169

"I don't have an appetite."

He looks at me. Sweet man. He wants to help. But what can he do? He's just a tech. If he really wanted to help, he could crawl into bed and cuddle me.

"What's going on, Mimi? Talk to me, Sugar."

"I don't know," I admit suddenly, stirring close to tears. I sit up and scoot back to let the wall support me. "I'm just thinking about everything. It's torturous."

He exhales.

"You need some fresh air," he declares, "Put on some warm clothes and a coat."

Yes, fresh air sounds nice.

I pull the covers off and slowly drag myself out of bed. I'm shaking a little. I need to move slow or who knows what might happen. Loss of control.

I take a sweater from the closet, a lime green one I had bought at a thrift store in Richmond, and slip it over my head. Donny chastised me for only buying used clothes. He said I acted like a poor woman and that we weren't poor. He thought I should shop at Ross or Walmart like the other women. But I like buying used clothes. Where else could I get such a pretty, warm, lime-green mohair sweater for two dollars? Even the pilling, the tiny hole on the cuff; personality, some sense of humanness that new clothes just don't have and take years to acquire. And it's all I ever knew. We never bought new clothes when I was young. They seem so sterile to me, untouched and unfriendly, fresh off some machine. I don't want to wear something that just came off a giant clothes-making machine in some dark factory in Bangladesh.

I grab my coat and follow Nigel down the corridor. He unlocks the door to the stairwell and we descend the one flight to the ground floor. He holds open the door leading to the first floor hallway. I start to walk towards the front entrance; not our destination.

"This way," he says using his head to point to the back of the building. We walk side-by-side down the long corridor past

170

doctor's offices, meeting rooms, bathrooms. Nigel uses his keys again and opens the back door for me. Ugh! The cold.

I sit on one of the stone benches that line the walkway down the middle of the grounds, one that is closer to the building, closer to the warmth of inside, though not at all affected by it.

The cold presses against me on all sides. The stone bench is like an ice block. I won't be able to handle this for long, but the cool, clear air in my lungs and the open blue sky *is* refreshing. Nigel sits next to me, on my left, creating a little warmth.

I look up. The sun is bright, but unable to warm us here, now. The effects of the slightest tilt of axis. I breathe out. "You know, Nigel, there was a time in my life when I wasn't all fucked up. I was happy."

"I'm sure there was," he nods.

"I actually felt like I was in harmony with the universe. It was alive. And good."

He turns to look at me. I can't read his feelings because he's put his sunglasses on. Do I smile? Do I cry and lay my head down on his shoulder? Do I change the subject? He faces forward again and sighs. Breath comes out of him visible, like a living wraith. And then it dissolves. Gone.

"Maybe it still is," he says.

"Still is what?"

"Alive and good. The universe."

I breathe in. Maybe it is.

But why can't I see it?

"Mimi, I'll tell you something. Working here these past few years I've learned some things. In fact...I would say I had a revelation." He pauses. He slowly surveys our artificial geometric landscape. "The mind is a strange thing," he continues, "People got no control over their minds. After being here a few months, I started noticing my own mind, how it doesn't shut up, like half the patients here, but they just do it out loud. I started looking around, observing people, my family, folks around town. You can see it. Everyone is lost in their minds. Constant mind chatter." He nods slowly, puts his hands together in his lap to keep them warm. "Animals don't think. They seem more content."

What would that be like, to stop thinking so much? Probably boring. Empty. Like living alone by a still lake in the Canadian tundra. Maybe that's when I'd really lose it to the ghost, with my defenses down.

Doctor Westland doesn't want me to believe in the ghost. I am trying to just see it as my wound, my own anger.

"I bet you're even thinking about what I just said." He looks at me. "It's like real life is always there, a miracle, waitin' for us to notice it, but we can't notice it 'cause we're too busy payin' attention to our thinking."

"A miracle?"

"Yea, a miracle! Life. Out of nothin'. Somethin' outta nothin'. The fact of existence. That's a miracle."

Yes.

But can I do that? Stop thinking?

I breathe in.

I breathe out.

I breathe in. I can't do this.

I breathe out.

Not think? That's impossible.

Breathing in.

My back hurts. I should lie down. Urgh. There's that fucking feeling.

"I can't do this!"

"Do what?" Nigel asks, his forehead all crinkled.

"Not think."

"Oh," he laughs, "Were you trying not to think?" He slaps his thigh. "You're funny, Mimi."

Uncomfortable. Like I need to run somewhere. I always feel like this…without the meds. It's like the moment when two dogs meet and you don't know and they don't know if they are gonna play or fight. That tension. I always have that.

Without the meds. But at least it's mine. It's me. The meds aren't me. This grating agitation is relentless, but at least it's me.

"Mimi, calm down. You're trying too hard." He flashes a big, white grin. "Chill out, lady."

I laugh.

"There ya go."

"Maybe you should be a doctor here," I say.

"Naw. I'm fine with this. Besides I don't want to peer too deep inside everyone's minds. No thank you."

His lips look so soft.

I reach out with my pointer finger and touch his bottom lip. So soft, like satin, it sends chills down my lower back. He pulls his head away.

"What the hell you doing?"

"Feeling your lip."

"Why?"

"'Cause I wanted to touch it. It looks so soft. Do you mind?"

"Well, first off, Mimi, that's a breach of our no touch policy. Second, you and I bat for the same team, just so you know." He pulls up his glasses, winks at me, and lets them drop back down on his nose.

Huh? Ah. He's gay. Duh! How didn't I know?

"You judging me?" he asks, staring again at the manicured garden.

"No. I think it's sweet."

"Wish my mama thought that."

We both sit quietly. The grounds are bare. The few trees within the stone walls just dark scratches upon the canvas. All the rest of life seems to know what to do with itself.
Nigel shifts a little.
"Maybe we'll both end up in San Francisco," he says elbowing me in the side twice.

"I don't think so. There's nothing for me there."

"What about your brother? He seems like a real nice guy."

"Ethan? How do you know Ethan?"

"What do you mean how do I know him? He was here for a couple of weeks soon after you arrived. You probably don't remember 'cause you were totally out to lunch, nothing but bats in the belfry. He was very concerned about you. And he calls here all the time."

Here a couple weeks? I shrug and shake my head.

Nigel looks at me, straight-mouthed, eyebrows curling in.

"I needed him when he came to visit me in Richmond. But he betrayed me."

Nigel nods, understanding. "Well," he says, "people do that. That's why the good Lord invented forgiveness."

Forgiveness?

But why should I be the one to reach out like that? I'm the one that's all fucked up. I'm the one that everyone's fucked over.

Forgiveness.

Ethan should apologize first, though. A chilly gust swirls around me, a cruel gift from the arctic. My hands and face have gone to ice, the muscles can barely move. I try to close and open my right hand, but the red, boney fingers are frozen stiff and bent, looking like a monstrous claw. I tuck my hands under my arms and start rocking back and forth.

"Tell you what, though," I say with a smirk, "It never gets this damn cold in San Francisco."

"That's the spirit," he says, slapping my knee.

Don't get the wrong idea. I can't actually go live there. That feels like going backwards. Like I failed. I can't do that.

"C'mon. Lets go back inside and get warm. Not that it's *all* that cold out here." He stands up. "You ready?"

I nod. What is he talking about? It is miserably cold out here. I look up and see the black circles of his shades, and I see myself reflected in both lenses, all hunched up and rocking.

"C'mon," he prods, waving his hand in a scooping motion. I put my claw-hands on the frigid stone bench and push myself up to standing.

27

Global warming. The apocalypse. It's not supposed to thunderstorm in winter here.

I am sitting on my bed, slippered feet on the floor, fire all inside my body, turning me red, I'm sure, pressure all over squeezing up my throat, trying to burst out my mouth, my ears. Linda is facing me, sitting in the chair in front of my desk. Her pale purple lips, worms, pressing tightly together. The little pill vile, loudest of all, on the corner of my desk in front of me with the little round blue pill and the big ovular pink one. She knows I didn't take my medicines again, that I haven't been taking them. I just don't want to. Linda is more pale than usual, almost translucent blue; evil ice queen. I have drawn her many times with my crayons, usually standing, wrapped in black furs, in front of a castle of ice and stone, crows circling the towers. And she has some pretty severe crows feet for someone her age, a few years younger than me, I think, the lines now pronounced as she scowls at me. Nigel is standing in front of the closed door, arms folded under his chest, a sentinel. The clear plastic cup next to the pill vile, full of trembling water.

Thunder crashes loudly outside, like to shatter this corner of the earth, to shake me to dust.

"Mimi," Linda demands, contorting her face as she does, "you take your meds right this instant or you will have no TV privileges this week."

"I don't care!" I shout, "Those pills are killing me! What's the point of me taking them if I don't even feel alive? That is a waste of my life!" Heavy rain like pebbles begin to hit the window.

"Mimi," Linda snarls through her pulled purple worms, jaw not moving at all, "You don't have a choice. Take the meds."

A cold light crosses her steel grey eyes, lightning. She is a vampire.

"Mimi," Nigel chimes in from the doorway, "sometimes you get all angry and awful difficult when you don't have your meds. We can't be fighting with you no more. It's grinding our nerves."

"I haven't been acting up in months! I've been controlling my anger," I protest. I turn to Linda. "You provoke me."

"Mimi, I'm not gonna argue with you, and I'm not gonna listen to you accuse me for your outbursts. Now take these pills or you'll have to be sent to a confinement room."

Wind rattles the window. Ghosts everywhere.

"Nigel, don't let them do this to me. You're my friend."

"I'm not your friend, Mimi. I'm your psychiatric technician. And it's my job to see that you're taking good care of yourself." He looks at me like he thinks he's my mother. "Do yourself a favor and just swallow your meds."

Thunder, planets colliding, just above the building.

A little, cold tear forms in the corner of my left eye and with a blink it is tossed into this fluorescent light and concrete world. Never had a chance.

Rain chatters loud, frantic on the window.

Lightning.

Suddenly there is a knock on the door. I jump. Nigel turns and talks with someone. He turns back to Linda. "I gotta go help Beth bring folks into the dining room. You gonna be okay?"

Linda nods slowly. Nigel gives me a look. Pity and condemnation and pleading all in one. I thought we were friends. His job. It's his job to play cards with me and talk with me. If I wasn't in here, if I met him on the street, he couldn't care less about me. Fucker! Fake!

He turns and walks out the door, shutting it behind him. The room is dark, only lit by the dim yellow-grey evening making its way past the blinds. I don't like the overhead florescent light, and the bulb in my desk lamp went out two days ago and hasn't been replaced.

Thunder. Lightning.

Linda looks like an apparition, like a figure in a dream. If I turn around and turn back, she'll be gone. She is barely here. I twist my torso around and face the wall behind me. I turn back. Linda is still here. I knew she would be. Maybe it is me who isn't really here. The grey light makes me tired, makes me feel like I could slip away, like everything is made of fog, and I could just slip into some dormancy, out of this world. I lie back on my bed and turn towards the wall, away from Linda.

"Oh, no," Linda says as she grabs my shoulder and turns me back around. "Sit up! Sit up right now, Mimi."

I let out an angry groan and sit up quickly. Linda is scrutinizing me with narrowed eyes.

"Mimi, I'm gettin' tired of this. Take your pills right now or I'm taking your paints away."

The ghost is here. Fills me quickly, like a breath. Sour almost chocking me, my whole insides just gastric juices, acid. I want to dig my nails into her face. Do it. No. I should breathe. I can't! I can't breathe! I'm suffocating! I stand and bolt for the door, swinging it open. Brightness all around me. I dash down the corridor. Bright mint green. Bright, bright light. There is nowhere to go. Keep running. The Activities Room? I'll hide. The common room, the couch, there under the table. A hand on my shoulder, nails digging in. I turn suddenly, knocking into Linda. She falls to the floor.

I am standing over her. A loud crash of thunder, shaking the building, the fluorescent lights flicker then go completely dark. Only the sound of the thunder's reverberation, and the beating of my heart. Lightning flashes from outside the window. I am breathing. Panting. I wonder if I could escape from here right now. Where would I go? My eyes begin to adjust to the dark grey light. Linda on the floor, holding herself.

I did have a life. I did with Jared. And sometimes even after Jared was gone.

Linda looks up at me. The white of her eyes much brighter than the rest of her. She props herself up on her elbows. I didn't strike her. Is she gonna say I struck her? I look into her eyes. Anger? Blame?

No. Her eyes looking up at me, not the same eyes. A sad little girl. This is the real Linda, in black and white like an old photograph. A sad, scared little girl.

I offer her my hand.

28 —

A month after Jared's visit, in summer, I hatched my big plans to my family.

"I'm moving to New York," I said one night at dinner. Everyone went quiet, with jaws slightly ajar. Sadness crept over their eyes like a shadow.

Ethan stood up. "No," he whined.

I could have cried. Mom patted his hand planted on the table.

"Ethan, it's okay," she said.

"Why?" he continued.

I took up my chest like a robin. "I just need a new life."

Ethan couldn't understand. He stormed off to our room.

"Why New York?" Dad asked.

"I don't know. Lots of reasons. I want to develop my painting more. I want to explore the art scene."

"San Francisco has a thriving art scene," Mom insisted.

"Not really," I sighed. "Besides, I just need to be somewhere else. My life here is so stale."

How could they argue, the way they've led their lives? But they wanted to.

"Are you done with school then?" Dad asked.

"I don't know. I just don't feel inspired by it right now. I don't know what I want."

Mom was fidgety in her chair, looking like she needed to pee.

"When do you plan to go?" Dad asked.

"Maybe September."

And that was that. We had a few more conversations and Dad arranged for me to stay with his cousin Michael and Michael's wife Lisa in Brooklyn for a month so I could get my feet on the ground. The months leading up to my move Ethan was in turns doting and overly affectionate, and sullen and moody. I took it in stride, knowing he couldn't understand. I needed to find my happiness.

New York was all that I hoped it would be on a surface level, full of new experiences, interesting characters and everything was art. I attended art openings, went to all the museums, saw off-Broadway shows and experimental performance pieces and found the most quirky little cafés to do my reading and thinking. I loved the tornado of magic that was New York. I lived in a small studio in queens paid for by my job at a used bookstore. I spent a good deal of time in that little studio painting. As my world and my thoughts became more random and abstract, so did my paintings. One day I found myself laughing at how my work was looking more and more like Jared's did back in high school. Maybe he really was a genius.

Some people I called friends came and went from my life. I would meet them at an exhibition or a café, but they each eventually evaporated like a cloud on a hot day. Phone calls went unanswered; chance meetings in public were politely rushed. I also got involved with men, and even a woman: Tammy. But these didn't last either. Everyone got frustrated with me. Thatcher broke my heart. Called me cold. I was so into him, too. He was a blonde clarinet playing punk, always wearing his leather jacket and tight black jeans. He made his money playing gigs, but mostly from tutoring kids in Brooklyn. He said it was sad how mothers stood by as sentinels while their pimple-faced kids plugged away at a simplified Bach melody, obviously under practiced. If med school didn't pan out, at least there would be klezmer. He was funny. We had fun together. The sex was great too. But in the end, he said he didn't feel connected, not like we should be after six months, said I didn't make prolonged eye contact. I was shocked. And wrecked.

I have been petrified of people. I blame my parents for not socializing me like a normal person. My contempt of them grew over the years, as did my estrangement from everything. Sometimes I wonder how I ended up like I did, institutionalized. How did it happen? When did it happen? Truth is I can't point to any particular time or place. The whole thing just feels like a slow descent, punctuated with moments of tumbling sharply and deeply into what I can only call hell.

After Jared, I never again had any deep, lasting connections. Ever. My whole life. Feeding on solitude, the ghost grew in power. Anger. Loneliness. It all seemed normal. The ghost convinced me this whole world is bleak. It still does. I see selfish, judgmental people in a meaningless world.

After ten years I decided that New York really was a zoo, and a heartless place, filled with cold and pretentious people. So I moved to the City of Brotherly Love, hoping that it would be all that its name promised. But I found it to be worse than New York. Not only could I not find any true friends, I also couldn't find an art scene to speak of or interesting cafés. I lived in a seedy part of town and was mugged twice. Again, I worked in a bookstore. Depressed and lazy, I started having trouble with time and would always be late.

The ghost grew even louder in Philly and I was always sweating and getting sick and found myself getting into yelling bouts with people: servers at restaurants who I felt were ignoring me, women at the laundromat who would take my clothes out of the dryer if it was done when I was across the street having a coffee or grocery shopping, people who smoked in bus stop shelters when it was raining, subjecting everyone to that vile and harmful stench. Everyone was an enemy. Everyone was horrible, disgusting and so goddamn ignorant. Me against the world. I was losing.

Five years and three jobs later I moved to Baltimore, still hunting like a hungry beast for contentment, but instead only going deeper and deeper into the swamplands. In Baltimore I would spend hours walking around the harbor, Fells Point, meandering through the aquarium, envying the fish for their simple minds. I often awoke to myself, noticing that I was chatting aloud, sometimes spitting angrily. Children stared at me; the ghost hated them. It didn't take long for the owner of the bookstore I was working at to take notice of my unsavory behavior, and I was, of course, fired. That was the last time I worked with the public, and before Poolesville the last time I worked at all. I lived off of unemployment and food stamps. At home I spent most of my time watching TV, a world I could escape to and usually not feel threatened by. I painted less frequently and the work took on more of the ghost's visions than my own: dirty, dilapidated buildings crooked and haunted, people were skinny and pale, wide eyes with dark rings, the living dead. I decided I had to get away from all these people. So I moved to DC.

In DC, I tried to get a job but no one would hire me. I thought about moving back to San Francisco to live at my old home, but I reviled my parents too much. I thought about asking Ethan for help, but couldn't. That's when I ended up on the street. I don't remember much about that time. I remember noticing how dirty I was, one time just staring at my filthy hands in horror. I would have cried, if I could, but I didn't cry then. I remember having sex, being raped by men also living on the streets. I would hide in the shadows, behind shrubs, for days after being raped or when the ghost was wild. I had a bag of clothes that I was obsessed not to lose as well as one smaller painting I had kept, the one of Three Birds. I begged for money so I could eat.

Fortunately I was put into a shelter, cleaned up and saw a counselor who helped me. I was dead then. I was dirt. So dead, in fact, that there was little fodder for even the ghost and she began to lay somewhat dormant. I didn't speak much, felt like I had had a lobotomy, my brain, my soul sucked out by the vacuum of life on the streets.

I told my caseworker, don't remember her name, that I wanted to get out of the city. Over a couple months she worked with Montgomery County and set me up in Poolesville, a small town about 45 minutes northwest of DC in Maryland, and got me a job as a custodian for the government buildings, like the town hall and libraries. I was put in a small, one-window apartment. No one at the shelter could understand how I got housing. I guess it was a miracle.

I called Ethan and gave him my new phone number. He asked me where I had been for the last eight months. I told him that I didn't have a phone for a while. He called me at least once a week after that.

After a year in Poolesville, I picked up the ringing phone and Ethan, crying, could barely croak out the news. Dad died. He had had a heart attack. I was a little sad, but mostly just felt guilty for being numb and not feeling sadness like I knew I should, like a normal person.

I went home for the funeral. Ethan paid for my plane ticket.

Ethan picked me up at the airport. It had been a few years since I last saw him, when he visited me in Baltimore. I felt somewhat uncomfortable for the first time around Ethan, like I didn't want him to see me. 'Yes,' I would say meekly, 'I was sad about Dad.'

When I got to my parents' flat, things looked pretty much the same, except the chairs around the old kitchen table were now a set; four simple wooden chairs. Also the old couch had been replaced, and now there was an electric scale on the coffee table to measure out the merchandise.

Mom looked so different to me. Her hair was now dreadlocked, down to her waist and streaked with grey. Her skin looked pale and without its glow. A face now drawn with

182

lots of tiny wrinkles around the eyes, lips and cheeks. She greeted me with a simple hug, not her usual shriek. But Dad had just died. And I had basically cut her out of my life only having a few phone conversations over the years. Besides, her mood suited me.

My old room was familiar, yet I couldn't find comfort in it. Who I had become was not the person who once occupied this room with her dear little brother. I felt strange in there, alien to myself.

Two days later at the funeral, I sat there in the black dress I had bought the day before at a thrift store. The sky was dark, the air cold. Mom and Ethan, Matilda, Grandma Rose, Aunt Sadie, Uncle Carl, were all there in the front row with me, all of them crying or sniffling. The rabbi approached to tear the piece of cloth from our clothing, so we stood. All of us had ribbons pinned on that the rabbi had given us. This is a modern take on the tradition so people won't have to rip their actual clothes. But mom refused the ribbon. She said the whole point is to feel the tear, the loss. The rabbi in his black suit stood over mom, her head slanted down. He made a cut with scissors along the seam of her sleeve, put the scissors in his pocket, took the sleeve in both hands and yanked. Mom let out a scream like a wild animal, like her own flesh had been torn. And then she cried. When the rabbi came to me, I also looked down to the ground. I became one of the small grey rocks lying there on the dirt. The rabbi cut the ribbon pinned to my chest. Then he ripped it. I didn't make a sound. I didn't feel a thing.

The next day, I returned from an outing at a café, after convincing myself that I should spend a little time with my mom. That night I would be flying out of SFO on a red-eye back to DC. I found myself sitting at the old kitchen table. Mom came in the house, from I don't know where, and walked into the kitchen looking sad. She stood there, looking at me. I couldn't look back. I looked around the room.

"I don't understand you, Mimi. You've always been so standoffish. Ever since you were able to walk, you've been walking away from me."

I became stone. My teeth clenched and I tasted metal. The world flipped upside down and I got dizzy. I ended up in Antarctica, freezing, alone on an expansive ice shelf. I could not argue with her accusations. She knew how I felt about hers and Dad's parenting. There was no denying I was loved, but for some reason I have been unable to return any tenderness, to see them beyond my own anger. I had been cold and now my mother stood over me as a giant mirror and I felt all those years of coldness in my body. I sat at her table keeping myself from shaking. Her eyes were not wet with tears, as I thought they would have been, but looked at me hard. She was done crying over me. She stood there not my mother at all, but as herself, telling me her truth.

I could have said so many things in that moment. I could have cried. It even crossed my mind to stand up and give her a hug. But all of that was too scary for me. My teeth began to chatter. I pushed the chair away from the table, stood up and walked past my mother without looking at her. I went to my old room, grabbed my little duffle bag and left.

I decided to go to the airport where I would wait for my flight. I walked all the way to 16th & Mission BART. The sky was a dark grey-blue, streaked with silver. The wind whipped my hair about, tossing it, pushing me, taunting me. I heard a clap of thunder, not thunder like the East Coast gets, but still there it was: a distant, muffled rumbling in the beast of heaven's throat. Rain came down suddenly and with dedication. I walked fast, my hair getting soaked, my face completely wet, my shoes drenched. It was like walking the floor of a turbulent sea.

I finally made it to the station, a wet and shaking animal. I took the train to the Daly City station, and then got on the bus to the airport. When I got to the airport, I looked a mess. But who fucking cares. I changed in the ladies room, lay down at my gate and fell asleep. When I woke, there was a wet spot where my head had been. My shoes were still squishy and wet. Eventually the plane came and I boarded, sleeping most of the way home.

Back in Poolesville I found my apartment bare and sad. Once again, I decided to move. I waited two years, saving money and toying with ideas of where to go. Poolesville was tiny, but in its spaciousness I had began to rediscover some of myself again. I had started painting and reading again. I still felt empty and sad, and the ghost always carried on in the back of my mind, gnawing away at anything inside me it could, a doubt in the solidity of things. But I persisted.

I decided on Richmond, Virginia as a new home. It wouldn't be as crowded as the cities, so full of chaos assaulting the senses, but it would have some history and culture.

29 ➝

It's him. His glowing face, light, eyes of love, inches away. A sensation in the middle of my chest, like opening, like tiny moths flying all around the opening. I look down and the Saint has two fingers touching me there, in the middle of my chest. I gasp. The feeling grows into a vibrating pleasure, an orgasm pulsing from my chest, radiating, growing. My back arches slightly. This feeling, this sweet feeling growing, deepening, coursing all through me. Cloudy yellow-white light everywhere, alive, the marrow of the cosmos, inside of me, inside everything, beautiful mystery, beautiful. My eyes water, mouth agape. I am part of this.

I have been hard on myself.

Everything is vibrating, is vibration. It is intelligent. It knows me. Soothing me.

Everything is humming, my throat, my jaw. I want to sing. I want to swim in this ocean of energy.

God. The sweet silent nothing at the center. Sacred. Every flower, every heart. Silent nectar, everything sings with its sweetness. Everything is the singing. It is me. I am…

My chest still radiating…supernovas into a million new universes, ecstasy, crying countless new oceans, sighs new worlds, creatures, elements, dancing.

Something is happening.
Pulling
   me down.

It is leaving.
Dimming.
Where is it going?

Where did it go?

Nothing.

My body, heavy.
I am lying down.

A noise.
A lawnmower.

My body is hard.

The blanket on top of me.
Warm.

I take a breath. Bittersweet; the remnants of bliss still here.

But not like it was, the place beyond the dark purple mountains of death.

Energy still courses through my body. Aftershocks.

I open my eyes.

This room. Sharp with its white walls, white linoleum floors. It stabs. Bloodless. I have been here for eternities. Did I ever really live in San Francisco with a family? On the road with Bertha? What is memory?

* * * * * * * * * * * * *

I must have fallen back asleep. The light is different. More yellow. Less blue.

That saint. It isn't a dream. It is too real. I understand things there that I couldn't possibly understand here, the meaning and workings of everything. I can't even remember what I realized there. But it was beautiful. It's what is really going on.

So why this pain? Why this human drama?

My stomach tightens. My throat is scratchy.

I breathe steadily. There is still a sublime energy in my body. The soft blanket rubs against my skin. The sunlight in my room is alive. It is the most real thing in this world...a direct emanation of the other world, the truer world. No wonder people everywhere used to worship it. Light; truly the language of the Divine. Do people see this? Somehow, I feel like I've always known.

I stretch my legs out, pointing my toes, smiling, groaning in pleasure. I want to get up, go get breakfast and see Nigel and everyone, but I also want to stay here in bed. This is so cozy.

What if this feeling goes away?

Last time I was visited by the Saint, the blissful feelings faded, although some of it lingered behind. Maybe the memory of it is enough, a little ember emitting just enough warmth if I stay close to it.

The fabric of me is made of light and there are no holes. The mind creates holes when it seeks them out.

Is that what I do? Look for holes?

What does that mean?

Ugh! It doesn't make any sense.

I shut my eyes and let myself be still. I take a deep breath. I exhale slowly.

I breathe in slowly again, through my nose and when my lungs are filled, I gently hold the breath. Peaceful. And exhale slowly.

I can do this. I can steady myself.

I kick off my blanket and sit up at the edge of my bed.

I stand up and walk across the room and take panties, socks, jeans and a t-shirt out of the dresser. I dress quickly. I want breakfast.

I start towards the door, but I'm chilly. I open the plain plywood wardrobe, yank my yellow sweater off its hanger, which swings back and forth, and pull the sweater over my head. That's better.

I walk down the corridor towards the dining room.

"Come on little mama, let me light your candle, cause you know I'm sure hard to handle...da dada dada bum bah bah."

I open the left door, walk in and stop suddenly because of all the eyes on me.

"No need to bust the door down, Mimi," Linda says coolly, "There's plenty of food." She smirks, amused with herself.

Did I really come in with that much energy?

I walk over to the counter where the food is left out, buffet style. Yum. Scrambled eggs. I put some on my plate. Toast. Bacon, yuck. Fruit salad, yes. I put some on my plate. I wish it wasn't the canned kind. It always tastes kinda funny, and nothing is fresh and crisp. Maybe I should get a job cooking for this place, when I'm no longer a prisoner. What am I talking about? I'm gonna get as far away from Virginia as possible.

With my small plate full, I turn around to find a seat. No Val.

No Nigel. Is it his day off? Wait! He's not my friend anymore. A phony!

I guess I'll sit next to Daryl. He is usually quiet in the morning.

Daryl is alone at the small circle table. I sit down in a chair across from him. He smiles and bows his head chivalrously. "Mimi," he says, "Good mornin'."

"Good morning," I say back. That's as far as this conversation can go.

I look down at my plate and dig into the eggs. I'm starving. Maybe going to heavenly realms takes a lot out of a person. I look up at Daryl. I want to tell somebody about the Saint and the dream. He is studying his plate, chewing slowly, a knife in one large, dry black fist, a fork in the other, both utensils pointing up at his face, his chewing jaws.

So I eat my breakfast gingerly, humming made-up tunes between bites.

Linda comes by and sits next to me.

"Well, Mimi, you're awful chipper this morning."

I measure her demeanor.

"I guess I am."

"What's causin' that?"

Should I tell her? Will she believe me?

Who cares.

No, it will suck if she gives me a hard time.

"I had a vision last night."

"A vision?" I can't tell if she's patronizing me or not.

"What kind of vision?"

"Well…" why am I telling her this? "Sort of like a visitation."

189

"A visitation? By what? Aliens?" She chuckles her squeaky parrot laugh. "I've heard that one before. They seem to like the residents here."

"By a saint," I inform her proudly.

"A saint? Well, that's something. Which one?"

"I don't know."

"You don't know?"

I shake my head, "No."

"Well, how do you know he was a saint?"

"I could just tell. He is the sweetest thing." Why am I telling her this? "Like an angel. But he doesn't have any wings so I don't think he is an angel."

"And this all happened in your room?"

She doesn't believe me. I pause. "In my room? No. Not really. It was in my sleep. In another realm."

Linda gives me a crooked disapproving look. "Mimi," she shakes her head as she pushes herself up to standing and crosses her arms over her chest. "We call those dreams. They aren't real." And she turns and walks away, off to gnaw on someone else.

There is a walnut shell lump in my throat. I feel empty. I sit up. She doesn't know. What does she know? She is a prisoner of her own rigidity. I did have some hope. The look in her eyes when I pulled her off the floor two nights ago, during the storm. The little girl there. I did have some hope that things might change between us, might change in her. But I suppose a person doesn't change so drastically from just one such incident. I suppose a person has to want to change. That's what everyone says. There is some wisdom residing in the province of humanity.

I look back down at my plate and take another bite of eggs. They're pretty cold. And bland. I swallow with effort. I prod and squish the eggs with my fork. I'm done. I'll just have some coffee. Gotta have my morning coffee. Mm mm, so tasty. And helps me take my daily shit.

I push my chair back from the table, stand up and grab my plate.

190

"Mimi," Daryl says. He is smiling, as usual. He winks twice with such deliberateness, communication, like Morse Code, saying, "I believe you."

* * * * * * * * * * * * *

Back in my room I sit on the edge of my bed, enjoying the lightness I feel in my chest, the tingling in my face imploring the smile to just stay. I giggle to myself.

I sigh.

I wish Val was around. Someone to talk with. I look around the room: nothing of importance and nothing that is mine except the crayola pictures covering the far wall.

I squeeze my hand. The little smile now recedes with no one to show itself off to.

I go sit at my desk and draw up the blinds. The sky is grey and it looks cold out there. A cold front came in after the thunderstorm. It hasn't snowed much at all this winter, just a dusting a couple times, but the weather lady on the news said Smyth County could expect some significant snow. White Christmas lights are still wrapped around the bare branches of the two maple trees flanking the path outside the front door, just below my window. I have hardly celebrated Christmas in my life, but I have always liked those little lights, especially the white ones. They represent *some* human will to acknowledge and produce the better parts of our nature: kindness, peace, the ability to see beauty. But what really stands out, almost sings and hollers to me, is that path, that straight white line that starts directly under me and pushes forward like a dreamy midday stroll, towards the gate and beyond. How unfortunate to have been put in this room, where that path, that siren, calls, but like the sailors of old I cannot leap because that realm is not offered to me. People romanticize the sirens, the mermaids. But those are some tricky bitches leading people to a drowned doom, or at the least torture us by pointing to our hard confinements, contrasted to their songs of a watery world where we would float and fly, vertical movement granted us at last. No, we are obliged to accept gravity and the hard ground.

And what of the Saint? Is he merely a siren, or has he something to offer me?

He pointed to my heart. He touched it, with his two fingers extended. And I expanded, beyond all boundaries and became the Universe, again a member of that which exists. A component, like a pinky toe. Part of it all. Maybe only a molecule of the pinky toenail, but still, here I am.

The grey sky outside my window churns slowly, pulsates. It is breathing.

I am breathing.

Silence.

We are breathing.

Wow. And I think the Saint is there too, in those heavy clouds. He is in everything.

I open the top left drawer of my desk and pull out the painting I've been working on; the one of Bertha and Dad and Mom being pregnant in the parking lot at some concert, an image from several lives ago.

I open the bottom left drawer and pull out the paints and brushes that Shelly gave me. Water. I'll need water. I get up and make my way to the dining hall. I grab a coffee mug and fill it with water from the sink. And I'll need a palette. I take a paper plate out of one of the cabinets. I walk back to my room, water spilling a little over the edges of the cup. I should come back and clean it so no one slips. No, it's just a little bit. It'll be fine.

Back in my room. I set the mug down on my desk and plop in the seat. Now, what colors? I'm gonna paint Mom today. I'll put her in an olive green dress with yellow flowers. Titanium white, ivory black, chromium oxide, hookers green, green gold, cadmium yellow, canary yellow, dioxinine purple, raw umber.

I start with the dress, the green pregnant form. She is standing next to Bertha's open sliding door, looking at me, the viewer. I paint her small sandaled feet. I paint her head and her wild brown mane, and shade her shoulders and under her chin. It is midday. Time for lunch, or for the pipe or a joint to go around for the second time. I paint her arms, one holding herself up against Bertha, the other on her hip. I paint her face, her wild eyes, her gap-toothed smile. I have never painted my mother before.

I look up. Outside is even darker than just before. I take a breath. Something moves in the window. And again. Snowflakes. Floating slowly, zigzagging slowly down, having been shaken out from the sky above. I stand up a little to see the ground outside. Of course there is no accumulation yet. The snowflakes dancing wayward in no hurry to meet the earth and what changes await them there. They are breathing. I breathe with them. Me and the snowflakes.

I look back down at my painting. My mother. Why couldn't I breathe with them?

A knock. I turn and Nigel is standing in the doorway, smiling. Jerk. I show him my contempt and turn back to my painting.

"Well, that's some 'hello,'" he jokes.

My jaw tightens. My whole face tightens.

"Mimi?"

I turn quickly and snarl like an angry dog, "I thought you were my friend!"

Nigel's eyes widen, his mouth opens as if to speak, to defend himself or yelp, but nothing comes. I continue to glare.

He composes himself. "Mimi. I am…your pal. But primarily I am here to help you. You gotta understand that."

"You're a phony," I hiss, "You go on acting like we're friends, when all along you were just doing your job and that's all it is to you." I turn back to my desk and the dark grey sky and the snow flurries, still dancing, still breathing quietly, even without me.

"Mimi…"

I can feel him back there. The hair on my neck stands in response.

"Okay. I see how it's gonna be." And like a phantom carried away on a breeze, his presence is no longer there. I turn around to look anyways and the emptiness in the doorway validates what I already knew.

The dark grey sky is still breathing. The little dancing snowflakes, still breathing. I am unable to breathe with them now.

The weather lady said it might stick, that we might get a couple inches. Then I wouldn't be able to see the path below. There would no longer be some way out, some destination, but for a little while everything would be still, nestled together under the same cottony blanket with nowhere better to go.

30 →

Solitaire. Since lunch. Over an hour. Losing interest. But what else am I supposed to do? Joan and Barbara are on the couch watching TV, stiff as stiffs.

I look back down at the table. King, four, ten, diamond, red, jack, seven, club. Life is a riddle I can't figure out. How am I supposed to live inside of it? A hall of shattered mirrors, jagged pieces reflecting disjointed fragments of me and everything, that I can't make into some discernable whole. I float, flotsam and jetsam with energies, maybe radiated from the stars, emotions, images, ideas, but never ground to stand on.

Someone standing next to me. I look up. Daryl, wearing a faded yellow button-up shirt and an orange ascot with white polka dots, neatly tucked in above the top button. He's beaming his smile down at me.

I wrinkle my forehead. "Well, aren't you looking spiffy?"

He gets serious. "Let yo' walls down, Mimi. We could be friends." I scoff. "You got a sharp eye, Mimi. You can see all the bullshit. But you don't gotta be condemnin'. Soften yo' gaze a little bit."

My stomach, my whole torso, relaxes. Air escapes from my mouth, deflating.

"Mind if I sit?"

"I'm kinda playing solitaire," I squeak, not expecting to sound so meek. I wince.

"Oh, come on. Lighten up, girl."

I'm silent, looking blankly at the table.

Daryl pulls out a chair and sits opposite me.

"Why are you all dressed up?" I ask, staring down that two of hearts that hasn't budged, sittin' on top a whole pile of cards I need.

"Well, my first date with Mimi Rizner, I gotta look sharp."

"Date?"

"Friend date?"

"I'm not sure we'd make good friends."

"What? Your mouth is facing the table. Look up."

I look up, scowling. "I *said*, I don't think we'd make good friends." I stare just long enough to burn a hole in the old goat, then look back to the cards. I gotta find the ace of hearts. I bet it's under the goddamn two.

"Why not? The way I see it, we got lots in common. I'm in a mental hospital, you're in a mental hospital. I'm witty, you think you're witty." He chuckles. "I'm a witch, you're a witch."

"A witch? What the hell are you talking about? I'm no witch."

"Is that why you hear ghosts?" he laughs.

My stomach tightens into solid rock. "That doesn't make me a witch."

He's still laughing. "The way you carry on running around screaming to nobody in particular."

My throat tightens. The muscles in my forearms tense like they're gonna snap. The skin on my face is being pulled back like a rubber mask. A twitch just over the right corner of my

195

mouth. "That doesn't make me a witch!" I shrill, tears coating my eyes. "And neither are you! You're just a lazy old man who pretends to be deaf and crazy so he can be all taken care of in the mental hospital."

Daryl laughs, leaning back in his chair to let the fullness of it out. He slaps the table. He looks at me, eyes glistening with delight. "Now *that's* funny, Mimi."

"You're hearing awfully well right now, Daryl."

"Perceptive as you are, you can't see me at all. Or yo'self. No ma'am. You blind when it comes to seeing me or you. You don't let yourself see what ya can't handle. True of most people. So let me fill you in. You a witch. And I'm a witch. How did we get this way? Well, I believe it's carried in the blood."

"Will you shut up?"

"Now, Mimi, don't be rude. I'm telling you a story." He glares at me, making sure I'm under control. Then continues, "See, my grandmammy, she was a big witch in Talbot County, Georgia, a rural black area where people knew that witches are real. She was a powerful seer. They all called her Miss Willows cause she lived in a little house down by the creek, surrounded by willow trees. And all the town folk would come to her to learn 'bout their fortunes, askin' questions 'bout love and business and ailments and everything. But as you can imagine, just 'cause people believe in witches, don't mean they trust 'em. Grandmammy got knocked up and she was a good mama to my daddy, 'cording to what he tells me. But he was lonely. He was feared, not fully trusted by the folk, this child of the witch. His life was confused. There was even a rumor 'round town when Mr. Carter killed himself, he did it 'cause the witch was demanding he teach my daddy to be a man, and if he didn't she would let everyone know he was the father. Things got bad off, so when he was fifteen, my daddy left Georgia and come up here to start a new life. He found work, met my mama, got married. Never had any premonitions or strange speriences." Daryl puts his forearms on the table, leaning in. "I, on the other hand, got grandmammy's powers. Daddy knew when I was just a kid, my vivid imagination, voices and characters I would take on. He knew they were signs. But I didn't start hearing voices till I was almost twenty." His yellowed, bloodshot eyes widen. "Scared the dickens out of me." A chilly breeze up my arms, around my neck. Goosebumps. "Mimi, I been hearing voices for a long time. Most of them is harmless and some is downright friendly and teach me things. But at first, I didn't know how to handle it, all these voices…and the way my mind can transform me. Like I'd be by the river, looking for some peace, and I'd see a fish and suddenly it was like I became a fish. I felt like a fish, saw like a fish. I could feel and understand its movements down to my cells. Times I thought I'd never get back to myself; I'd stay a fish or the wind, or some other person forever. It was the scariest thing. I was haunted from being haunted. How would I ever be normal again? When it 'came 'parent that I wouldn't, I wanted to kill myself." He leans back in his chair crossing his arms over his chest. "But I was too much of a chicken. So instead, I started banging my head against walls. Whenever I heard voices or felt myself transforming, over and over, smashing my head against a wall, trying to get the voice out. And I was worried 'bout people finding out." He smirks at me. "It worked, usually, stopping whatever was happening. But it also caused me to lose my regular hearing too."

My mouth and eyes open, receiving this revelation. I want to say I'm sorry. Sorry for being a bitch. Sorry all this happened to you. What if he's lying? No, he's not. He's looking at me so raw. No one does that. Jared did. Ethan did. Raw like the shell is cracked open and the soft tissue begins to spill out. I give Daryl a little smile, the most I can muster.

We sit quietly for a moment. He looks comfortable in his chair, smiling kindly at me. My eyes move about, my body rigid and angular like a Picasso.

"So what's your story, Mimi?"

"My story? I don't know. It's long and convoluted."

He nods. "Just start at the beginning."

I tell him about Bertha. How my little family lived, like a tribe, wild creatures with tangled hair and eyes sizzling with the rapture of freedom (or was it the LSD?). Highways and byways. Beaches and woods and mountainsides where we would park and live for a day or a month. Daryl listens patiently, nodding with interest, letting me go on and on. I tell it all like a faerie tale. A dream. I was a quiet one. I liked my space. But this was the closest thing to home I've ever known. I stop there. Why tell him about landing in SF? About the torment. About Jared. And then beyond that. My unraveling. Maybe I was never raveled to begin with.

I let out a loud sigh. He smiles. He bows his head, pushes back from the table. "This has been a lovely first date, Mimi," he smiles and stands up. "Meet me for tea after dinner?" I nod my head. He smiles, lips not parting, and starts to walk off.

I grab him by the wrist. "Daryl!" I say, surprising myself, "I'm glad we're friends."

He gives me a dry smile, "It's gonna be a short friendship," and walks on, my arm falling back to my side.

* * * * * * * * * * * * *

Almost everyone has cleared out of the dining room. It was a raucous one this evening. Sort of like going to see twenty one-man shows all at the same time. I managed to keep pretty calm though. It feels so calm in here now, like after a summer afternoon thunderstorm.

Daryl is at the tea and coffee table making us our tea. The young men who work here, preparing food, serving and cleaning up, are now comfortable enough to talk and joke freely with each other. They don't do that when too many patients are around and the cuckoo-meter is running high. And most of them don't look us in the eyes. That's how you contract a mental disease.

Something's caught in my teeth. We had pork chops for dinner tonight. Fancy. And they weren't so bad either. A little piece of flesh caught between my teeth. I use my fingernails like pincers trying to grab it, while my tongue keeps track of its location. Tricky little bugger.

Daryl comes back to the table carrying two steaming mugs. "Peppermint tea," he declares, placing one down in front of me.

"I got something caught in my teeth."

"What?"

I take my hand out of my mouth. "I said I got something caught in my teeth."

"You got something caught in your teeth?"

"Yeah. I can't get it out." I try to pull it through inwards with my tongue. "It's buggin' the hell out of me."

Daryl walks over to the kitchen and says something to one of the guys working. He waits a moment, then the young man hands him a slip of paper. Daryl beams a smile, then comes back over to me, holding the paper in his hand.

"Here. Use this," he says, handing it over.

I take the folded paper and push it in between the two teeth in the corner of my mouth where the little piece of pig tissue is hanging on. The paper strikes my gums, painful yet satisfying. Something feels different. The pressure. I remove the paper and swipe my tongue against the back of my teeth. The thing is free and now on my tongue. I bite down on it with my front teeth, give it a tiny chew there, move it to the back of my mouth and swallow. Little bugger.

"Gone," I announce.

Daryl smiles.

He settles in his chair. "Thanks for joining me for another date, Mimi. Two dates in one day; I'm on a roll!"

I smirk, picking up my hot mug of tea, too hot to drink yet. He's still smiling at me.

"I suppose I could use a friend," I say.

"I can't hear you or read your lips behind that cup."

"I *said* I suppose I could use a friend." I practically shout.

He nods sympathetically. "Now that Val's gone."

I make a dismissive hiss. "She wasn't a good friend."

"Yes, well, in any case, you could stand to be around someone who smiles."

"Oh yeah?"

"Yeah, Mimi. You need to lighten up."

"Fuck that. How's a person suppose to lighten up when the whole world is mad? It's all fucked. There's no meaning to any of it."

"I got me a tattoo, Mimi," he says like telling me a secret.

"What? Did you understand a word I just said?"

"I think so," he chuckles.

"Well what the hell does a tattoo have to do with it?"

"It's my only tattoo."

I stare at him. He *is* crazy.

"It's on my left shoulder. On the back. I probably don't seem like the tattoo type, do I?"

I shrug. Who cares? What the fuck is he talking about?

"It's a skull. A human skull." His eyes widen as he leans towards me. "*My* human skull."

"Will you shut up?"

He settles back in his chair and laughs. I purse my lips and shake my head. He is an idiot. Why am I even here?

His laughter subsides and he looks at me intently. "Don't you wanna know why I got my human skull as a tattoo?"

"Not really," I'm not interested in your crazy-ass antics.

"To remind me my own death." He looks at me.

I swallow hard.

Why would a person want to be reminded of their own death?

"So, you're looking forward to dying?"

"No. But I am…curious."

"Then why the tattoo? I thought you said you didn't kill yourself 'cause you were chicken."

"'It reminds me not to take life so seriously. Yes, I'm also scared. But I have to face reality," he says. "Everything dies.

Every person, every moment, every thing. Including me." His eyes, like a bull's. "And you."

"That's awful," I say.

Suddenly I see my old painting 'Death' in my mind. The lady (me?) walking through endless rolling golden fields towards the mysteries of twilight.

"It's not awful," Daryl informs me, "It's liberating. Nothing to hold on to. Something I realized is that everything we got a hold on, got a hold on us. So you wanna be free, let go of everything."

"What could I possibly be holding onto, Daryl? I don't have anything."

"Not true," he smiles, "You got your self-pity. You got victimization. You got beliefs 'bout how unfair the world is. You holding so tight to lots of things."

I sniff. Sit up straight, knees together, feet together, wrists on the table. "If you got it all figured out, what are *you* doing in a mental institution?"

He smiles benevolently. "Mimi, you tenacious. That's how you is, tenacious." He gets serious, leans in, clasping his hands together on the table. He takes a breath. "Maybe the world don't know what to do with a witch." He raises his eyebrows, casts a dark sheet over us with his eyes. In a goat hair tent together, among sand dunes. A warm, dim light barely illuminating us, holding us. "Maybe I'm in here so that I could have this conversation with you." Wind ruffles the dark fabric. A strange bird calls out in the night. I shift. I slump a little. "God works in mysterious ways, Mimi." He leans back again, but still looking right at me. "I don't pretend to know His intentions. But here I am. And maybe that's *all* a person can ever really know."

His look softens. The tent is picked up from the top and whooshed away. We're in the dining room. Bright light. Dishes clanking in the kitchen.

"You so busy in your head, Mimi. "WAKE UP!" he shouts, clapping his hands together, making a thunderous noise, rattling me. He sees me jump and laughs.

201

The back of my head buzzing like a chainsaw. Him laughing.

"Shut up," I say.

"You shut up," he says, mocking me, sounding like a squeaky, rusty thing.

I giggle.

He nods his head while laughing. "There you go. There she is."

I start cracking up. Energy in my body, shaking me like a friend, reminding me of some great secret. A secret so secret I can't even understand it. But I know it's something about laughing.

An old well is bubbling up and I can't help it. Something shifts. Rotating just a little, the feeling. Now I'm crying. Full of crying. Nothing but sobbing. I sink my head into my chest. Daryl reaches across the table and wraps his big hands around mine.

"That's okay. We can make room for crying too. That's part if it too." He squeezes my hands tight and warm. "Sometimes it hurts. And sometimes it's rough; God trying to put so much God into these skin bags. It ain't easy. How does the clay respond to the light? Sometimes it's downright scared. Can drive a person crazy. Lost in a maze of fear."

I have been crying so much in the last few months. After years of not crying it feels strange to cry like this again, cry like I did when I was just a little girl and I knew how to sob. "I need a tissue."

He releases my hands, gets up from the table. I just cry myself to empty. Letting it go. Snot everywhere. I've been lost in a maze of fear. Completely lost.

He returns with a stack of white paper napkins. He puts the stack down on the table and places one of the napkins in my hand. I lift my head, blow my nose, fold the napkin and wipe my nose. I crumple it and put it on the table. I pull another one off the pile and use it to wipe the tears from my eyes. I crumple it and put it on the table. The last hiccups of crying moving through. Bubbles in a spring.

I look up at Daryl. Tenderness.

"You alive, Mimi,' he says eyes wide with excitement. "You gotta free yourself and do your own thing."

"What's my own thing?"

"Like you don't know. You an artist. A magician. A harbinger. You can see what others can't yet see."

Air, breezes moving around inside me, my torso. The knot in the pit of my belly still there. Always there. Will it ever go away?

Daryl smiling at me.

31 ➙

"I don't know why I'm telling you so much of my teenage years and my relationship with Jared." I sniff, and gently rub my fingers along the back of my hand, not the same hand as when I was seventeen. A hand that has held countless cups of coffee, and paintbrushes, pressed against cold, dirty sidewalks, but has not known enough of other things like wildflowers, or a baby's foot, or the hand of a dear friend. I picked up a book of poems by Mary Oliver, but I couldn't read it. She kept asking so many questions about how I'm living my life. No, Ms. Oliver, unfortunately I do not run out into the garden every morning, half naked, rushing to take up the fluffy white peonies in my arms. That has not been my life. Besides, try pulling off something like that here!

"I think so much about those old times, because they are the best times of my life. I don't want you to think I'm all bad."

The room feels so empty. The light coming in through the window is warm. Spring isn't too far off. Dr. Westland is the nicest person I have ever known. I take a breath and at the crest, the stillness between the in breath and the out breath, I feel a mild sweetness there like the fragrance of apple blossom.

"My life has been a tar pit with just a few sparkling jewels thrown in."

"Mimi you talk like you're an old lady."

"I feel like one."

"You're barely middle age. You have the second half of your life ahead of you."

I'm on a train, the track laid out before me, passing through endless white fields. White sky. Bright emptiness.

"And maybe you should focus on the jewels and not so much on the tar."

I want to protest. But forget it. Out of the whiteness I see Ethan as a little boy. A smile comes over my face.

"There you go."

I smile bigger and give Dr. Westland a wicked look as if to say, 'you devil.' The smile sinks away. If I leave here, I won't get to talk with Dr. Westland any more. Too bad he isn't my husband. I laugh.

"What's so funny?"

"Will you marry me?"

He smiles. "Well, you know, I'm already married."

I nod, smiling amusedly, noticing the picture of the blonde family wearing earth tones on his desk.

"But, Mimi, I'm confident you can make friends. You are fun and witty and more thoughtful than you realize.

Warmth moves up my face. Whoa. When was the last time I blushed?

"It's important to like yourself, Mimi. Even love yourself."

Little sparks, electricity crackling in my chest.

"Okay," I say, "and what about when the ghost comes back? And I know you don't want me talking about her like she's a living thing, but…"

"You can handle that ghost, Mimi. She's not so tough. She hasn't gotten you defeated. Just watch her. Love her. Listen to her. The trouble is in the resisting, the fighting. That's when you get absorbed. Just let the feelings be there when they show up. Ride it out, like the captain of a ship in a storm."

A deep breath takes over me, filling me up. I sit up straighter in my seat. Yes. I can ride out those storms. I already have over and over again. "Do you think she'll ever go away?"

"I don't know. But I know you can live a good life, either way."

A good life. Happy people smiling.

"What constitutes a good life, do you suppose?" I ask.

"I would say gratitude. When you are grateful to be alive. That sounds like a life worth living to me. And there doesn't need to be any absence of darkness or suffering for that to happen. You can include the suffering as part of the life that you are grateful for; it is part of the whole picture. The way I see it, the dark stuff always causes growth, some expansion, some opportunity. When we see its gift it's so easy to be grateful for it."

I feel like a swamp, only the dimmest light reaching the murky floors of bog, and drenched plants. "I can't see what use this torture has been, all my life."

"I can't tell you, either. But don't get lost in it."

Don't get lost in the swamp.

"See it as part of the whole picture."

It's just part of my world.

I nod feeling a command of myself for the first time in years.

"And don't forget to breathe. The mind can be slippery and scattered. Breathing is like an eraser on the chalkboard of your mind. It's good to keep the chalkboard pretty clear, not all cluttered up."

I take a deep breath. I smell my shampoo. The warm sunlight is hugging my arm. My body is sitting in this chair, sitting up.

"I'll see you again in a couple days, okay Mimi?"

I nod.

The little plastic orange chair is hard and cold pressing into my butt bones. Gail, watching me, wiggles her mouse nose, her whiskers. This feels hard.

"Do you want me to dial for you?" Gail asks.

I shake my head, "No. I just need a moment."

I have decided to call my mother. Gail tells me she thinks I'll be released soon, that Dr. Westland alluded to my time here being almost over. Gail told me this three days ago and all I have been doing is imagining. Excited. Breathing more freely. Green walls are retracting back, giving me space. But I've also been nervous. Excitement turns over to nervousness so easily. So what *will* I do when I leave here? Gail has made it clear that going back to San Francisco to live with Mom and to have Ethan nearby would be the best thing for me. 'What other choice do you have?' Gail said. And it's true. As much as I resent Mom for being an awful mother, she still does care about me some, I think. And it will be a place to live. I can live there until I get my feet back on the ground. And Shelly said she has a friend who owns a gallery in the Lower Haight who would probably be interested in me showing my work there. That's exciting!

Besides, what's the alternative? Some halfway house in the middle of Nowhere, Virginia?

What if Mom rejects me? Even the thought of it obliterates me into grey dust. But I wouldn't be altogether surprised. I have not hidden my resentments and harsh criticisms over the years. Mostly by just dropping out of communication, losing what bond we did have. I hurt her. The last time I saw here, or even spoke with her, was after Dad's funeral.

Gail is looking at her hand, maybe at the liver spots. She touches her wedding band, twisting it ever so slightly, adjusting it.

My own hands are clammy, cold. My heart is beating so hard. If she rejects me, she rejects me. I can survive on my own. But it would be in her best interest to have me back home. I could help with the cooking and cleaning. And she's not exactly young anymore. She can't sell that pot forever. Some young punk might rob her.

I pick up the receiver and start dialing. I know the number. It's been the same for thirty years. It's ringing. Everything collapses into thirty years ago. I can see the foyer of the old house. I see Dad and Mom sitting at the kitchen table laughing, smiling at me. I see Ethan looking up at me, his big sister. I smell old wood, and dust, and roses. The vein in my neck is pulsating, growing, about to explode. *Ringing*. I see my Mom smiling. I see Mom when I came home for Dad's funeral, streaks of grey twisting through her long serpentine dreadlocks, the light not in her face, the look in her eyes like being buried under the mountain, looking right at me.

"Hello?" It hardly even sounds like her, so sober. I try to speak, but my throat is clogged with twenty years of silence.

"Hello?" she repeats.

"Mom?" I squeeze out.

Silence.

"Mimi?"

Water comes up. "Yeah."

"Mimi!"

And crying. Warm spring water dripping down my face.

"Mimi, are you okay?" she coos.

I gather myself, sniffle. "Yeah. I'm okay."

"I can't believe it's you. Are you still at the hospital?"

"Yeah."

"Of course, yeah, Ethan would have said something if you had been released. I'm sorry, maybe I shouldn't be talking like that, I'm sorry sweetie, how are you?"

"Mm. I'm fine."

"That's good, that's good. They're treating you good there?"

"They treat me fine."

"Oh, good, good. 'Cause if something is wrong, you could tell me and I…"

"It's good to hear your voice, Mom."

"Oh, Mimi," The water is coming up in her now, "Mimi, I miss you so much. I can't even tell you. I'm so sorry about how I was after Dad died, I was just so…so sad and upset and I…"

"It's okay, Mom."

"No, it's not okay. I should have known that you've been struggling."

"Mom?"

"Yeah?"

"I think I'm getting out."

"You are?" she squeals, "That's great! When?"

"I don't know. But I think soon."

"Oh, Mimi, that's great. Oh that makes me so happy. Oh my god, thank god. The doctors think you're okay?"

"Well, I don't know if they'd put it like that exactly…"

"Oh, Mimi." She giggles.

"But I'm okay enough to get out of here."

"Oh, that's great news."

Silence. It's so hard.

"Mom?"

"Yeah?"

"Can I…" I sniffle.

"Yes?"

Cough. "Can I…"

"You want to come live with me?"

"Uh," more waters. "Yeah." Thrusting sobs, my belly contracting, beating like a bass drum.

"Well, of course. God, that makes me happy." She squeals anguish and delight. "Oh, Mimi. God, what's happened? I wish I understood everything. But I promise, I won't bother you. It'll just be nice to have you in the house. But I won't bother you or make you talk about anything you don't want to talk about."

"Okay." I say, just because I don't know what to say. I don't mind talking about things. I suppose I used to.

"You know, I can handle whatever it is you go through. I can. Your Dad had depressive tendencies. He was depressed a lot actually, more in the later years, once we stopped traveling and after you left, but he always had tendencies. He'd be driving Bertha and I wouldn't get a peep out of him through all of Montana, and that is a long time. He would just get so down for no reason at all. When do you think you're coming home?"

"I don't know. A couple weeks."

"Oh, that's so great, Mimi. Its like the Universe has answered my prayers. I have your room all clean and ready. The kids sleep in there when they spend the night."

"Who?"

"Leo and Maya. Ethan's kids. God, do I adore them."

Oh yeah. Ethan's kids. I met them when I went home for Dad's funeral.

"You are gonna fall in love with them, they are the sweetest things. And so damn funny! And they just love their crazy old grandma."

I hope they like their even crazier aunt.

"That sounds nice." I say. But it sounds scary, actually, so normal, life outside of here. "Mom. I should go."

"Oh. Okay. Oh, Mimi. Oh, I am just beside myself."

"I'll call you when I know the details."

"Yes. Ethan and I will come get you."

"That's not necessary."

"Well, we want to!"

"Okay, Mom."

"Alright, now you…take care, and…I'll talk to you soon."

"Okay. Bye."

"Bye, Sweetie."

And I put the receiver down.

Gail is smiling at me. "That went well, didn't it?"

I nod, "Yeah." Surreal. My head is a balloon, floating up to the ceiling. The room blurs. What if I can't do it?

"Well, I'm happy for you, Mimi. This is a big deal."

"Yeah."

32 →

Nigel came by to get me, to bring me to Dr. Jensen's office. I told him I didn't want to go with him, that I don't trust him. So he went off to go get Hillary. I sit here on the edge of my bed wearing my dress, my sky blue dress with the little flowers and opalescent buttons. And my sandals, my only shoes other than my tennis shoes. This meeting with Dr. Jensen is just a formality. I am to be released. But I thought that last time, 10 months ago, was it? I was sure that since I had my wits back and I could take care of myself and I wasn't causing too much trouble, they were going to let me out. But they didn't. So who knows? But this time is different 'cause Gail told me Dr. Westland had strongly alluded to the fact that I'd be released soon and she advised me on what to do when I got out and sat there when I called Mom and everything. And then Linda told me I was to have this appointment with Dr. Jensen. So it seems like that's what's going on. I'm getting out. I'm getting out. Wow.

Footsteps. Nigel appears in the doorway, green walls and florescent lights behind him. I give him a stiff look, nose up, lips tight.

"Hillary is busy with another patient. It's me or nobody."

I want to say nobody. I want to smack him. But if I don't go to the meeting with Jensen or if I make a scene, that could ruin everything.

I glare at him. He won't get out of this without feeling some heat. Asshole.

I get up loudly, blow air out of the side of my mouth, walk towards him and past him like a storm, wind blowing wild and hard. I keep going, briskly. He walks a step behind me. I chug and breathe, a locomotive.

"Slow down, Mimi."

I don't slow down. We get to the door that leads to the stairwell.

"You always gotta be mad at someone."

I glare at him. What does he know? He unlocks the doors and we go down the flight of stairs to the first floor. I wait for him to open the door. He puts his hand on the handle and looks at me. "You driving me crazy, Mimi."

I ignore him, just stare at his hand on the door handle, burning up inside. Teeth tight together.

He finally opens the door and we walk out and down the hallway with white walls, offices. Oh, shit. What is Jensen going to ask me? What am I supposed to say? And we're here. Right in front of his door. Nigel knocks with the knuckles of his first two fingers, his palm facing me, dulce de leche color, not the color of the rest of him, which is darker. Palms are stiffer skin, and creased with all that he's held. Fingers, wiggling tendrils, tools. Mysterious. All of it. All of this life.

"Come in." Dr. Jensen's muffled voice calls out.

Nigel turns the handle. He looks at me, catches my eye, holds me with his eyes, conveys what he needs to, our whole time together, his whole life. "Mimi, when he asks you how you're doing, remember to ask him back."

What?

He opens the door. Jensen sits behind his desk. Big man. Big desk. His smiling round head looks like a baby's.

"Mimi," he says, like it's some pleasant surprise, "Come on in." I take a few paces past the threshold. He looks past my shoulder, "Thank you, Nigel." The door closes behind me. "Come on in, Mimi, take a seat." He points to the grey chair in front of him with a big, fat hand. I walk up to it and sit down. His smile is huge, but he doesn't know me. He knows my diagnosis. He knows what medications I take and what my behavior reports say. But he doesn't know me. You can stop smiling, buddy. "Mimi! How have you been?"

211

"Fine," I say. I start to wring my hands. Dry. Cold. "How are you?"

"Oh, I'm doing good. Thanks for asking." A look in his eyes. A sly smile to himself. He writes something down.

"So I heard you spoke with your mother the other day."

"Yeah."

"And how was that?"

"It was good. It was really good."

"And you hadn't spoken with her in a while, is that right?"

"Yeah."

He waits for me to say more.

"It's been since Dad's funeral. A couple years."

He nods.

"And you plan on living with her?"

"Yeah. That's the plan."

"How does she feel about that?"

"Good. She's excited, actually."

"Oh, that's good."

"Yeah."

The air in here is stale. Scentless. Not like Dr. Westland' office. And no colors except smatterings here and there; books on the shelves, a framed photograph of a mountain with the word 'Stability' underneath.

The phone rings.

"Pardon me one second, Mimi. This might be an important call I'm expecting."

I make a smile. He picks up the receiver. "Hello?" He deflates suddenly. "Hi, Karen. Yeah, okay. No I can't. Well why don't you?" He rolls his eyes. "Alright, alright, I'll pick some up on my way home." He chews the inside of his cheek. Torture. "Look, I'm with a patient right now, I can't talk." He can't stand her. Must be his wife. He sighs heavily. "That's fine. Alright, I've got to go. Bye. Yeah. Fine. Bye." He puts the receiver down with a little grunt. Looks at me. Smiles. "Sorry about that. Now, where were we?"

I shrug my shoulders.

"Mimi, I'm going to be upfront with you. Do think you are ready to be released?"

"Yes. I do."

"Do you have concerns about being able to take care of yourself?"

"No."

"Do you believe you can control your actions?"

"Yes. I do."

"You know, Mimi, being released from the hospital doesn't mean the healing process is over. You would need to continue taking your meds, and we suggest continued therapy."

"I understand."

He sighs. "I would be lying if I didn't tell you that I have concerns. I am responsible in cases like yours to consider public safety."

I'm not going to hurt anyone you motherfucker.

Everything is tight. "I understand."

"But Dr. Westland is quite confident that you have control over yourself."

I nod.

"Mimi, it's one thing to have control here in this setting where you are being monitored and life is quite predictable."

I squeeze out a smile. "I understand."

He looks at me quizzically. He doubts. Silence clogs my throat. Fear.

"I will be fine, Doctor Jensen. I promise. I have learned so much from Doctor Westland about how to be aware when the anger is coming up, how to be bigger than it, how to stop. And breathe." I let out a breath. He is looking at me. I look back, still persuading with my eyes. He stares blankly. Not even looking at me. Where is he? His eyes slowly trail to my left. And down. He comes back with an inhale and looks at me again.

"I know that Gail has already alluded to your release. And that you are aware Dr. Westland has given the green light. He and your nurses and I will be having another meeting. A decision on a release date goal will be made then." He smiles, what seems like regretfully. He would keep me here forever. Like a pet gerbil that he doesn't love, but just wants in its cage to be looked at, examined as she runs and runs on her wheel.

33 ➤

Sitting at the table in Bertha with my watercolors. I was maybe nine. Ethan was five, I guess. I loved my watercolors. They were a present that year for my birthday, which was pretty rare. Mom and Dad didn't believe in rewarding us with material possessions. They believed experience was the greatest present. I suppose that doesn't sound so bad. They decided to get me the paints, though, because art is experience not an object.

I was painting a scene from the lake in Vermont we had just left. We were camped out there for about two weeks with a bunch of other vagabonds and travelers. There had been a music festival nearby and I guess a bunch of folks just spread the word to rendezvous at this lake in a nearby park. It was like summer camp. There were lots of kids and Ethan and I were out playing all the time. I met two girls around my age, Lizzy and Meadow, and we were inseparable, swimming, building mud castles, playing dress-up with our parents' clothes, giggling, telling stories, playing pranks on Ethan and his friends, who did their share of spying on us. It was the most fun I'd ever had and I felt like those two girls were the best friends anyone could ever want.

People slowly began to leave the park, as more and more locals harassed us and talk about permits started circulating. Lizzy left first and Meadow and I cried as her family took down their tent and pulled away in their station wagon. It wasn't long before Dad decided our time to move along had come as well. In all of our years on the road, I never heard Dad discuss leaving with Mom or lick his thumb and stick it in the air to see which way the wind was blowing. He would just announce suddenly that we were leaving. Usually I took this information as easily as him saying it was time for lunch, but this time something happened. I screamed. I cried. I pleaded. I loved the lake. Meadow and I didn't want to be apart. We were best friends. Why was he doing this to me? He explained that Meadow and her family would be leaving too, that everyone was leaving. The cops would be coming soon, he said. This isn't a free country, he said, we aren't allowed to just be somewhere. Not unless we are a slave to the system and continually pay for some little piece of land that we can call "ours and only ours." Meadow and I hugged each other and cried and said we would write. She gave me her address on a piece of paper. I had Mom write down our PO Box address and gave it to Meadow. I wrote to her twice and never heard back.

It had been almost two days since we departed and I was still pouting as I rendered Meadow standing by the lake wearing the orange dress she wore so often. We were somewhere in Indiana, on our way to another music festival in Wisconsin, then we'd have to go back to California because we needed more product from our supplier. Dad pulled off into a parking lot so we could have lunch.

"I don't want any," I whined as I moved the brush with purple paint over the top of the watercolor paper; perhaps a thunderstorm was coming.

"Mimi, you should eat," my mom said sympathetically, crouching down next to me.

"I'm not hungry."

She pressed her lips together and looked at me, a small, warm flame flickering behind her amber eyes. She placed her tan hand on my little one, dirt under all the fingernails.

"Mimi, you need to eat some food," Dad said, "How about a peanut butter and jelly sandwich? We have strawberry," he smiled, knowing it's my favorite.

I started to sob.

"Aw. Mimi." Mom frowned.

"I don't get it!" I cried, my face surely contorting, "Why couldn't we just stay at the lake?"

"Mimi, I told you, no one is staying at the lake. The government doesn't allow it."

"Why don't we stay anywhere? I want an address!" I screamed finally looking up at him.

Mom and Dad looked hurt. I've never been a parent, thank god, but I have heard that every parent questions the choices they have made from time to time.

Dad came closer and put his hand on my shoulder. "Darling, nothing lasts forever. Everything is impermanent."

I looked back down at my little painting, a half-created girl standing by an ephemeral lake, under dark purple clouds. His words only expanded my feeling of emptiness. I yanked my shoulder away from his hand.

"How 'bout half a sandwich?" Mom said. "I'll share one with you." She pressed her teeth between her lips and cocked her head, trying to pull me out, trying to coax me into a better mood.

"I'm not eating." I said resolutely.

Little Ethan, who had been sitting at the small table with me, drawing with his crayons, slid off his chair and crawled onto my lap. "I'm not eating eeder," he announced. I put my arm around his waist. His mess of pink and yellow straw hair still smelled of the lake, like blessed water. I started to get teary again. Ethan curled in tighter to me.

"Okay. A hunger strike then," Mom said. She stood and took a seat at the table across from Ethan and me.

Dad began to dig into the cabinets.

"Jack. We're on hunger strike." Mom repeated.

"Us too?"

"Yes. In honor of Mimi's grief. Solidarity."

Dad sighed. He wouldn't argue with her. "I suppose eating with such heaviness in the air wouldn't be much fun." He came by and kissed the top of my head and Ethan's too, then quietly pushed down the seat back that became our bed and lay down for a nap.

34 —

Why am I feeling nostalgic? Sitting here at this desk, not my desk anymore, bright midday light, looking down at the front lawn, a gardener putting down fresh mulch where the tulips will emerge. I imagine things will be the same. Poor Joan. Poor Ann. Sweet Daryl. I wonder if they will leave this place. The saddest thing here is the old people, with only death, their unacknowledged hero, to free them from anguish.

I wonder how Val is doing. Maybe I'll try to contact her, the little shit head. I bet Ethan can help me with that. My belly feels funny. Nervous. Too much hope is dangerous.

I walk down the corridor of the second floor for the last time. Goodbye mint-green walls. Nigel is escorting me. I have a duffle bag in one hand and a plastic Ross shopping bag with my painting supplies in the other. Nigel has been quiet.

"Sorry to see me go?" I ask.

"No. I'm glad you're leaving."

My mouth opens, my stomach sinks. But there is only tenderness in Nigel's eyes. Of course he wants me to go. He is happy for me. I smile, drop my bags and hug him. He hugs me back. His body is hard, warm. Should I plant a big wet one on his mouth? No, that's not what a sane person should do. I smile to myself. Besides, this is good enough. This is perfect.

He loosens his hold, so I do too. I pick up my bags and Nigel opens the doors leading to the stairwell. I said all my goodbyes at breakfast. Daryl, Joan, Ann, even Linda. She told me to 'be careful out there.' Nigel and I descend the stairs and enter the first floor hallway. White walls. Empty, blank white walls. We walk into one of the conference rooms used for staff meetings, meetings with families. Dr. Westland is here, and Gail, both smiling when they see me.

"There she is," Gail says. I just stand, frozen. "Say your goodbyes, Mimi."

Dr. Westland opens his arms for a hug, and I practically fall into the embrace. I wrap my arms around his neck, standing on my tiptoes.

"Thank you," I say softly in his ear, my eyes closed, golden-orange light inside.

"You're welcome," he whispers back.

My head on his shoulder never wants to leave this animal warmth. This is my second hug today. I don't even remember the last time I had a real, soul-embracing hug. Maybe not since Jared. Maybe. I can't remember.

"The marriage proposal still stands," I say softly.

He laughs a hearty laugh. His belly shaking like a firm Jell-O mold, shaking me like I'm on a ride at the carnival, making me laugh too.

"What's so funny?" Gail chimes in.

"Oh, nothing," says Dr. Westland as we let go of each other, "Just that Mimi takes me for a polygamist." Everyone in the room is smiling except Gail. She doesn't get it.

"Go enjoy yourself, Mimi. And good luck with the painting."

"Thank you." I wipe a tear of laughter from my eye.

"Alright, Mimi," Gail says picking up the bag with my painting supplies off the floor. I grab my duffle bag.

"Take care, Mimi," Nigel says.

"I will. And I'll be waiting for you in San Francisco."

He chuckles. "Alright, you do that. I'll have to talk it over with Lucy."

Gail nods. "Well, alright then, Mimi. Your mom and brother should be here any minute. Let's go outside and wait for them."

I take a last look at Dr. Westland and Nigel and walk out the door with Gail. We walk down the hallway to the front doors, the doors I never remember coming in through. Doors that have tormented me. Confused me. Told me stories of hope. I put my hand out as we approach, a little too early, but finally it touches a cold steel knob. I shoulder, then push the heavy metal door open. Blinding sunlight consumes me and I disappear. Air almost warm. Almost April. The smell of mulch and things budding. My eyes adjust to the light. I am holding the door open. I walk through and keep the door open for Gail.

I walk on the path briskly, slightly ahead of Gail. The air has never felt like this, so clear, so empty. There is ringing in my ears. My heart is flickering wildly. I hear Daryl's last words to me. Don't just be free of these walls. Go be free. Go do Mimi.

We arrive at the bench halfway down the driveway and sit. We will wait. Mom and Ethan will be coming through the gate in some rental car from the airport. They will drive down the driveway here and scoop me up. Tonight we are going to sleep in a motel together, because it would be too much for them to fly both ways in one day. It feels a little scary, the idea of sharing a motel room with them, of being in such close quarters, but it also excites me, makes me think of all of us in Bertha. Too bad Dad won't be with them. Too bad I didn't get to say goodbye to Dad. I can smell the ganja and the dust of his bookstore. I can see his mustache, his large excited eyes. I look up to the sky, past the bare budding trees. Just a few wispy clouds dancing way high up. "I love you, Dad," I say. Gail turns to me. I forgot she was here. She puts her hand on my back and starts rubbing. I put my hand on her back, almost expecting to feel a layer of mouse fur underneath the sweatshirt. But it's just flesh. Boney shoulder blades.

I breathe in the fresh, clear air. The sun is shining like a crystal. Birds singing, feathers brushing lightly inside my chest, on my cheeks, drawing up a smile.

Movement. A car at the gate, silver. The mechanical gate glides open. Is it them? My heart jumps, races, doesn't know what to do. I wring my hands and watch the scene moving slowly: the car coming down the driveway now, silver glistening, new green leaves on the maples, light in color, translucent with sunlight, trembling with the breeze.

I hope Mom grabs me, pulls me into one of her twisting, squealing hugs.

Made in the USA
Lexington, KY
17 March 2014